MW00774247

BORROWED

The MacLellan Sisters Trilogy

LUCINDA RACE

MC Two Press

This book is a work of fiction. Names, characters, places, and incidents are the product of the author's imagination or are used fictitiously. Any resemblance to actual events, locales, or persons, living or dead, is coincidental.

Copyright © 2019 by Lucinda Race
Published by MC Two Press

All rights reserved, including the right to reproduce, distribute, or transmit in any form or by any means. For information regarding subsidiary rights, please contact the author, Lucinda Race.

Edited by Mackenzie Walton
Cover Design by Jade Webb, Meet Cute Creative
Manufactured in the United States of America
First Edition 2019

ISBN Paperback 978-0-9986647-7-4
ISBN E-book 978-0-9986647-8-1

For my Mom:
We are always connected to the ones who came before us.

For my readers, who encourage me to keep writing.
Thank you.

Karen: thank you for correcting me on the difference between
sneakers and running shoes.

Magic is everywhere.

CHAPTER 1

Kenzie bumped the hallway table and dropped her luggage, scattering mail over the entryway. She caught the jar of wildflowers midair. With a tired smile, she murmured, "Robbie Burns, you always know what I need after a long trip."

She buried her nose in the blooms, drinking in the fresh scent of sweet pea, lavender and daisies. Carrying the jar into the living room, she placed it on the table where she could see it and flopped on the soft leather couch. Her cell buzzed. It was Robbie.

Putting a smile in her voice, she said, "Hello there." She closed her eyes and pictured his easy, crooked smile.

"Welcome home, Kenz. Good trip?" His voice was smooth, like aged whiskey.

"It was. You'll never guess what happened." Not waiting for him to ask, she shrieked, "Jamie and Caleb got engaged!"

With a low whistle, he said, "Wow, that's a shocker. The first MacLellan sister to tie the knot."

Kenzie propped her feet up and sighed. "I'm going to

finally have a brother. He showed up in Scotland our second day there and popped the question."

"How did he ask her?" Kenzie could picture Robbie slouched in his comfy chair.

"It was so sweet. We were having tea and he dropped to one knee. Jamie freaked out, said no and ran from the house. Of course, Caleb went after her, and when they came back from the field an engagement ring was on her left hand and a smile as bright as the sun shining over the Highlands in our beloved Scotland."

"That sounds special for the both of them."

Kenzie laughed softly. "Right out of a romance movie."

"When are your parents coming home?"

"Sometime before the holidays." She twirled a short strand of chestnut-brown hair. "You know, one of these days we need to stop talking about you coming with me and make some definite plans. Scotland's like no place else on earth. After all, you do have Scottish blood in your veins."

His deep, rich laugh made her smile. She had missed him, and said, "Before we do that, I'll need to hire someone to keep the gym open while we're trip-tropping through the Highlands." She stood up and stretched one arm overhead, changed the phone to the other hand and worked out the kinks on the opposite side. "Or we'll shut down for ten days."

"Whoa," he chuckled. "Am I talking to Kenzie MacLellan?"

With a small laugh, she said, "Chalk it up to me being overtired, but I'm serious we need to hire someone." Kenzie tousled her hair. "I'll open tomorrow."

"Sleep in—I've got everything covered. I didn't expect you until late."

She grinned. "Robbie Burns, you really are one in a

million." She thought, *I could use a man like you around all the time.*

"Oh, and I put a few essentials in your fridge so you don't need to go to the store, at least not today."

"Hey, did you go hiking?"

"I came back early it wasn't as much fun without you." Kenzie could almost hear the shrug in his voice.

Teasing him affectionately, she said, "Well, in that case, I won't forget your present. You deserve something extra special."

He chuckled. "Until tomorrow, Kenz."

She noticed a layer of dust on the glass table. Padding into the kitchen, she grabbed a bottle of vinegar and water. She polished every surface in the condo until it gleamed. Feeling more lighthearted than when she walked through the door, she made her way around her ultra-modern digs opening windows to freshen the air.

Curious to see what Robbie had bought, she wandered back into the kitchen and peered in the refrigerator. Greens, cooked shrimp and some fresh fruit. On the counter was an avocado. Dinner. Silently she thanked him again.

After adding some shrimp to her tossed salad, Kenzie carried her plate into the living room. After being with family for the last two weeks, the silence was deafening. She grabbed her phone and started to dial Jamie but stopped. She was with Caleb, in Boston.

I'll call Grace. One sister is just as good as two for an impromptu dinner.

On the second ring, she heard, "Hello?"

"Hey, Gracie, I was wondering what's for supper."

"Takeout, I guess. You?"

She toyed with her salad. "Robbie stocked the fridge."

Grace sighed and said, "He's a sweetie."

"I know, right? Do you want to come over? I have plenty."

"Absolutely! See you in twenty." Grace disconnected, but not before Kenzie heard a faint *"YES."*

Kenzie set her plate on the coffee table and went into the kitchen to fix one for her younger sister. After it was ready, she slipped it in the fridge.

I wonder what will happen now that Jamie's getting married. She kicked back on the couch and closed her eyes, drifting off. The door banging jarred her out of her tired stupor.

Grace stuck her head into the living room. "Hey, long time no see, sis. It's been, what, three hours since we got home?"

Grace as well as Jamie looked very similar to Kenzie. Their heart-shaped faces were just the start. They had the same coloring; crystal-blue eyes and auburn hair. Except Kenzie's was short and spikey, Grace wore her hair long with tough-to-tame curls and Jamie's was long and sleek.

Grace's eyes twinkled mischievously as she held aloft a pink-and-white striped paper bag. "Technically we're still on vacation, so I picked up sundaes."

Kenzie joked, "Good to know you're upholding the long- standing tradition—vacation ends when we go back to work." She peeked inside the bag. "Did you get me hot fudge on peppermint stick with extra sprinkles and whipped cream?"

"But of course," Grace chuckled. "Sans the cherry."

Kenzie wrinkled her nose. "What a way to ruin a sundae. At this very moment, you're my favorite sister."

Grace snorted. "Only until Jamie does something extra nice for you."

Kenzie dug in the bag and pulled out a container. She handed it to Grace. Grace's eyebrow spiked.

Salad forgotten, Kenzie licked whipped cream from the edge of the sundae cup.

Frowning, Grace said, "Don't you think we should put these in the freezer?"

With a lopsided smirk Kenzie replied, "No. The fudge is never the same after it freezes."

Grace furrowed her brows. "Kenz…" She dragged out her name. "Do you believe Gran's wedding dress is enchanted?"

"Maybe." Kenzie looked at her from under long eyelashes. "Do you want to try it on?"

Grace smirked, "You should be next."

"I don't want to jinx it."

Ignoring her response, Grace dropped her face. "Will Jamie have time for us after she's married?"

Kenzie closed her eyes and basked in the decadence of the fudge sauce. "Ah, this hits the spot."

Sharply, Grace said, "Kenz, did you hear me?"

"Gracie, of course she will. Jamie's getting married, not going to the moon. We may need to knock before just walking into her place after Caleb moves in."

Grace stirred the ice cream. "I'm happy for her. Caleb's a great guy."

"Me too."

"Who knew Jamie could smile all the time?"

Kenzie laughed. "Love does seem to bring out the best in a person."

The girls' phones buzzed and they looked down. "It's Jamie," Grace announced.

Hey—we'll be home tomorrow. Let me know you got home okay.

Grinning at Grace, Kenzie said, "I guess we have our answer—she's always going to be our big sister."

Grace took a picture of her sundae and texted Jamie, adding a caption: *Dinner. Yum!*

Moments later, their phones chirped. *Peppermint stick? Save me some.*

Grace's face perked up and she put her phone on the table. "I don't know about you, but I'm feeling better."

Kenzie beamed. "Me too. Now let's finish our dessert so we can eat our salads."

Jamie held up her cell so Caleb could see the picture. "Guess what my sisters are having for dinner?"

Caleb studied the small screen. "Ice cream?"

Jamie chuckled. "Technically we're still on vacation, so we can have ice cream too."

He pulled her into his arms. "Is this a MacLellan tradition?"

Jamie's bright blue eyes batted in his direction. Feigning innocence, she said, "And if I said yes?"

He pecked her lips and said, "I'll be right back." Caleb hurried from the room. While he was gone, Jamie unzipped her travel bag. Before she had time to decide if she should completely unpack, Caleb opened the door. "Good news. I told Mom we were going to miss dinner."

Jamie's brow wrinkled. "Huh?"

He flashed a flyer in front of her face. "We're going out for ice cream."

In two short steps, she flung her arms around his neck, showering his face with kisses. "I promise, you're going to love this tradition."

He chuckled. "I can't wait to discover more family traditions."

She stopped kissing him and looked in his eyes. "Can I ask you something?"

Caleb searched her face. "Of course."

Jamie chewed her lower lip and pulled him down on the bed next to her. "I can't wait to marry you, but I can't lose my sisters. We're not just related to each other, we've chosen to be best friends too." She unconsciously picked at a loose thread on the bedspread. "We have keys to the other's homes." Her voice dropped. "Do I need to ask them to return theirs?"

Caleb smoothed back her hair. His eyes held hers. "Absolutely not. The only thing I ask is the master bedroom and bath are off limits."

Jamie let go of the breath she was holding. Laughing she said, "Thank you for understanding."

"Sweetheart, they're going to be my sisters too, and you need to realize I don't want to change your life just become a part of it."

Jamie's lips hovering over his. "When I think I can't love you any more, you do or say something so sweet." She kissed him lightly. "Now you said something about ice cream?"

Caleb said with a laugh, "Absolutely. I'm not breaking a MacLellan tradition."

Robbie prowled around his apartment. Kenzie was home and tomorrow couldn't come soon enough. The last two weeks dragged on forever.

He'd attempted, many times over the years, to pry her from his heart. She'd never see him as more than her best friend and coworker, but he loved her. For better or worse, she'd captured his heart a long time ago. She was in his blood. Maybe now that Jamie was engaged, there was hope Kenzie would let go of her foolish idea that a long-term relationship would take something away from her.

He leaned his head against the cool glass of the window, his body unmoving but his mind racing. *How can I make her see I'm the man who will love her for a lifetime but never ask her to change?*

CHAPTER 2

With her eyes squeezed tight, Kenzie swatted the air and finally made contact with the alarm clock, silencing the annoying morning DJ.

She mumbled, "The first day after vacation sucks."

She lay back in the pillows, pulling the soft down comforter over her head. She was already missing Scotland, where she got out of bed after the birds, not before. Sticking her hand out from the cozy covers, she flicked a switch on the lamp, and a warm, rosy glow filled the room. She moaned, "I can't lollygag in bed all day," and threw back the blankets.

After a quick shower, she toweled-dried her hair and dressed in form-fitting workout clothes with a fleece hoodie that sported the gym's logo.

Then, whipping up a smoothie, she filled two insulated mugs and grabbed her lunch bag. It was time to open the gym for early morning exercise enthusiasts.

The front windows blazed with light. Unlocking the

door, she strolled inside, and with a rush of pride she flipped over the OPEN sign.

She pushed open the men's locker room door. "Robbie?"

A muffled, "Be right out," answered her.

She let the door close and fired up the desktop computer. She thumbed through the sign-in logs and saw the gym had been busy while she was gone.

"Hey, Kenz, it's good to see you." Robbie moved with cheetah-like grace, fast and powerful, and gave her a warm hug. His grin was irresistible.

"Robbie." She held him tight. "I missed you." *This feels good. Now I'm home.*

His dimples deepened and he held her at arms-length. "You're looking fantastic. How was Scotland?"

She handed him a mug and cocked her head. "Bitter-sweet, but overall fantastic. I'll always miss Gran's perky smile, but going there made her seem like she was with me, if you know what I mean."

He dropped a friendly kiss on her cheek and lightly tapped her chest. "She's always with you." He moved away from her and beamed, "You should see the logs."

"I scanned them before you came out. It looks like you were busy, and I noticed you signed a new personal training client."

"Some woman Grace works with. A new therapist."

"What plan did she take?" Kenzie took a sip of her shake.

"Three months of gym with personal training twice a week."

"Wow." She teased, "You had your salesman's hat on."

With mock seriousness, he said, "Maybe it was my charming smile and sleek physique." He pumped his biceps and grinned broadly.

Kenzie flashed him a huge grin. "You're too much." She held up an index finger. "Hold that thought." She rummaged in her tote and pulled out a paper bag. "For you."

His eyes softened as he set down his smoothie. "I didn't need a gift."

"If it wasn't for you, I'd never be able to travel with my sisters."

He took the bag and shook it. His eyes sparkled with mischief. "What's inside?"

She poked him. "Open it."

Tearing off the top, he reached in and pulled out a folded swatch of plaid. His eyebrows shot up in surprise. "The MacLellan plaid?"

She chuckled, "Of course. Keep going."

He folded back the fabric. It held something that resembled a small dagger.

"It's the traditional *sgian dubh*. It's made from walnut, and see?" She pointed. "On the top, in pewter is a thistle. You know, it's worn in a man's kilt sock as backup protection, but nowadays it's just for looks."

Robbie turned it over in his hand. "It's amazing." He kissed her forehead. "Thank you for thinking of me."

For a half second, she thought his lips lingered a little longer than normal. "I always do." Their eyes locked.

The bell on the door jingled and broke the moment. She greeted a regular with her trademark smile. "Good morning, Pete."

"Hey," he grumbled. Without a backward glance, he hurried into the cardio room.

With a shake of her head, she said, "Don't you just love clients who are *not* morning people?"

Robbie continued to look at her with an intensity she

hadn't seen before. "As long as they keep coming through the door, what does it matter?"

She nodded, unnerved by the way he'd looked at her. "True. Do you have a class this morning?"

His demeanor shifted to business. "No. You have spin first, then yoga. This afternoon I'll take spin and I have my client at the end of the day."

"Anything else I should know about?"

He reached around her and grabbed his mug, his arm grazing hers. A warm glow rippled through her as they touched. "You might want to check on the new vendor for the replacement mats. If you get them and order before the end of the month, there's a discount."

Slightly breathless she said, "I'll get right on it." She was thankful Robbie was on top of everything. *What is going on with me? All these jitters around Robbie. It must be a carry-over from spending so much time with Jamie and Caleb while on vacation.*

"Oh, thanks for the smoothie, and one last thing—we talked about taking a couple of days to go hiking. We should check our calendars so we can get coverage for the gym, unless you really were serious about closing it down for a few days."

Kenzie looked down at the screen, distracted, and said, "Pick a couple of dates and we'll talk at lunch."

Robbie's hand hovered on the door handle to the cardio room when Kenzie called out, "Wait! I almost forgot—Jamie and Caleb will be home today."

Robbie looked over his shoulder and said, "We should get together and celebrate." He leaned against the door-jamb. "Any idea what he'll do about his job?"

"He's going to open a culinary school, right here in town." Kenzie thought she saw a flash in his eyes before he turned away. "Robbie?" she called out as the door closed behind him.

Does he have a thing for Jamie? She shook her head. Nah. If he did, he could have asked her out a thousand times.

"Earth to Kenzie," Grace whispered. Her bag slapped down on the counter, jarring Kenzie from a jetlag-induced haze.

She gasped. "Sorry, when did you get here?"

"I just walked in. Where were you?"

"Longing for sleep." Kenzie stretched her neck from side to side and said, "How do you look like that?" She waved a hand around her sister's face. "Well-rested and ready to go."

Grace smirked. "It's a special brew I call coffee, strong, and lots of it."

Kenzie grimaced. "That boost fades. At least mine did long ago."

Grace laughed. "Not before my workout and dinner. Then it's crash time and a good night's rest. Tomorrow I'll be raring to go again."

Kenzie slid off the stool and trailed Grace into the locker room. "Did you hear from Jamie today?"

"Yeah, she sent a text and asked if we could have dinner with her tomorrow night." Grace laid out a tee and shorts on a bench. "I said I'd pass along the message. I don't have anything going on, do you?"

With a shake of her head, Kenzie said, "I thought she'd be spending every free minute with Caleb."

"My guess is we'll be talking wedding plans and she needs our help." Grace finished dressing, locked her bag and keys in her locker, and gave the dial a twirl.

Kenzie frowned and grabbed Grace's water bottle. "Right, the wedding."

Grace sighed and got a dreamy look in her eyes. "She's going to make a beautiful bride and Caleb is so handsome, in a tall, dark, slightly scruffy sort of way. Do you think she'll wear Gran's dress? After all it's the reason she met him."

"Of course, she'll wear it. She can't break with family tradition and remember its enchanted so maybe some magic spills over to the marriage." She tilted her head. "Ya know, I always pictured Jamie with a lawyer or banker."

Grace snorted. "Like Steve? I think she needed someone who's more chill. Isn't that what they say, opposites attract?"

"So I hear." Robbie's smiling face popped into Kenzie's head. She really was lucky to have him as her best friend. "What are you working on tonight?"

Grace looked torn between the cardio and weight rooms. "Cardio."

"I'll join you. I could use a short run. Hopefully it'll give me an energy boost." She held the door open for Grace.

Grace hopped on the bike and pedaled at a steady pace and Kenzie nudged the speed up a little on the treadmill. "I think Robbie has a client soon. Ally Evans." Kenzie broke into a slow jog. "I'd like to meet her."

Grace kicked her machine into gear and conversation stopped as she worked her way through a punishing routine. When she finally went into cool-down mode, she pointed to the mirror in front of her. "Ally's here."

Kenzie stopped the treadmill. She turned as Robbie greeted Ally with a warm handshake and half hug. "Huh, that's a little out of character," she mused.

Grace drained her bottle, toweling off her forehead and arms. "What is?'

Kenzie flicked her head toward the lobby. "He's wearing his *charming* smile."

"He's being polite, that's all."

"Yeah, right." She studied the newcomer. She said, "Refill your water before we move to weights."

She stalked from the room with Grace hurrying after her. "Kenz?"

Concentrating on Robbie, Kenzie couldn't hear the conversation, but the look on Ally's face annoyed the heck out of her. *This woman is looking at Robbie like he's the last bottle of water in a desert.*

"Ready?" Grace demanded her attention.

Kenzie positioned Grace across from Robbie's client. On autopilot, she put Grace through a tough upper-body routine while trying to not be obvious she was eavesdropping.

Grace set the weights down. "Kenz." She snapped her fingers in front of Kenzie's eyes. "Do you want to meet her?"

"Huh? What?" Kenzie focused on Grace. "Yeah, sure."

After Ally finished her set, Grace said, "Hi, Ally." She flashed a huge grin. "I'm glad you found the place."

Ally smiled and said, "I'm surprised you're working out tonight. Aren't you exhausted?"

"I'm going to wait until the weekend before caving in to sleep deprivation. I'd like for you to meet my sister, Kenzie. This is her place."

The petite, curvaceous redhead extended a hand. In a soft southern drawl, she said, "Nice to meet you, Kenzie. Robbie's told me all about you."

Kenzie cringed. Giving Ally an overly firm shake, she said, "I hope you find the gym to your liking."

Ally glanced at Robbie. "I already do."

Kenzie gritted her teeth and grabbed Grace's arm. "You need to cool down."

Grace allowed herself to be pulled from the room, calling over her shoulder, "See you tomorrow, Ally."

"Pleasure to meet you, Kenzie, and have a good evening." Ally turned her attention back to Robbie.

Kenzie stormed over to the open door. "Grace?" She flipped on the lights to the yoga room.

Grace gave Robbie a confused look. He shrugged his shoulders. Quietly closing the door, her voice low, she said, "Kenzie, I think you're the one that needs to cool down. What's wrong with you? If I didn't know better I'd think you were a tiny bit jealous."

Kenzie's annoyance was moving towards an unfamiliar sensation. She ignored Grace's comment. "Did you see her fawning all over Robbie?"

"Sis, he must get that a lot. He's a good-looking guy..."

"I've never seen him react to a client like that."

Grace's eyebrow arched and she set her hands on her hips. "You are jealous!"

"Of Ally? No." *What's wrong with me?* "Robbie and I've been best friends for almost thirty years."

Grace chided, "It's like you've never seen another woman interested in him."

"He's dated a lot of girls. But this Ally chick, she's totally wrong for him."

Grace reminded Kenzie, "Hasn't he thought the same thing about some of your boyfriends."

"Exactly my point." She jabbed her finger toward the weight room. "I'm going to keep my eye on this situation. If little Miss Southern Freckles thinks she's going to get Robbie, she's barking up the wrong tree."

Even as she heard the words come out of her mouth,

she didn't understand why she was so angry. *I must be really overtired and overreacting to every little thing.*

Grace's eyebrows shot up. "Ally's just being friendly; after all, she's new in town. I seem to remember you and Robbie dated briefly. When was that?"

Kenzie sniffed. "The summer between high school and freshmen year of college. But we both decided we were better off as friends. Why?" Her stomach did a funny flip.

"You seem awfully irritated over nothing."

"I don't want anyone taking advantage of him." *Was that all there was to it?*

"If that's what you want to call it." Humor flashed across Grace's face.

Kenzie ignored the annoying comment that came out of her sister's mouth and flicked out the yoga mat. She snarled, "Let's stretch."

CHAPTER 3

K enzie pulled up in front of Jamie's garage door. She grabbed a large tote bag filled with takeout containers from the passenger seat. Walking through the back door, she called out, "Anybody home?"

She heard a muffled response from the patio. Poking her head out the slider, she saw Jamie wandering around with a notepad and pen in hand, pausing every few feet. "What are you looking for?"

Jamie gave her sister a sunny smile. "The perfect spot to get married."

"You're tying the knot here?" Kenzie scanned the tidy yard with flowerbeds spilling into the grass. "There's not much room."

"I want to keep it simple and cost effective. That's why I wanted to run some ideas by you and Grace. If you agree, I'll talk to Caleb tomorrow."

Giving her an indulgent smile, Kenzie continued, "Who would have ever thought you'd fall in love with someone as awesome as Dad? And if we're talking wedding plans, I need wine."

Jamie laughed and pointed to the house. "You know where everything is—crack open a bottle and pour glasses for all of us."

Muttering, Kenzie walked into the kitchen.

"Kenzie?" Grace appeared in the kitchen. "Did you say something?"

"Oh, hey, Grace." She held up a stemless glass. "You were right. We're planning Jamie's wedding. I don't know about you, but I am going to need at least one."

Grace's eyes lit up and she clapped. "Sounds like fun."

Kenzie's fingernail tapped the bottle of wine. "Only you would think planning a wedding would be fun."

Folding her arms across her chest, Grace frowned. "Come on, Kenzie, don't rain on Jamie's parade just because we said we'd never do it. Be happy for her."

"Now you sound like Mom."

Grace smiled. "The apple didn't fall far from the tree, for any of us."

"I know." Kenzie grumbled just a tad. "We support each other no matter what." She handed Grace a glass, picked up the remaining two. "Lead the way."

Grace latched the screen door after Kenzie stepped onto the patio. Jamie squealed and seemed to float across the lawn. "Now we can get down to some serious wedding planning."

Kenzie handed Jamie a glass and took a sip. "So, let's hear your ideas for the big day."

Jamie glowed. "Well, it's going to be four weeks from Saturday."

Kenzie coughed and sputtered as her wine went down the wrong pipe. Grace pounded Kenzie's back.

"What's the hurry?" She waved a hand for Grace to stop. "Mom and Dad are still in Scotland and you've only been engaged for two weeks." She dropped heavily in a chair.

Grace's eyes widened. "They'll be home soon, and Kenzie, if Jamie and Caleb want to get married, we *will* make it happen."

Jamie laid her hand over Grace's. With a small smile, she said, "I knew you would understand." Her expression brightened. "Kenz, I've found the man I want to spend my life with. Why do we need a long engagement?"

Kenzie could hear the steely determination in Jamie's voice, and when she really looked at her older sister, it was clear she was over the moon for Caleb. She mumbled under her breath so her sisters wouldn't hear her. "Who am I to argue with true love?"

Grace stated, "You've missed the two-month window for invitations."

Kenzie cocked her head. "Where did you learn so much about wedding timelines?"

With a sniff she said, "I read." Grace focused her attention on Jamie. "How many people are you inviting?"

Jamie looked at her sisters, her eyes dancing. "Just our immediate families."

Grace's brow arched. "Jamie, that's not really practical. You have a lot of friends that would love to be a part of your special day. Your backyard is not big enough."

Kenzie snorted and, with a touch of snarkiness, said, "Especially since you've said for years you're never getting hitched."

Jamie's eyes narrowed. "Kenzie, do you have a problem?"

She held up her hands in defeat. "Not at all. It just seems like you're rushing into this wedding as if Caleb's going to vanish in a puff of smoke."

Jamie pulled her chair closer to Kenzie. "All right. Do

you want to know why I'm *rushing*, to use your word, this wedding?"

Kenzie nodded. Had Jamie thought all this through?

"For the first time, I finally understand what real love—combined with respect, compassion, compatibility and yes, physical attraction—feels like." She laid her hand over her heart. "In here. I'm hoping you and Grace can see I'm truly happy." Her eyes bored into her sisters. "Kenz, it's okay to let down your guard and let someone love you. You're worth it, we all are, and I've discovered there are good men, just like Dad, out there waiting for us." Her eyes pleaded for understanding as her gaze moved from Grace and then Kenzie. "I didn't realize but I've been waiting my entire life for Caleb, so why do we need to wait when it's what we both want."

"Oh, Jamie." Tears sprang to Grace's eyes. "That's beautiful."

Kenzie leaned forward, never breaking eye contact, and asked, "Do you love Caleb with all your heart? You're not just letting the emotion of Gran's death cloud your judgment? Or the fact that we inherited an enchanted wedding dress that is supposed to show us our future?"

Jamie nodded, tears dampening her lashes. "I really do love him and I get it, what Gran used to say. That when a good man walks into your life, don't slam the door in his face." She wiped the tears from her eyes. "If it took me trying on the wedding dress to see what I really longed for, then I'm glad I took the chance."

Kenzie wasn't convinced. "But you thought Steve was the guy too."

"I thought Steve was *the one* because I tried on Great-Gran's dress. After reading the stories about her and Gran falling in love with the next man they met, I thought that's how the magic worked."

Grace perched on the edge of her chair and clutched her heart. "The magic did work because meeting Steve led you to Caleb."

Jamie grinned. "Twins. I guess that's something to write down for future generations."

Kenzie heard a difference in her sister's voice, and seeing Jamie's smile light up her crystal-blue eyes, something inside softened. "So, what do we need to do first?"

"Oh, Kenzie…" Jamie hugged her tight. "Do you mean it, you're all in?"

Kenzie wouldn't allow her bias toward marriage put a damper on Jamie's happiness. She said, "You can count on us, for anything."

Grace held her glass high. "To a MacLellan sister wedding."

The girls clinked glasses.

Jamie set her glass down and picked up her pen. With a gleam in her eye, she said, "With the date set, we need a time of day."

"Does Caleb have a preference?" Grace grabbed the pad and pen from Jamie. "How about getting married in the evening? A simple but elegant wedding seems to suit you both."

Jamie looked surprised. "It does?"

Grace tapped the pen cap against the pad. "I picture you getting married by candlelight, your hair piled high, and your groom is wearing a black tux."

"You do, do you?" Jamie laughed. "Anything else?"

She gushed, "Of course, a lovely and elegant supper afterward, in a garden with fairy lights. Kenzie, what do you think?"

"I have to admit it does sound lovely, and Grace does have the dramatic flair for all things romantic."

Jamie leaned back and closed her eyes. "I can see it now.

The ceremony at seven under the stars with dinner and dancing." Her eyes popped open and scanned the yard. "Do you think we can do everything here with fifty guests max?"

"Wait!" Grace's face brightened. "I've got it! You can have the ceremony at Racing Brook Stables. Jo has a beautiful spot on top of the hill that overlooks the valley. We could set up a couple of tents and a flower-covered arbor."

Jamie's smile widened. "I'll ask Caleb, but I know he'll love it."

Kenzie asked, "Can he take care of the catering?"

Jamie pointed to the pad. "Grace, are you taking notes?" She nodded, and Jamie continued, "That's right up his alley —he has plenty of contacts in the restaurant biz that would do it."

Kenzie said, "I hope he doesn't skimp on the wedding cake. I firmly believe that is the best part of the meal."

Jamie laughed. "I'll make sure to tell him the cake has to be the best money can buy, just for you."

"Jamie, are you going to wear…"

Jamie didn't give Grace a chance to finish her question. "Of course I'm wearing Gran's dress, but I'm thinking about having a few modifications to modernize it, just a bit."

"You are?" Grace glanced at Kenzie, worry lines popping up on her forehead.

"Let's go in and I'll show you what I'm thinking. After all, it's our legacy and I won't do anything unless we all agree."

The girls' chairs scraped the stones. Grace linked arms with Jamie and Kenzie. "You're going to be a beautiful bride."

Once they were inside the house Jamie flicked on the

overhead lights as they entered her bedroom. Grace sucked in her breath as they saw the dress.

"Here it is." Jamie spoke in a hushed, almost reverent tone.

Kenzie and Grace's eyes popped—everything seemed different about the gown, as if it had a new purpose. In a few weeks Jamie was going to wear this gown at her wedding.

The lighting enhanced the exquisite gown. The aged lace was like rich cream, the soft folds revealing the intricate design of thistle and heather lace.

Jamie lifted the hanger off the door and held out the dress. Kenzie's fingers grazed the fabric. "It is so soft." Her eyes met Jamie's. "Put it on for us."

Jamie shed her T-shirt and shorts and kicked off her sandals. "Loosen the back so I can step into it."

Grace held the skirt as Jamie carefully pulled the dress up her willowy body, slipping it over her arms. She turned so Grace could secure the back, taking care with the delicate lace.

Jamie pivoted before her sisters.

It sounded like the side door banged. "Wait!" Grace raced from the room.

Kenzie asked, "Are you expecting someone? Caleb?"

Jamie shook her head. Kenzie poked her head into the hall. Turning towards Jamie, she flashed a huge grin. Jamie gathered the chapel-length train in her hands and padded across the soft carpet.

"Mom! When did you get home?"

Olivia MacLellan was a petite blue-eyed woman with short blonde hair, and her slender figure was pure genetics. Her smooth, fair skin was a testament to wearing sunglasses and big floppy hats whenever she was outside. She opened her arms to her daughters and kissed their cheeks and teased, "Did you think I was going to let you plan your entire wedding without me?"

Stepping back, she took in the sight of Jamie in the dress, a smile slowly spreading across her face. "I see I arrived in time for the big reveal."

"Grace, I can't believe you didn't tell us," Kenzie admonished.

With eyes twinkling, she said, "It was more fun this way."

"It's like the dress was made for you." Mom pulled a tissue from her pocket and dabbed the corner of her eyes before she adjusted the capped sleeves.

"I'm surprised, since Gran and I have totally different figures. Grace is curvy like Gran."

Kenzie jumped in. "She needs to wear her hair up."

"Yes, I'll have an updo and I'm thinking long gloves."

Grace's head bobbed up and down. "Oh, Jamie," she gushed. "It's perfect for an evening wedding."

Jamie laid her hand over her heart. "Mom, can I wear your pearls?

Mom's eyes grew misty. "Of course. They'll be your something borrowed and the dress is your old. What about the new and blue?"

"I'm not sure, but what if I took our plaid, since it has blue in it, and had bows made for the back of my shoes? And my garter too. That covers the blue and new. It'd feel like Gran and Grandad are with us."

Aghast, Grace's hand flew to her mouth. "You can't cut up the MacLellan plaid Gran sent to us!"

Startled, Jamie said, "Of course not, but I can order fabric from Scotland and have it air shipped. And if either of you want to wear the shoes next, you can."

Mom and Jamie looked at Grace and Kenzie. Kenzie took a step back. Holding up her hands in protest, she exclaimed, "Don't look at me, I'm not jumping into the pool. Maybe Grace will."

With palms upturned, Grace chimed in, "I'm not saying anything. Right now, it's all hands on deck to get you and Caleb married in four weeks."

"Jamie? I knew you wanted to have a short engagement, but that's hardly enough time, sweetheart."

Jamie took her mom's hands. "Breathe. We're talking a small wedding with family and a few close friends. We're looking at maybe forty to fifty guests, tops. Think of it like a holiday dinner—it's not really that much more."

Looking unconvinced, Mom said, "It's the same amount of work if it's for fifty or five hundred."

"Caleb's taking care of the catering. As long as Jo agrees, we'll get married at Racing Brook Stables."

Kenzie grinned. "You know she'll be thrilled. She is a romantic down to her bones."

"Before we start talking specifics, I'm going to change and we can have dinner and make a ton of lists."

Mom kissed Jamie's cheek. "Your favorite thing to do."

"Uh, Mom, we all got that little quirk from you."

"Okay, you didn't get all your odd habits from me, some are from Dad, like your fondness for scotch." She made a face like she had just bit into a sour lemon. "Yuck."

Kenzie laughed. "We can tell you don't have a drop of Scot in your veins."

Jamie looked at Grace from the reflection in the full-length mirror. "Grace, if you can unlace me, I'll get dressed. We can continue this conversation over two fingers of the good stuff."

Kenzie said, "I'll pour." *It might be three fingers for me.*

∼

26

As the bride-to-be requested, four compact whiskey glasses sat on the counter, each holding a splash of rich amber-colored liquid.

"Are those glasses new?" Mom picked up one and swirled the contents. She wrinkled her nose. "This smells like a peat bog."

Jamie took the glass from her mother. "Aren't they pretty? I found them online." She swirled the scotch in her glass and held it aloft. "Ladies? I'd like to propose a toast." She waited while Mom, Grace and Kenzie lifted their glasses. "To the best sisters and mother a girl could have. Thank you for helping me make the journey to the next phase of my life memorable."

The ladies took a sip. "This is smooth," Kenzie said.

Mom took a tiny sip and set the glass down. Grace set her glass aside and grabbed a tissue to dab her eyes.

Jamie smiled. "Who would have ever thought we'd be planning a wedding?"

Mom held up her hand. "I did."

The sisters' eyes grew round. "You did?" Kenzie said.

"Of course, I did. Despite what the three of you said, I never thought you'd stay single forever. You're wonderful, warm, loving women, and any guy worth his salt would see it and never let you get away."

Kenzie slung her arm around her mother's shoulders. Planting a kiss on her cheek, she chuckled, "Be honest, Mom—you're just hoping for grandkids."

CHAPTER 4

Beep. Kenzie glanced at her phone and saw a text from Grace. *Stop over. Need to talk wedding stuff.*

"It's only been twenty-four hours since we started working on Jamie's big day." Kenzie set the phone on her desk. "I don't know how much help I can be, I never thought I'd be planning my sister's wedding."

Robbie arrived at work seconds later, his broad grin a welcomed distraction. "Are you talking to yourself again?"

"I guess so."

Robbie leaned on the counter and flipped open the training book. "One appointment today."

Kenzie was slamming desk drawers. Robbie looked at her, his eyebrow arched. "What's bugging you?"

Rapping her fingers on the countertop, she said, "I don't want to bore you."

"That's never stopped you before," he teased. "What's up?" He came around the desk and collapsed in a chair.

Flapping her hands in the air, she grumbled, "Jamie and Caleb are getting married in less than a month."

Robbie grinned. "I heard. He asked me to be a groomsman."

"Isn't that just swell?" Her voice was tinged with sarcasm.

He scowled. "Kenz, what's the matter with you. Are you jealous?"

She pushed back from the desk and stretched. "No. It's not that. I'm thrilled for her. But I wish they'd slow down and enjoy being engaged. It's been, what, a couple of weeks?"

"It's not like they're teenagers," he reminded her. "They're adults who've had other relationships and they know this is the person they want to spend their life with; I'm surprised you don't find it romantic."

In a quiet voice she said, "I love my sister and I want her to be happy."

Robbie smacked his palm on the desk and grinned broadly. "Now what do you say we get back to business?"

Slowly nodding, she said, "You're right. You always have a way of putting things in perspective. How do you do it?"

"Lots and lots of practice and patience." He messed up her perfectly spiked hair.

"Hey!" Kenzie held up a hand to protect her head. "Don't mess with the 'do."

Robbie said with a laugh, "I've got things to occupy my time." He sauntered from the room.

"That's good." Kenzie's laughter rippled through the air. She called after him, "It's why I'm paying you."

Kenzie picked up her cell and, with fingers flying over the small keyboard, texted Grace. *I'll bring dinner. Six?*

YES!!!

With no one around to hear her, Kenzie said, "Since

Grace is on wedding detail, maybe I should organize a shower." She flipped open her laptop and started a new Excel sheet. Typing in a list of names was easy, and choosing the food, a snap. She opened the internet browser and typed in a search window, wedding shower themes. She scanned through many ideas and typed, *HOLIDAY SHOWER?*

She composed a hasty message to Grace and Mom, as it was her habit she talked out the email as she typed. "Let's give Jamie a holiday shower. Every guest is assigned a specific holiday."

Kenzie hit *send*. "This might be fun after all."

She jotted down the holidays one might decorate for, adding emphasis to Christmas and Thanksgiving, and assigned those to several guests.

The gym phone rang and she paused to answer it. "Mac's Fitness."

A cheery voice answered her. "Hey, sis."

"Jamie. Are you working today?"

"I'm on my way into the office, but I wanted to tell you Jo said we can have the wedding at the stables." Hesitating, she said, "I know this is short notice, but I was hoping we could all go out there tonight, including Robbie, and take a look around."

"Sure." Kenzie hoped her voice sounded enthusiastic. "I was going to run over to Grace's after work, but we'll meet out there instead."

"Thanks, Kenz. Can you call Grace and let Robbie know too?"

"Not a problem. I'll see you later?"

"Yeah." Jamie gave a small snort. "I'm so excited I can barely focus on work."

Kenzie laughed. "We have a lot to do, so make lists, check things off as we go and above all, relax and enjoy."

"Oh, Kenz," she gushed. "I have to pinch myself this is really happening to me."

"Aren't you glad things didn't work out with Steve?"

"Yeah, I've got the best guy." Jamie said, "You know, it's your turn next."

Kenzie's mouth went dry. "For what?" she croaked.

"To try on the dress. You know Great-Gran said we each needed to do it."

"Um, I don't remember that in the letter…" Her heart hammered in her chest.

"Kenz." Jamie drew out her name with a light warning tone.

Slowly Kenzie said, "I'm listening."

"As your wedding gift to me, will you promise to put the dress on and look in the mirror?"

Kenzie fell silent. She was at a total loss for words. After several moments, she heard Jamie ask, "Are you still there?"

"Yes." She took a ragged breath. The idea of trying on the dress scared her to death. What if no one was in the mirror waiting for her?

Finally, she answered Jamie. "If you promise to stop talking about it, I'll do it. But how long do I have to keep it on?"

"As long as you want." Kenzie could hear soft laughter.

"Then can I give it to Grace?" *Please say I don't have to keep it in my house…* she thought.

"Nope. You have to hang onto it. You'll know when it's time for Grace to take ownership."

Robbie strolled into the lobby and Kenzie crooked her index finger in his direction. "Jamie, I gotta run, but I'll see you at six."

Before she disconnected, she heard Jamie say, "Don't forget: call Grace."

"Bye." Kenzie laid the phone down. "That was the bride-to-be."

"And?" Robbie hovered over her.

"She's asked if we can meet her and Caleb at the stable. Jo agreed they can have the wedding and reception there."

Robbie gave a low whistle. "That sounds awfully romantic, don't you think?"

Playfully, Kenzie threw a pencil at him and Robbie ducked, laughing. "So, are you going with me tonight?" she demanded.

"You won't abandon me out there, will you?"

"Nah, I'll drive you back to town. Besides, I've been driving you around since I got my license."

"You *are* a month older than me," Robbie teased.

"You should respect your elders, young man." Kenzie swallowed a laugh while pretending to look annoyed.

"Yes, ma'am." Robbie gave her a smart aleck salute. The door opening caught his attention. He swiveled around. "Ally, did we have an appointment today?"

Ally was wearing tight leggings and a sports bra under a low-cut tank top. "No, but I thought I'd swing in and book something for tomorrow."

Kenzie narrowed her gaze. "Robbie, if you're booked I can work with Ally."

Ally drawled, "Oh, I'm happy to work around Robbie's schedule. He's such a good trainer, I really don't want to make a switch now." She gave him a warm smile. "We've developed a rapport."

Kenzie feigned indifference. "Whatever."

Robbie looked from one woman to the other. "Ally, let's see what I have free." Giving Ally a couple of options, she chose one and he handed her a card. "Thursday it is."

"I'm already looking forward to it." Beaming, she strolled out of the gym.

After she was out of earshot, Robbie asked, "Why were you brusque? That's not like you."

Kenzie twitched. "She rubs me the wrong way, acting like she owns the place and you."

"We've both had those kind of clients, the ones who develop a little crush on the trainer, and we know how to handle them. We keep to the three Ps: pleasant, polite and, above all, professional."

Kenzie flashed Robbie a smile. "I'm sorry I'm so cranky. I'm not sure what's bugging me…"

He tweaked her nose. "It's cool Kenzie. I'm going to get ready for my next appointment."

"I'm running out to pick something up for lunch. Are you hungry?"

"Sure, get whatever and I'll pay you later."

Robbie left the room and Kenzie propped her elbows on the desk, her chin cupped in the palm of her hand, watching people drifting down the street. Why was she so wigged out over Ally? Robbie had lots of pretty clients in the past, but what was it about this one that drove her nuts.

Kenzie went back to her shower plans, and then stopped to shoot Grace a text. *Change of plans, we're meeting at Jo's. See you there.*

Seconds later, she received a *K.*

Another tone chirped from her laptop. "Now what?"

She tapped a few keys. Mom loved the shower idea and said she'd get addresses for the guests, and when did Kenzie want to hold it.

Kenzie shot back, *Two weeks, and let's have it at your place. More room.*

A string of smiley faces was her response. Kenzie closed the laptop. She picked up a slip of notepaper and jotted down more ideas for the shower.

Satisfied with her progress she said, "I'll run these by Grace tonight." Tucking the note paper in her wallet, Kenzie stood, stretching her arms overhead toward the ceiling. She did this several more times, deep breathing and focusing on stretching a little further each time.

Feeling centered and more relaxed, she glanced at the clock. Plenty of time before she needed to pick up lunch. She grabbed a bottle of vinegar and water to spray down the furniture and moved around the room, saving the front windows for last.

She was wiping it dry when her dad came jogging across the street and burst through the door. "Ah, Kenzie."

She stood on tiptoes and kissed his cheek. "This is a surprise, Dad, you usually don't stop in without calling first. Why didn't you stop over with Mom last night?"

"I thought it was more of a mother-daughter thing. And does a father need a reason?" He averted his eyes and glanced around the room.

She wagged a finger in his direction. "Mom sent you, I can tell just by the way you're avoiding looking at me."

"Not at all. Did you change paint colors?"

Kenzie shook her head. "No. Dad?"

He chuckled. "I confess, your mom did ask me to stop in." He looked at her. "Did you know we didn't wait long between her saying yes and our wedding?"

"I remember you telling us you didn't want to give Mom a chance to change her mind." Kenzie laughed and arched an eyebrow, her lips pursed. "But I don't understand—how does Jamie go from not wanting to get married to falling in love and jumping in with both feet?"

Dad slung his arm around Kenzie's shoulders. He kissed the top of her spikey-haired head. "It's a leap of faith and love, lass." His thick brogue had the words rolling off his tongue.

"So, you're suggesting I stop worrying?"

He nodded. "Aye, I do."

Kenzie wrapped her arms around her dad and laid her head against his broad chest. "You can count on me to be Jamie's right hand for all the wedding prep and festivities."

Hugging her tight, he smiled, "That's my girl."

She looked up at him. "Are you going out to Jo's tonight?"

Dad winked. "I wouldn't miss it."

Robbie came into the lobby. "Hello, James, good to see you. How was Scotland?"

Dad stuck his hand out, giving Robbie's a vigorous shake. "Bittersweet, but it's good to be back in Vermont. Nothing like fall in the Green Mountain State."

"I agree."

"I'm going to run out and pick up lunch—can you cover the desk? Robbie needs a few minutes to get ready for the afternoon."

Dad grinned. "I thought you'd never ask."

Kenzie's foot tap, tap, tapped on the floor. Impatiently she glanced at the clock for the umpteenth time. Robbie was worse than any girl when it came to getting ready to go someplace; too bad he wasn't as speedy as she was.

She pushed the door open to the men's locker room and called out, "If you don't hurry, we're going to be late."

Robbie's voice was muffled. "Kenz! Give a guy a break. I'll be right out."

She let the door slam and dug her phone out of her backpack. She jotted out a quick text to Grace. *Waiting for Robbie, be there soon.*

Kenzie grasped her keys in one hand and glanced at her

watch. She yelled, "I'm going to start the car! Meet me out back!"

Robbie appeared in the hallway as Kenzie rushed past the locker room. Smoothing his hair into place, he said, "What's got you in such a rush?"

She grimaced. "This wedding stuff is overwhelming, so much to do in so little time."

"True but we've got this." His tone was definitely cheery.

"Thank heavens it's not my wedding. I'd be so stressed out with a short engagement."

Robbie laid a hand on her arm and took a step closer. "Are you saying you're thinking of changing your mind?"

"About getting married?" With a shake of her head, she said, "It's not something I need to think about today." She clicked the car door locks as they crossed the parking lot. "Son of a…" She swore and pointed to the back tire. "It's flat."

"Pop the back and I'll change it."

Frustrated, she groaned. "We don't have time."

"Come on, we'll take the truck." He pulled the keys from his jeans pocket. "Later I'll drop you at home then pick you up in the morning, and I'll change the tire then."

"I don't really have much of a choice." She looked at him sideways. "You're always looking out for me."

"I always will."

Kenzie climbed into the truck and buckled up. Looking out the window, her mind wandered. She was confused; her feelings toward Robbie weren't as straightforward as they had been. *Why does my stomach flip when he gives me that quirky smile or when he touches my arm? Stress—that explained it.*

$\approx$

The drive to Racing Brook Stables was over all too quick. After being cooped up all day in the gym, driving down a country road gave her time to look at the trees changing colors. Robbie parked, and she noticed several familiar cars. "We need to hurry."

He pointed to an ATV. "I can get us to the upper pasture in a jiff."

Kenzie settled on the seat next to Robbie. The engine roared to life. He gunned it as the wind teased Kenzie's short locks. Bouncing on the seat, she smirked. "Do you need to hit every bump?"

"It's half the fun." He grinned and hit the brakes, screeching to a halt. Kenzie slid forward in the seat, and he put his arm out to stop her and announced gleefully, "We're here."

She glared at him. "Shush, everyone is staring at us."

With a wink, he said, "We're making a grand entrance."

Kenzie gave a half-hearted wave to her family. "Hey."

Jamie sauntered over. "Kenzie, is everything okay? It's not like you to be late."

"Nothing major, I had a flat tire."

She breathed a sigh of relief. "I'm glad you're here safe and sound."

Kenzie linked arms with Jamie. "Let's see what we need to do to get this place ready for your wedding." She flashed everyone a huge smile as she and Jamie strolled over, with Robbie falling into step next to them.

Grace said, "Hey, Kenz. You didn't miss much. So far we've talked about two rows of chairs on either side of the aisle, number to be determined based on the guest list. Jo found an arbor in the shed, which George is going to repaint. We'll have pots of flowers on either side and over here"—she walked across a stretch of grass—"the pastor will stand here, and to the left, the guitarist."

"Robbie, that's sweet of your dad to paint it." Jamie wiped away happy tears. "Everything sounds perfect, Gracie."

She beamed. "That's just the beginning. Next, we should go down to the barn and decide how to set up tables for the reception."

"Wait." Kenzie spun around. "I hate to be a wet blanket, but what happens if it rains?"

"I'm glad you asked, my pessimistic sister. Jamie and I talked, and if it rains we'll have umbrellas to hand out to all the guests."

"Please tell me you're kidding. I don't think anyone wants to stand in a cold October rain. We'll be popsicles before the *I do's*."

Robbie struggled to keep a straight face. "Um, Kenz, they're teasing. We'll have an area in the barn for the ceremony if needed. Let's send good vibes for a clear, star-filled autumn night, shall we?"

Kenzie kicked the ground. "I should have realized Grace was attempting to be funny at my expense."

"Everyone, we'll meet you at the barn," Robbie poked her arm and grinned. "They do it because you always take the bait." He slung an arm over her shoulders. "I have something I want to show you."

She kept pace with Robbie's long stride. "What do you have up your sleeve?"

He flipped her a grin. "You'll see."

Bouncing along on the ATV as they approached the barn, Kenzie sulked.

"Penny for your thoughts?" Robbie asked.

Frowning she said, "Don't you ever get tired of old-fashioned sayings?"

"Nah, but you can blame Mom. They were her thing and I guess since she's gone I like to spout them off occasionally." Giving Kenzie a sidelong glance, he continued, "I miss her."

"Yeah, me too. I still think she's going to step out the back door, wipe her hands on a towel and let me know what's cooking, enticing me to stay for dinner." With a faraway look she said, "She tried to teach me to sew one summer, remember?"

Robbie laughed. "Clearly it was not a good fit; if I remember correctly, your skirt ended up in the quilt pile."

Kenzie sighed. "How's your dad?"

"He's keeping busy helping Jo. In fact, look." He pointed toward a paddock. "There he is now."

Her eyebrow arched. "He's in motion every time I see him."

"I think that's what makes him the happiest, working with the animals and spending time with Jo, and of course riding around on the tractor."

"And you." Kenzie poked his shoulder and gave him a sideways glance.

He gazed up toward the sky. "You know we've been at odds for most of my life. I wasn't cut out to be a farmer and that was a huge disappointment to him."

Kenzie wanted to wrap her arms around him and chase away the sadness she heard in his voice. "That's not true. Your dad loves you and he's proud of you."

"I'm not cut out to farm."

"Well, that is definitely not true. You can do anything you set your mind to, but Jo's taking care of things here while you follow your passion."

Robbie snorted. "If you say so."

Kenzie's head snapped in his direction, her eyes searching his. "Are you unhappy at the gym?"

"No, it's just I don't know if it's enough..." His voice trailed off.

"What are you talking about?" A shiver ran down her spine. "Are you looking for a career change?"

"Nah, don't worry, I wouldn't leave you high and dry."

"But…" Her stomach went rock hard.

"Here we are." Robbie cut the engine and avoided looking in her eyes. "Are you coming?"

Kenzie sat dumfounded; *was he really thinking about leaving and if he wasn't, why did he bring it up?* Robbie walked toward the shed door. *We will be chatting later.*

"Wait for me." She hurried after him.

He held open the door, letting Kenzie step inside ahead of him.

"It's dark in here." A tremor ran through her voice. She hated pitch-dark spaces. She put her hands out in front of her so she didn't stumble into something nasty like a spider web; that would be even worse.

"Wait for it." Robbie's voice held a catch and was close to her ear. He flipped a switch and light filled the room.

"Oh wow, Robbie you've outdone yourself." Kenzie let out a low whistle. Slowly she crossed the space. "Did you do this for Jamie?"

He nodded and haltingly said, "My mother rode in this buggy to marry Dad. With Jamie and Caleb getting married here, it only seems fitting. Jo and I don't plan on getting married anytime soon, so someone should put it to good use."

Kenzie hugged Robbie. "There is a lucky girl out there for you."

Robbie rested his chin on her head, then extracted himself from her embrace. He ran his hand over the side rail. Kenzie wondered what it would feel like to have a man's hand caress her with similar care and tenderness.

Robbie asked, "Do you think Jamie will like it?"

Snapping back to the present, she breathed, "She's

gonna love it. When do you plan on showing her and Caleb?"

"We should keep it a surprise from Caleb. Kind of like the dress being a secret."

"I like how you think." She tilted her head back and gazed into his eyes. "You've got quite the romantic streak, Robbie Burns."

"Guilty as charged. Now, if you can keep Caleb occupied, I'll whisk Jamie out here and unveil the surprise."

"Do us both a favor—have a tissue on hand because the water works..." She blinked away a tear. "Heck, you've got me choked up."

Kenzie and Robbie hopped back on the ATV and zipped over to the barn. She stepped through the large double doors and gasped. The interior was flooded with a harsh glare. Her heart sank. "Oh, we've got work to do in order to transform this into a wedding venue."

The family gathered and everyone started talking at once. The noise was overwhelming.

Jamie scrambled onto a bale of hay. A shrill whistle cut the air. Silence. In a clear, authoritative voice, she ran down a list of to-dos and motioned for Caleb to come closer. "Sweetheart, you've been pretty quiet—what do you think?"

"The only thing I need is great music and a smooth floor. I want to dance with my bride at our wedding." Grasping her around her waist, he twirled her down to the floor. "Everything else is just window dressing."

Kenzie noticed Jamie's eyes danced and her cheeks flushed. Deep down, Kenzie felt an unexpected pang of longing. *What would it feel like to have a man hold me and look at me like that?*

To the casual observer, Kenzie wouldn't have seemed to be studying the happy couple, but Robbie winked at her.

She mouthed *What?* in his direction.

He held up his hands. She pointed to Jamie and jerked her thumb toward the door. Robbie took the hint and strolled over to the bride-to-be. "Hey, I need your help for a couple of minutes?"

Caleb fell into step next to them, but Kenzie slipped her arm through the crook of his. "Can you settle a disagreement between me and Grace?"

Robbie ushered Jamie out the door as Caleb was effectively redirected.

Robbie and Jamie walked toward the shed. "I want to show you something."

"I gathered that..." Jamie laughed. "You're being awfully mysterious."

He pulled open the wooden double doors and stepped aside.

"Robbie!" Jamie rushed forward running her hand along the smooth black rails and then rested them on the plush velvet cushions. "Where did you get the carriage?"

"Dad gave it to Mom on their wedding day. Jo and I talked it over and we'd like for you to use it."

Her eyes widened, "Oh, Robbie. That's too much. This is a family thing."

"Jamie, we've known you our entire lives, and we're like family. Jo will drive the carriage with you and the girls up the hill and then return you and Caleb, as husband and wife, to the reception." He scuffed the hard ground and looked over her head. "If you'd like to use it, that is."

Jamie squealed, threw her arms around Robbie's neck and kissed his cheek. "You know, there's another girl who'd look great in this carriage."

He took a step back and felt heat flush his cheeks. "I…
I'm not sure what you're talking about," he stammered.

Jamie grew serious and cupped his face. "I'll let it go,
for now, but don't wait too long before letting Kenzie know
how you feel."

He rubbed his hand over his chin and watched Jamie
seemingly float back to the barn. *How the heck does she know
how I feel? Has everyone figured it out except Kenzie?*

CHAPTER 5

The shower was upon them and Grace was waiting when Kenzie pulled into the parking lot of her apartment building. She looked fantastic in a deep purple floral skirt and matching pale lavender sweater set. Kenzie laughed to herself. She had picked out a similar outfit in pale gray.

Opening the car door, Grace said, "Are you ready to be a hostess with the most-est?"

Kenzie winked. "Co-hostess."

"Who's picking up Jamie?" Grace buckled herself in.

Kenzie drove the two miles to their parents' place. "Caleb's dropping her off in about a half hour."

"Good. When he picks her up, he can haul the loot back to her place." Grace grinned. "Who would have thought just a few months ago that we'd be throwing a bridal luncheon for our big sister?"

Kenzie's hands clutched the steering wheel. "Better Jamie than us, right?"

Grace looked out the window. "Well..."

"Are you seriously starting to think about a trip down

44

the matrimonial aisle?"

Wistfully Grace said, "Maybe. Haven't you ever wondered what it would feel like"—she laid her hand over her heart—"to have someone who loves you completely?"

"Sure. I guess." Kenzie chewed her bottom lip. *It would be amazing to have someone so head over heels for me too.*

Slowing, she pulled up the long, winding driveway to her parents' home. Grace said, "Maybe you should really think about it." Kenzie turned off the car. Grace's hand lingered on the door handle. "I, for one, am giving it a great deal of thought."

Grace left Kenzie sitting behind the wheel. "Jeez, she didn't even give me a chance to say I agreed to put Gran's enchanted dress on." She snapped down the visor and checked her makeup. Closing the car door, she stopped to smooth her skirt before grabbing bags from the backseat. She noticed Robbie's truck coming up the drive.

"Hey, Kenz." Robbie jogged over, his smile filling his eyes as he took a bag from her.

A grin tugged the corners of her mouth. "This is a nice surprise. What are you doing here?"

"Jo asked me to deliver her gift—it's a tree. She knows it doesn't go with the theme, but she wanted to give something that would endure."

"That's sweet and unique."

Robbie's eyes ran from her toes to her face. "You look beautiful."

She felt a flush of heat rush to her cheeks. "Thanks, just something I threw on."

Smiling, he said, "I like your hair." He reached out and touched a stray lock. "You should do you hair like this more often."

Surprised by the compliment, Kenzie patted the soft waves which replaced her usual spikey do. "I've let it grow out a bit, but sadly this would never hold up in spin class."

"Too bad." He touched his brow in a mock salute and grinned. "I'll see you later."

"Robbie?"

He stopped mid-step and turned. "Yeah, Kenz?"

She pointed to the bag.

"I've got it."

They continued toward the door. She took a deep breath to calm the unexpected flutter of butterflies.

"After the wedding, let's go hiking." A wave of shyness blanketed her. "We talked about it but didn't firm it up yet."

He did a double take. "You're closing down the gym?"

"I'm hoping to hire someone, but if I don't, we deserve a break."

A slow smile went from his lips to his eyes. "I'd really like that."

Relieved she was able to ask him, she said, "We'll finalize plans on Tuesday."

Robbie tapped his watch. "You'd better hurry up. The bride will be here soon."

Breaking the moment, she said, "Oh, shoot." She ran up the walkway despite the three-inch heels strapped to her feet, certain he was watching her every step.

Standing at the sink Kenzie ate another piece of cake. If she was any judge the shower was a huge success. Jamie received lovely gifts and was overwhelmed when Mom gave her Gran's antique cameo necklace. It would be the perfect accent to the dress.

Grace strolled into the kitchen. "Are you ready to go yet? I'm whipped."

Kenzie put the plate and fork in the sink and wiped her hands on a towel. "Let's say good bye to Mom and head out."

"Sounds good." Her cell phone rang. "Grace, give me a minute."

Several times in the hours after seeing her, Robbie was kicking himself. He'd had Kenzie's attention—why hadn't he asked her if she wanted to go riding after the shower? He checked the time and figured he could leave a message. She answered on the third ring.

"Hey, Kenz, it's me, Robbie."

"Hey there." He could hear the smile in her voice.

He hesitated. "Any chance you want to go for a horseback ride? Unless you have to do something with your sisters." He paced around his living room.

"How did you guess I'd be keyed up?" Her voice sounded like warm honey. Sweet and leaving this man wanting more.

He said lightly, "Just lucky?"

"Do you want to swing by and pick me up before you head out to the stables?"

Keeping his voice steady he asked, "How much time do you need to change clothes?"

"Thirty minutes?"

He fist pumped the air. "Sure, it's a date."

Kenzie said, "I'll be ready."

He disconnected and let out a, "YES!"

Keep it cool dude, it's just a trail ride. But it's with Kenzie.

Whistling, he went to change into boots and jeans.

~

Robbie pulled up in front of Kenzie's condo at the exact moment she skipped down the steps looking cute in her cowboy boots and tight-fitting jeans with a long-sleeve tee. Her hair was a short jumble of waves and her blue eyes sparkled like the late summer sky.

She hopped into the truck and fastened her seatbelt. Leaning back, she said, "This was a fantastic idea and long overdue."

"You're right." Dropping the truck in drive he asked, "How was the shower?"

"Jamie cried a bunch of times. Mom was happy— most of the food was eaten and there wasn't a drop of punch left."

He glanced sideways. "Did Jamie like the tree?"

"She loved it, and of course she bawled." Kenzie looked at him. "You didn't tell me about your parents. I thought it was really sweet."

"Yeah, my parents planted a tree just a few days after they tied the knot."

She asked, "Do you think if you ever got married you would do the same?"

"Plant a tree?" He slowed the truck and turned into the stable driveway. He pointed to a large maple. "See that tree right there?"

She put her hand over her eyes and squinted into the late day sun. "Yes."

"That's their tree. Mom said when the shovel sank into the earth, she felt the connection to my dad and the family farm go to her very core."

Kenzie gave a heartfelt sigh. "And it still stands as a testament to their love for future generations."

He grinned. "Kenzie MacLellan, *you are* becoming a romantic!"

Her face lit up. "I'm looking at things a little differently these days."

His heart quickened. "Anyone special come to mind?"

With a shake of her head, she said. "One step at a time, Burns."

Easing his foot off the brake, he drove toward the paddock. Jo peeked out from the barn and gave a wave. Kenzie raised her arm too. "She got home from the shower really fast."

"As much as she loves to go into town, the horses are her life."

Walking side by side, their arms brushed. His blood hummed. *Maybe this wasn't the best idea. All I want to do is pull her into my arms.*

"Robbie?"

His gaze whipped to hers. "Sorry. What did you say?"

"I asked who you're riding today."

"Oh, Pirate."

"Darn." Her lower lip jutted out in a tiny pout. "I was going to claim him as mine. He's such a challenge."

Chuckling, Robbie said, "You're two of a kind. Do you remember when Dad brought him home and you announced he was your favorite?"

She laughed. "What I remember is I hopped up and trotted around bareback until he decided I wasn't *his* favorite and tossed me to the ground."

He tweaked her nose. "Dad told you to wait until he got used to you."

She placed her hand on his shoulder and joked, "Are you insinuating I'm stubborn?"

After waiting a half beat, he grinned. "That's exactly

what I'm saying." The sound of her laughter was music to his ears.

The door to the barn stood open. Robbie held his finger to his lips, pointed to his ear and then toward the door. They could hear Jo talking to the horses. Robbie smiled and placed a hand over his heart. It proved his point that this farm was his sister's life.

"Hey, Jo," Kenzie called out as they stepped inside. "How's it going?"

"All good here. Are you guys ready to head out?"

Robbie pulled two bridles off the peg. "We're going to take Pirate and Snowflake out."

"I thought as much." She held out her hand to take a bridle. "I'll help you saddle up."

Kenzie heaved her favorite saddle off the stand and placed it over the blanket on Pirate's back.

Taken aback Jo asked, "Kenzie, you're riding Pirate today?"

She nodded and winked at Jo. "Robbie's going to take Snowflake."

"Really." Jo smirked. "Interesting choice."

"It's not the name of the beast but the heart inside." Robbie patted the horse's neck and she nickered softly under his touch. A look crossed Kenzie's face that he couldn't read. "Everything okay?"

She took the reins and led Pirate to the door. "Burns, if you don't get moving, we'll lose the light and be taking a night ride."

Kenzie and Pirate ambled out the barn doors. Jo lightly punched his shoulder. "You heard the lady, get a move on."

Robbie tugged at Snowflake's reins. "Come on, girl, we've got a couple of spunky ones to keep up with."

CHAPTER 6

Kenzie woke to sounds of kitchen cabinet doors slamming. She groaned and glanced at the clock —glowing green numbers indicated it was not quite six.

More annoyed than afraid, Kenzie slipped her arms into her soft chenille robe, dropping her cell phone in the pocket. Cautiously, she tiptoed to the doorway. "Jamie! What are you doing?"

Her sister turned, eyes rimmed red. Her voice cracked. "I can't find the sugar."

"I'll get it." Kenzie glanced at the coffeepot—dark rich liquid dripped into the carafe and the carton of cream was sitting on the counter. Out of Jamie's line of sight Kenzie shot a quick text to Grace: *Jamie's here!!!*

On my way… was the response.

Kenzie took the sugar bowl from the cabinet and handed it to Jamie. Soft hiccupping followed by a snuffle broke the silence. Kenzie understood; she, Grace, and Jamie took comfort in each other's presence. There would be time for an explanation once a mug was in her hands.

Kenzie poured coffee and added a dash of cream and a spoonful of sugar to a mug, and just cream to another. She waited until Jamie made eye contact, and then handed her the coffee. Kenzie grasped the back of the wooden chair and scraped it over the ceramic tile, then sat down and took a sip. Waiting.

Her patience was rewarded. "Sorry I woke you." Jamie stared at her mug.

Kenzie waved her hand. "It's fine. I'm glad you remembered your key and didn't call first."

"I just wanted to hide, at least for a little while, before I call Caleb."

Kenzie cocked an eyebrow. "You'll see him later, and isn't it bad luck to talk to the groom before the wedding?"

Tears slipped down Jamie's cheeks. "That's just it. There isn't going to be a wedding." She abruptly set the mug down, coffee sloshing over the rim. She jumped up to grab a paper towel and blotted up the mess.

Kenzie remained quiet until Jamie sat back down. "Did something happen?"

Kenzie could tell Jamie was antsy when she hopped up and threw the paper towel away. "We're not the marrying kind of girls."

Softly Kenzie pointed to the chair, "Sit down. You're hopping around like you're walking on hot sand."

Jamie pulled her feet up on the chair and tugged the oversized T-shirt over her knees. She hiccupped. Her perfectly pink painted toes peeked out from the hem. "Your floors are cold," she said, pointing out the obvious.

"Do you want a pair of socks?"

Ignoring Kenzie's question, she cried, "Have you ever been in love? Heart-stopping love? I haven't."

Kenzie shook her head while Robbie's smiling face popped into her head. Quickly dismissing it, she said, "I've never been lucky enough to find a man who I could love like that."

Jamie's voice trembled. "How do I know this isn't just a passing phase?"

"You've never felt about anyone the way you feel about Caleb, and he's totally in love with you. To be honest, I envy you."

A gleam shone in Jamie's clear blue eyes. "I know what you're doing."

A smile twitched Kenzie's lips. "You do?" she asked innocently.

The front door banged and footsteps hurried toward the kitchen. Grace burst in. "Morning."

Jamie smirked. "You called in the cavalry?"

"Just a text, and it was in case I couldn't make you see that you have an old-fashioned case of cold feet."

Grace said, "What'd I miss?"

"Pour yourself coffee and bring the pot. It's going to be a long day. Our sister's been having an anxiety attack or something and I could use a refill."

Grace slid into a vacant chair and took her first sip. "Yummy." She set the mug on a napkin and said, "Let me guess. Jamie let herself in and made coffee, just loud enough to wake you up." She looked at the bride-to-be. "Have you been up all night fretting?"

Jamie hiccupped. "Maybe."

Grace snorted. "And then Kenz did the whole logical thing."

"Maybe." Jamie looked at her toes, avoiding their eyes.

"And now that I'm here, you can see how silly you're being and there *will* be a wedding tonight as planned."

"Gracie, what if…"

Grace held up her hand. "Stop right there." She grasped Jamie's hand. "Do you love Caleb?"

Jamie bobbed her head. "I love him more than I thought I could ever love anyone."

"And do you believe, with all your heart, that he loves you?"

Her smile was like a brilliant ray of sunshine. "I know he does."

With a curt nod Grace said, "Then the only question I have left is—Kenz, do you have cucumbers in the fridge? Let's pamper ourselves."

"Before we do that, let's start with wet teabags." Kenzie pointed to the living room, thankful it hadn't taken Grace long to get Jamie to calm down. "Go relax on the couch, and Grace, put on some soothing music. Make sure she doesn't take up all the room on the sofa. We're going to join her."

Grace flopped on the kitchen chair. "Jamie's going to take a quick shower. But I'm curious. Do you think if this was our wedding day we'd have gone off the deep end too?"

"I don't know. Jamie's always been a control freak, and falling in love is totally outside of her plan. Heck, it's outside all our plans." Kenzie handed Grace a banana. "And then Great-Gran's wedding dress arrived, and she met Steve, who led her to Caleb. It was fate."

Grace perched on a stool. "You believe in the magic!"

"Don't you think it was because of the dress that Jamie met Caleb?"

Grace laid the peel aside and studied Kenzie. Her voice was wistful. "You know me, I love the idea that magic plays a role in our lives, but I think it's more than that. It's still up to us to see what's possible. Don't you agree?"

"I don't know what to think." Kenzie chomped on her

banana. She threw the peel in the garbage and said nonchalantly, "I promised Jamie I'd put the dress on."

Grace's mouth dropped open, her eyes wide. "Is she pushing you?"

"No. It's fine." Kenzie wiped down the counter with a sponge, anxious to change the subject, and asked, "Can you go check on the bride again?"

"Sure." Grace wandered down the hallway.

Alone with her thoughts Kenzie leaned against the counter. *Maybe the dress has limited magic and if I try it on, it won't work. That'd just be my luck.* Her thoughts drifted to Robbie. *He is certainly looking handsome lately. I wonder if he'd let me borrow him for the wedding.*

She shot off a text: *Hey, want to be my date today?*

In moments the answer came back: *Sure.*

Staring at the screen her pulse quickened, she was taken aback at the intensity of her response to a single word.

Grinning from ear to ear, she opened the fridge and pulled out a mini bottle of champagne and orange juice. She selected three crystal-cut fluted glasses from the cabinet. Popping the cork, she filled the glasses half full and added a splash of juice. She set them on a tray and carried it into the living room. She tidied up the room while waiting for her sisters.

Jamie and Grace came in. Jamie's hair was pulled up in a messy bun to await the hairdresser. They were reclining on the couch, soft, soothing music played in the background. Jamie smiled. "Mimosas? You think of everything."

"Nothing but the best for my sisters." Jamie took a glass and handed one to Grace. Kenzie set the tray aside and held up her glass. "I'd like to make a toast."

Jamie linked arms with Kenzie and laughed, "You're

always making toasts." They held their glasses high, grinning like cats that got into the cream.

"Although I never dreamed this day would come, I'm glad you found Caleb. He's a good man who's lucky and smart enough to have fallen in love with a MacLellan. Jamie, live the best life possible."

Jamie laid a hand over her heart, her eyes misty. "Don't make me cry."

"Kenz…" Grace jerked her head toward Jamie. "There's not enough home remedies to fix her eyes if you really get the water works flowing."

"All right, I'll save the rest of my speech for tonight." Kenzie clinked her glass with her sisters and said, "To Jamie and Caleb."

The girls took a sip, and Jamie grinned. "Kenz, you do have a way with champagne."

Kenzie glanced out the window—the sun was low in the sky and it was almost time for the wedding to begin. Her gaze lingered on the buggy waiting to take the girls to the ceremony site. She looked at the clock and out the window again. The hillside was aglow with torches.

Impatient to get Jamie going, she called up the stairs, "Are you dressed? It's time to go. Jo's waiting."

Beaming, Jamie seemed to float down the stairs. She wore three-inch heels as if they were flip-flops. She paused in the hallway and tugged on the top of her long, ivory gloves. Her chestnut hair was artfully arranged with tendrils cascading over the ribbon and eyelet holes on the back of her wedding dress.

Awestruck, Kenzie breathed, "You're gorgeous."

Grace sniffed and pulled a hanky from the belt of her

sapphire-colored gown. "Oh, Jamie," she sighed, overcome with happiness. Dabbing her eyes, she requested, "Twirl."

Jamie giggled like a school girl. Swishing the skirt from side to side, she said, "Do I really look okay?"

Kenzie said "Caleb's jaw's gonna hit the floor when you walk down that aisle." *The dress will never look this good on me. It's as if it was made for Jamie or maybe Grace.*

Jamie nervously smoothed her hands over the skirt. "I feel like a princess."

Kenzie and Grace wrapped their arms around her. Kenzie whispered with a catch in her voice, "You look like one."

Jamie glanced toward the door. "Where's Dad?"

Kenzie gave her a reassuring smile. "Robbie took Mom and Dad up a few minutes ago. They thought we'd like a minute together."

Grace picked up their bouquets from the sideboard and turned the doorknob. "Ready?"

Jamie took one final look in the mirror. Her reflection made Kenzie think, *So, that's what true love looks like.*

Grace climbed into the carriage and held out her hand, carefully helping Jamie step up. Kenzie took the seat next to Jamie without crushing her dress. Grace handed them their bouquets.

From the driver's seat, Jo spoke into the walkie-talkie. "Robbie, we're leaving now." With a flick of the reins, the horses moved at a slow, steady pace.

Jamie leaned forward. "Don't go too fast, Jo. I want to savor every moment."

Jo flashed her a grin. "I'm not taking a chance messing up your hair, and in case you forgot," she teased, "they always wait for the bride."

The sisters rode in silence, hands clasped tight, as the sun hovered on the horizon. These were the last moments it was just the three of them. Kenzie knew her sisters were feeling the same joy as she did as they made the short buggy ride. The tree line was a riot of fall colors ranging from bright yellows to fiery reds into a deep shade of purple. Stars were tiny pinpricks in the sky.

The buggy slowed to a stop. Jamie strained to catch a glimpse of Caleb.

"Hey, if you can see him, he can see you," Kenzie murmured. "Don't go spoiling the first look."

Jamie squeezed Grace's hand. "Did you remind the photographer to get the shot of Caleb the moment he sees me?"

"I've taken care of everything. Oh, look." Grace pointed. "Here comes Dad. Doesn't he look handsome?"

The girls watched their father, head held high, his kilt swishing around his knees. He was sporting a traditional black-tie look complete with kilt hose and black dress shoes.

"Ah, my beautiful daughters." He helped Kenzie and Grace from the buggy. "My darling Jamie, you're a vision." A catch could be heard in his voice, his brogue thick with happy tears. He extended his hand to the bride. "Are you ready to become a Sullivan?"

In a light brogue she responded with a smile, "Aye, Dad. But I will always be a MacLellan." Jamie glanced to where the guests were seated. "Where's Mom?"

"Your future husband escorted her down the aisle."

Jamie's face shone with happiness. Kenzie's heart flipped. *This is it, all our lives change.*

She touched Jamie's arm. "I'm going to have the guitarist start to play.

Jamie slipped her hand through the crook of her father's arm. Standing on tiptoe, she bussed his cheek. "Now I'm ready."

Grace sashayed down the flower-strewn aisle. She took her place across from Caleb, who was focused on the aisle.

Kenzie's dress brushed the floor and caressed her legs as she took her first step in the simply tailored gown. Her eyes were fixated on Robbie, standing tall and devilishly handsome next to Steve. His eyes smoldered and locked with hers. Kenzie felt an unfamiliar but thrilling sensation zing through her. She looked away and then back as his lips curved into a slow, seductive smile. Her heart jolted and blood warmed.

As the tempo of the music changed, Kenzie took her place next to Grace. She turned to watch Jamie glide arm in arm with Dad. Then her head swiveled. She wanted to see the exact moment when Caleb saw his bride.

Kenzie let go of the breath she hadn't realized she was holding. Caleb's face radiated pure bliss. *That's love that will last a lifetime.*

A shimmer to the left of the pastor caught Kenzie's attention and she did a double take. *Gran?* She stared as the filmy image of Gran glowed briefly, smiled in her direction, and faded away. A warm glow spread through Kenzie. She knew Gran was with them on this very special day.

The ceremony was brief, and before the final pronouncement of man and wife, Jamie turned to Kenzie, who handed both bouquets to Grace. Mom handed her a braided cord, a mixture of the MacLellan and Sullivan plaids.

Kenzie took her place in front of the pastor. Grace had laid the bouquets aside and joined her. "The hand-fasting ceremony is traditionally done by the pastor. However, I ask your indulgence as my sister Grace and I handle this part of the ceremony."

In a clear voice, Kenzie blinked back tears and said, "Jamie, Caleb, please join hands."

They did, and turned to face Kenzie and Grace.

Kenzie looked at Grace, who was beaming and nodding. Kenzie continued, "Hand-fasting is a Celtic tradition. As two families become one, the happy couple wanted to combine our Scottish and Caleb's Irish heritage.

Kenzie and Grace placed their hands on the couple's. In unison they proclaimed, "Because love is a light to guide you and love is a blanket to warm you and love is a wonder to cherish and hold forever dear, with this symbolic entwining of your hands, we ask that you forever pledge your life to the other."

Caleb tenderly kissed Jamie's lips. He spoke just loud enough for the MacLellan sisters to hear him. "Does this mean I need to start wearing a kilt?"

Jamie threw her head back and her laughter rang out. "It's open for negotiation."

The pastor stepped between the sisters and said, "To conclude our ceremony, I would like to introduce, for the first time, Caleb and Jamie Sullivan."

Amidst cheers and clapping, the bride and groom sealed their love with a smoldering kiss.

The newly married couple sailed up the aisle as flower petals rained down on them. Caleb helped Jamie into the buggy for a ride back to the reception.

Robbie's gaze slid from her eyes to her toes with a deep *hmm* of approval. He took Kenzie's elbow and escorted her down the aisle. For her ears alone he said, "You look amazing."

Her heart fluttered in her chest and she looked into his eyes. "You clean up pretty good yourself." She grinned. "I'd kill for a pair of flats, though."

Her heel caught in the hem of her dress as she began to tumble. Robbie slid his arm around her waist. His grip on her elbow tightened. "Don't worry. I've got you."

Her breathing hitched. "Thanks." She looked at him, unsure why she felt a touch nervous. What was it about today that had her feeling all jumpy inside?

He helped her into the ATV and jogged to the other side. "I'll get you down below and come back up for the others."

She glanced over her shoulder. "We could squeeze in a few more for this trip."

The ATV roared to life and Robbie zipped down the lane, taking care to avoid the ruts. "I wanted a few minutes alone with you. It's going to be hectic for the next hour or so until your duties are complete."

She leaned against him, his body warming her, and she caressed his hand. "Look."

Robbie slowed the vehicle to a stop. His eyes followed the length of her arm past her fingertips. "A harvest moon."

"It's huge." Her voice was awestruck. "It's late this year." Kenzie turned in her seat. "Do you think it's a good omen for Jamie and Caleb?"

"I've read the Celts consider the full moon to be a blessing. So, it's appropriate the harvest moon appears tonight."

Kenzie shivered and Robbie put his arm around her, pulling her close. "Let's get you down to the barn before you freeze to death. What made you choose a sleeveless dress?"

She could smell his cologne. Musky and oh so appealing. "When I picked it out it was for looks and dancing. I conveniently forgot about being outside in October."

Robbie pulled as close to the door as possible. "I tell you what, when I get back I'll buy you a drink and we can hit the dance floor to get your blood moving."

With a playful poke in his ribs she said, "There will be

no dancing until the bride and groom grace the floor—tradition, you know."

"Right." Robbie hopped off and lightly held her hand as he escorted her to the door. "After you."

"What's gotten into you tonight?" She stepped over the threshold and looked over her shoulder. "The compliments and holding doors."

He laughed and gave her a deep bow, releasing her hand. With mischief in his voice, he said, "Can't your date use his best manners once in a while? It's a special occasion and the night is full of possibilities."

A shiver raced down her back and she could still feel his touch on her bare skin. With a toss of her head, Kenzie said, "You should go back and I'll get the party started."

The door closed tightly behind her and Kenzie slowly turned taking in every detail. *It doesn't look or feel like a barn tonight.* Ivory semi-translucent panels of fabric were draped from the beams. Fairy lights trailed alongside each panel and gave a soft glow to the tables below. Intimate tables for six were set with a table for two in the center of the room.

The flowers were exquisite. She was surprised to see bluebells in the center of each vase surrounded by white lilies with a touch of green. With a shake of her head, she said, "Where on earth did she find bluebells at this time of year? They're out of season."

Grace came up behind her. "Doesn't it look beautiful?"

"It's unbelievable. The meticulous attention to detail, right down to the flowers."

She slipped her arm through Kenzie's, hugging it tight. "You know Jamie—when there's something she wants, she gets it. Hence the bluebells."

Kenzie softly laughed. "It's absolutely perfect."

Guests drifted in. The guitarist took his spot with the

other band members and soft music wafted through the room.

"Look." Grace pointed to their parents. "Mom and Dad are here." Excitement filled her voice. "Are you ready for your big moment?"

Kenzie said, "Wait!" She latched onto Grace's arm. "I've prepared the toast, but aren't we doing it together?"

In a shaky voice, Grace said, "Kenz, can you do it? I hate speaking in front of large crowds."

Hesitantly she said, "Okay then. But..." The last thing she wanted to do was add any stress to the evening. Relief washed over Grace's face and Kenzie was happy to help out her sister.

Grace announced, "I'm going to watch for the happy couple, and you can take care of the maid of honor duties for us."

Kenzie teased, "You're saying I have to do the hard work and make sure everyone has fun."

"You are the older sister, so by default it's you." Grace flashed a grin and hurried to the door before Kenzie could protest. Calling over her shoulder, she said, "I'll give you a high sign so you can cue the band when the bride and groom step from the carriage."

Kenzie casually strolled to the bar and asked for a glass of white wine, then mingled her way across the room to the band. She kept one eye on Grace. When she raised her bouquet above her head, Kenzie nodded to the band. At just the right moment, Jamie and Caleb glided into the barn and twirled onto the parquet floor, installed for the sole purpose of dancing.

Shocked with an intense stab of envy, Kenzie knew she wanted to find love. Watching Jamie sway to the music with Caleb, making their way across the room, she finally understood what Jamie tried to tell her. She wouldn't have to give up her independence to fall in love and be loved in return.

She grabbed a bottle of pink champagne and made a beeline to the new Mr. and Mrs. Sullivan. After filling their glasses, she set the bottle down on the table. Jamie picked up the glass, handed one to Caleb.

Kenzie beckoned Steve to join them. He crossed the short space and stood behind Jamie and Caleb. Kenzie whispered, "The best man usually goes first."

Steve cleared his throat and in a booming voice said, "Hello, everyone." The din in the room fell quiet. "On behalf of the Sullivans, I'd like to welcome you to my brother's wedding. And for those of you who don't know, I take full credit for introducing these two."

Steve placed his hand on Caleb's shoulder. "Jamie MacLellan is a rare combination of grace, strength, intelligence and beauty." Heads bobbing rippled across the room. "I know without a doubt that today she has married the best guy I know, my brother Caleb." He raised his glass high. "Please join me in toasting Caleb and the newest addition to the Sullivan family, his bride, Jamie." He took a sip of champagne. "To love, laughter and happily ever after."

Glasses clinked as Jamie and Caleb leaned in to kiss.

Kenzie took a deep breath to steady her nerves and turned to face the guests. "Welcome, everyone." She smiled, wishing the butterflies would take a hike. "On behalf of the MacLellan family, I'd like to welcome you tonight and thank you for being a part of this very special day."

She beamed at Jamie and Caleb. "Grace and I are thrilled to be a part of your wedding." She pointed at Caleb. "Just for the record, when you married Jamie, you got Grace and me as a bonus." Laughter bounced around the room. "Anyway, I don't want to talk too long, but I wanted to say to you both, we're excited as you take the next steps in this journey of life together. Caleb, it will be you who takes care of her when she's sick." She winked at him. "Thank you, by the way—she's a horrible patient."

Laughter rippled through the barn as Kenzie continued, "Before Grace and I bust through the door, we promise to have called first…" More laughter. "Seriously, we"—she gestured to Grace and their parents— "couldn't be happier to have a new branch on our family tree." Kenzie raised her glass and smiled through happy tears. "To our sister and our new brother. Have a long and happy life."

Robbie winked at Kenzie.

Kenzie grinned at him. Air-clinking their glasses, she announced, "To family."

CHAPTER 7

R obbie could tell Kenzie was itching to dance as her head tipped side to side in time to the music. As the tempo picked up, her gaze swept the table. "Who's ready to kick up their heels?"

Jo and Grace hopped up, and Kenzie turned to Robbie and said slyly, "Are you coming?"

He smiled. "Absolutely." He had been waiting all night for this moment.

Kenzie laid her napkin on the table and took a sip of water. "Think you can keep up?" she challenged.

He gave her a wicked grin, and winked. "The bigger question is, can you?"

"Burns, just watch and see how it's done."

Robbie danced with Kenzie as she shimmied and twirled around the floor to the driving beat of the music. They moved in sync with the racing of his heart, not from the exertion of the dance moves but the deep feelings he had for her. *I'm dancing with Kenzie.*

At the end of a long set, the band announced a short

break. Kenzie pointed to the bar. "Buy me a drink?" she teased.

They meandered to the bar. Robbie ordered her wine and a beer for himself. Propped against the counter, he said, "Jamie and Caleb seem to be having a blast."

Kenzie's eyes followed her sister and new husband as they made the rounds to everyone in the room. "She looks like she's walking on air."

He brushed her cheek with his hand. "That was a really nice toast you gave. Just the right amount of tear-jerking and humor."

Her eyes widened and she said, "I've never given one before and Grace didn't want to, so I spoke from my heart, for both of us."

Totally focused on her, he said, "From what I've heard, that's always the best."

Kenzie pushed a stray lock of hair from his eyes, and his heart quickened. "Have you ever thought seriously about taking the plunge?"

He looked down at his beer. "Yeah, from time to time I think about a wife and a couple of kids, but I'm waiting for the right girl to notice me."

She cocked her head. "How will you know she's the one for you?"

Robbie gazed into Kenzie's eyes. *I already do.* His heart beat faster. He laid a hand over his chest. "When I'm with her, no matter where we are, I'll feel like I'm home."

Kenzie sipped her wine. "I'm surprised a girl hasn't claimed you yet."

He couldn't look away. She had him mesmerized. "It'll happen, in due time."

"Well, I hope you find the girl of your dreams."

You're in my dreams and when I'm wide awake...

Parump pump. Drumsticks rapped a snare drum. Kenzie

grinned at him. "Sounds like the band is starting up. Dance with me?"

He looked over her head and stated, "Actually, it looks like Jamie and Caleb are getting ready to leave."

Kenzie set her glass down and called over her shoulder to stop Jamie. "Wait! I want to say goodbye." Robbie fell in step next to her as she raced across the room.

"Are you leaving?" Kenzie pulled her sister into a bear hug.

Jamie squeezed her tight. "We are. Are you going to stay or go home soon?"

"I'm headed out soon—my feet are starting to ache from wearing these heels all day," Kenzie replied.

Caleb shook Robbie's hand and dropped a brotherly kiss on Kenzie's cheek. "You did an unbelievable job with everything, Kenz—thanks for helping us out. It couldn't have been a better wedding. And Robbie, it meant the world to us to start our married life on your family's farm."

Robbie clapped Caleb on the shoulder. "Trust me, it was our pleasure."

Jamie looked at Kenzie's feet. "You're still wearing your heels? Didn't you bring something to change into?"

"You mean like sneakers?" Kenzie laughed. "No, once the shoes come off, so does the dress."

Robbie's heart nearly stopped dead. He blinked hard and refocused on Jamie, who was saying, "Robbie, thanks again for everything. This farm has always been special. When we get back from our honeymoon, we'll have everyone for dinner." She snickered and pulled her new husband close. "And Caleb will cook."

Robbie shifted his gaze to Kenzie. "We're going hiking for a few days and I would hate to miss it."

"Not a problem. Kenzie gave me the dates." Jamie kissed her sister's cheek. "Okay, Kenz, we're off."

Robbie noticed Kenzie's parents cross the dance floor. "Here come your mom and dad."

Caleb stuck out his hand, "James, Olivia, it was a wonderful evening, thank you for everything."

"Yes, it was, son." James clasped his hand. "You two have a wonderful holiday."

"We will." Jamie threw her arms around her parents. "See you in two weeks, okay?"

James slung his arm around Caleb's shoulders. His voice thick, he said, "Take care of my daughter."

"Sir, with my life."

Olivia hugged Jamie. "Have a wonderful honeymoon. I'm assuming brunch is planned right after Kenzie and Robbie get back from their hike."

With an impish grin Kenzie said, "You know us, Mom. We love any excuse to have breakfast foods any time of the day."

Grace skidded across the dance floor, shoes in hand. "Hold on!"

Jamie laughed, "Don't worry, I wouldn't have left without saying goodbye." Amid tears and smiles, Jamie held tight to her youngest sister and opened her arm for Kenzie. She exclaimed, "You are the best sisters! I wouldn't have been able to pull this day together without your help. And when it's your time I'll return the favor."

Caleb tugged Jamie's hand and said, "Mrs. Sullivan, we need to go."

With one last squeeze, Jamie sailed out of the barn on Caleb's arm into the crisp, star-filled night. Robbie stood next to Kenzie, watching them.

Olivia asked, "How much longer are you girls staying?" She looked at Kenzie and then Grace.

Robbie held Kenzie's hand. She said, "I'll stay until

everyone leaves if you and Dad want to go home. You too, Grace."

Shaking her head from side to side, Olivia said, "Since you girls were up early with the bride, you can take off."

"Are you sure?" Kenzie looked at Robbie. "I'm sure I can twist Robbie's arm to stay."

Olivia nudged them toward the door. "Go home. Dad and I have this under control."

Grace looked longingly at the dessert table. "I'm going to grab a slice of cake to go. Kenzie, I'll see you at the gym tomorrow?"

Picking one foot up and wiggling it and then the other, she said, "Don't make it too early; I'm not sure my feet will be up to working out bright and early. I don't know how anyone wears heels all day—they're pretty, but torture."

Grace grinned. "Maybe you need an excuse to dress up and don them more often. I'll bet if you got used to them, your feet wouldn't ache quite so bad."

"If you say so." Kenzie grimaced. "I'll see you around eleven?"

"Sure." Grace skipped away. With a quick look over her shoulder, she said mischievously, "See, my feet are just fine."

Kenzie slipped her heels off and gingerly tiptoed across the old floorboards holding onto Robbie's arm, her heels dangling from her fingertips. "I need to get my handbag."

Taking her shoes, he said, "I'll walk out with you."

They crossed the room and she picked up her bag. "Stay. Have fun."

He knew the moment she left the night would lose its sparkle for him. "Nah, I'm ready to head out. It's been a hectic but really fun day." He looked at her out of the corner of his eye. "Don't you think?" He held the door for her, wishing the evening wouldn't end.

Kenzie stepped out and shivered. "It got cold."

Robbie took off his jacket and slung it over her bare shoulders.

"Thanks, but I'm okay." She shrugged from underneath the silky fabric. He frowned as she handed it back to him.

His shoes crunched on the gravel and Kenzie picked her way to the grass. Leaping from foot to foot, she said, "The frost is like icy slivers in between my toes." She sighed deeply. "My feet are burning like they're on fire. But this feels so good."

"Kenzie, would it hurt you to let me do something nice for you?" He held out his coat again.

He was surprised to see the hurt in her eyes. "What are you talking about?"

He sighed and said gently, "I know you're cold—you're always cold, and that dress you're wearing is pretty flimsy and you *said* you're cold. And here we are taking a stroll through an autumn night, and you're barefoot to boot."

"I'm sorry if I insulted your manly pride."

He gave her a sharp look. "You're exasperating."

She rolled her eyes. "What? I'm nothing of the kind."

"You just don't get it. Smart people know the difference between a kind gesture and a threat to their independence."

"And you're over reacting." Kenzie stumbled. "Ouch!" she cried out as she almost fell to the ground.

Robbie caught her arm. "What happened. Did you trip on something?"

She thrust her foot in his direction. "Can you tell if I'm bleeding?"

"No, the lights aren't bright enough. I'll check when we get to the car." With ease Robbie swept her into his arms holding her safe against his chest.

"What are you doing? Put me down!" She wriggled as he tightened his arms around her.

"Walking without shoes with a cut on your foot isn't exactly smart. You could get a nasty infection and then we wouldn't be able to go hiking."

"Fine." Kenzie's lower lip jutted out. "But I do have one foot still working."

"Shoeless. Give me two minutes." With a few long strides, Robbie stood at the back of her car. "Can you reach the latch?" He didn't want to put her down, savoring the rare moment of holding her in his arms.

Her fingertips grazed the hatch, not quite able to release it. "Can you bend down?"

Robbie leaned over and Kenzie pushed the button. The hatch slid open. He set her down, dug into his jacket pocket and pulled out his phone.

Shocked she stated, "You don't need to call an ambulance."

He laughed. "I have a flashlight on my phone."

"Sorry. I wasn't thinking."

"Can you hold your foot out?"

Kenzie did as he asked. Robbie took a closer look. Her small foot fit into the palm of his hand. "It's just a small cut. Do you have a first aid kit? I can clean it, and when you get home you'll need to soak it."

Kenzie grabbed a red canvas bag from the back of the car and handed it to him. "I've got all sorts of emergency supplies."

He dug into the bag and pulled out a bottle of water, some gauze and bandage. Kenzie pulled the bag to her. Pulling a few more items out, she said, "There's alcohol in there."

"I'm going to rinse it with water, wash out as much dirt

as possible, dose it with the alcohol and then cover it with the bandage."

He felt her eyes watch him as he carefully poured water over the bottom of her foot, his hand cradling her heel for support. Using a gentle touch to not inflict any additional pain, he patted it dry and took one final look. Ripping opened the Band-Aid, he placed it over the wound. "When did you last have a tetanus booster?"

Softly, she said, "My checkup last year."

He held out a hand. "Let me help you get behind the wheel, or I can drive you home."

"No, I'll be fine." She hopped down from the hatch on one foot and promptly tripped.

He inhaled her soft floral scent. "Don't worry, I've got you."

Flustered, she straightened and mumbled, "I'll see you Monday."

"If you want, I can cover tomorrow."

"No. Take the day off, it should be slow."

Annoyed that she seemed to erect a wall between them, he said, "You're the boss."

Kenzie sat behind the wheel and Robbie closed the door. She slid down the window. "Thanks for…"

He tapped the door. "Forget it. That's what friends are for."

With a heavy heart, he watched her taillights disappear down the long gravel driveway.

CHAPTER 8

Kenzie had her foot propped on the desk when Grace came through the door the next morning looking fresh as a daisy. Her grin faded when she saw Kenzie's injured foot. She dropped her bag and came around the desk. "What happened to you?"

"I stepped on something last night and it's kind of hard to walk."

"I want to take a look. Take off your sneaker and sock."

Kenzie waved her hand in the air. "Grace, it's fine, really."

Ignoring her, Grace asked, "Tetanus up to date?"

"You should know—you're the one who jabbed me last year during my physical."

A wicked gleam came into Grace's eyes. "Consider it small payback for picking on me when we were kids."

"So that's how it is?" Kenzie's voice held steady as she kicked off her untied sneaker. Wincing, she pulled off the sock.

Grace bent over her foot. Concern filled her eyes. "I saw your face—how much does it hurt?"

"It's just tender." If she was being honest, it hurt like hell. But she had a lot to get done and no time to baby a tiny cut.

Grace scowled. "Shoot, Kenz, this looks infected. Did you soak it last night?"

"Robbie cleaned it at the farm."

Grace prodded the spot, causing her foot to throb.

Holding steady Kenzie continued, "And when I got home I soaked in the tub for a while, so I figured that was good enough."

Using a penlight, Grace exclaimed, "I see what's going on! There's a small piece of hay or something embedded in the cut."

Kenzie tried to pull her foot away, but Grace held firm. "Ew. Can you pull it out?"

"I'll grab my bag from the car. You"—Grace jabbed a finger at her—"stay put."

Kenzie's phone rang as Grace hurried out the door. A smile tugged the corners of her lips. "Good morning, Robbie."

"Hey there."

Kenzie played with a pen on the desk. "Were your ears burning?"

"No, why?"

She knew his worry lines would be crinkled as soon as he said those words. "I was telling Grace how you took care of me last night."

"I guess we're on the same wavelength. I was curious to see how it feels today."

Frowning, she said, "From what Grace saw, there's something in it. She went to get tools to operate." She sighed. "You know how she loves being in control."

"What? I'll come in so you can go home."

She knew that tone too. "Robbie, hold on." Kenzie sat

up straight. "I'm kidding. She's going to pluck it out and give it another cleaning. It's no big deal."

"You should be home with your foot up. I'm coming down."

"I'm…" Click. The line went dead. "Damn it."

Grace came back inside. "What's the matter?"

"Robbie called. I told him you're playing doctor. He's decided I need to go home."

"It's not a bad idea." Grace adjusted Kenzie's foot on the desk so she could get a closer look. "Hold still."

Kenzie paled at the sight of the large tweezers in her sister's hand. "Be careful. I'm kind of attached to my foot."

"Har har." Grace's poker face was in place as she prepared to irrigate the cut with something in a clear bottle.

"What's that?" Kenzie narrowed her eyes as she studied the bottle in Grace's hands.

"Saline, it's sterile." Exasperated, Grace snapped, "Now stop, and for heaven's sake, keep still."

Kenzie crossed her arms over her chest and her lips formed a thin line. "Fine," she huffed.

Grace brought the instrument closer. "Almost done."

"Ouch!" Kenzie jerked her foot. Tears smarted her eyes.

Grace held the oversized tweezers aloft. "Look." She showed Kenzie a small piece of metal. "It was bigger than I thought."

Kenzie leaned forward and peered at the tweezers. "That was in my foot?"

"It was." She dabbed the cut with some cream and covered it with an oversized bandage. "I'm going to put you on a short course of antibiotics just to be safe."

With a salute, Kenzie said, "Yes, Dr. Grace."

A grin tugged at the corner of Grace's mouth. "When Robbie gets here I'll take you home, but first we'll swing by the pharmacy, pick up the script, and then we can have a movie day."

Kenzie brightened. "Aren't you working today?"

Grace shook her head. "I'm on call next weekend. How does Chinese food sound?"

Resigned, Kenzie said, "Sure, what's one more day of splurge after all we ate during the last week?"

Grace was storing items in her bag when Robbie arrived. "Is everything okay?" His eyes studied Kenzie with concern.

Grace smirked. "She's going to be just fine."

Kenzie gave him a reassuring smile. "Don't worry. Our hike is still on as planned."

Robbie leaned on the counter and grinned. "That's good. I was worried."

"All right, well then," Grace zipped her bag. "we're going to Kenzie's to watch movies."

"Want help to the car?" Robbie came around the counter and held out his hand.

Kenzie waved it away. "No, I can walk or hop." She put her foot on the ground. "Thanks for closing up today. If it doesn't get busy, close early and head home."

Grace picked up their bags and Robbie rushed to hold the door open. "I'll call you later, just to check in."

"No worries, I've got a junior doctor in the house." Kenzie winked. "And I just might make her pay for lunch for causing me some pain."

Grace laughed. "Believe me, the pleasure was all mine."

Kenzie was on the couch with her foot propped up on a pillow. After standing in line at the pharmacy, Grace had insisted. Rather than fight, she gave in.

Grace handed Kenzie the remote and settled into the overstuffed chair. Kenzie announced, "We're watching *Star Wars*. Nothing resembling weddings or romance." She pointed to her foot and said sweetly, "Since I'm on the DL, can you put the movie in the player?"

Grace jumped up and started the DVD.

"Don't forget to turn on the surround sound. I want to feel the rumble under my butt when the Death Star rolls across the screen."

"You're such a geek." Grace pushed a few buttons, and they settled back to be swept to a galaxy far, far, away.

Princess Leia had just witnessed Aldreaan destroyed when the doorbell rang.

"I wonder who that is." Kenzie started to get up, but Grace gently pushed her back onto the sofa.

"I've got it, you sit."

Kenzie mumbled, "I'm not helpless, you know."

"Did you say something?" Grace's voice dripped with honey as she left the room.

Kenzie strained to catch a glimpse in the edge of the hallway mirror. Rustling bags and laughter were enough to push Kenzie off the couch. Hobbling into the hallway she discovered Robbie hovering near the door.

Her heart skipped a beat. "This is a surprise. But what about the gym?"

"It was dead, so I closed up." He directed a look her way. "Don't worry. I'm not staying. I just wanted to drop off Chinese. I heard that was the plan for the afternoon." He held up the bags. "Here I am."

Walking on her heel, Kenzie limped over and took the bags. "Hold on, let me get you some money."

Robbie held up his hands. "Forget it."

Grace said, "I'm paying." She pulled some bills from her jeans pocket and thrust them at Robbie.

Kenzie hopped toward the kitchen. "Do you want to stay and have an early dinner with us?"

Robbie looked from Grace to Kenzie. "No. I'm going to head out. Enjoy your movie. I'll see you tomorrow."

Kenzie smiled at him. "Stay."

He took a few steps towards her and pecked her cheek. "Take care of that foot."

She felt her cheeks grow warm. "Thanks for dinner."

Robbie stuffed the cash in his pocket, smiled and started towards the door. He paused, "When do you think we're going to hire someone? When one of us is sick, on vacation or when we want to escape for a few days together, we're kind of stuck."

"I know." She bristled. "We'll have enough time to get someone trained before we go." Kenzie slowly made her way from the kitchen to the sofa. Realizing she was being snarky, she conceded, "I'll place an ad tomorrow."

"Okay, have a good night." He left, quietly closing the door behind him.

Grace followed Kenzie into the living room. "What just happened here?"

Kenzie pulled a plush blanket off the back of the sofa, tucking it around her.

Grace perched on the edge of the couch. "Kenz? What's going on with you and Robbie? Did you have a fight? Are you mad he reminded you about hiring someone?"

"No, it's nothing like that." Kenzie smoothed out the wrinkles in the blanket.

"Well, you're obviously bothered by something, so fess up."

Kenzie chewed on her fingernail. "Did you get any odd thoughts yesterday?"

"What do you mean?" Grace leaned back into the cushions.

Kenzie stared at her hands in her lap. Silent.

"Kenz?"

In a rush, she said, "All right. Well, a couple of times yesterday during the wedding festivities, when I was around Robbie, I got a fluttering feeling in the pit of my stomach. Then my heart beat faster." She could feel her cheeks grow warm. "And I felt it again as he carried me to the car." Her voice grew soft. "He was so sweet."

"He's always been a nice guy." Grace studied her sister. "Do you think it's something more?"

Kenzie squirmed, uncomfortable under Grace's penetrating stare. "I don't know. I guess with all the hoopla of the wedding, my emotions were in overdrive." With a dismissive wave of her hand, she said, "Just forget it. Let's watch the movie."

She closed her eyes and pinched the bridge of her nose. What was she thinking, noticing the cute way his hair slipped over his forehead and those green-gold eyes? They warmed her from head to toe.

"I'll grab the food." Grace crossed the room and paused. "When you go hiking, you can see if you still have those feelings."

Something clicked in Kenzie's mind. "Yeah…the White Mountains are the perfect place to clear my mind."

"Sounds like a lot of fun for you. A day hike is fine, but give me a hotel with a spa—that's my idea of a getaway." Grace laughed her way into the kitchen.

Kenzie called after her, "You should come with us sometime. You might just like it." She brightened. "We could do some easy trails, and sitting by a campfire at the end of the day is just, well, heavenly, and the views are spectacular."

Grace walked in carrying two plates, napkins and the bag. "I'll pass." She set out the containers on the coffee table. "You know, I was thinking about it. I'm surprised Robbie hasn't found someone by now. I've always pictured him with a wife and a few kids."

"We talked and he does want the picture-perfect life. When I asked him how he'd know he found love, he tapped his chest and said he'd just know."

Grace clutched her fork to her chest and sighed. "Wow."

Kenzie laughed. "Sometimes I forget you're the sentimental one."

"You'd be doing yourself a favor to be a little more flexible."

"That's not true," Kenzie protested. "I can be *very* flexible."

Snorting, Grace choked on her noodles. "Name one instance you've shown at least a little bit of a bend."

"I will not defend myself, Gracie." Kenzie speared a shrimp. "I thought we were going to watch a movie, not pick on how I live my life."

"You're protesting way too much, sis. I think maybe you need to take time on your little adventure and do some soul searching."

"Robbie's my best friend, always has been and always will be. Yesterday I must have got caught up with wedding day mania."

"If you say so." Grace smiled. "But I think you're spending a lot of energy protesting."

CHAPTER 9

Kenzie pushed open her front door with her hip, dropped two grocery bags on the foyer floor, kicked the door closed and sagged against the wall. The last two weeks had flown since Jamie's wedding. A white garment bag hung over the coat closet door, catching her eye.

"What the..." She breathed one word: "Jamie." Kenzie extended her hand and snatched it back as if the bag were on fire. Admonishing herself, she said, "This is silly—it's just a dress."

Grabbing the groceries, she carried them into the kitchen to put them away, her eyes drifting back to the garment bag each time she walked past the hall. She muttered, "It would have been nice if she'd given me a heads-up she was dropping it off today. I've got a lot to do to get ready for the hiking trip tomorrow."

Her cell phone buzzed. *Speak of the devil.* "Hey, Jamie."

"Hi Kenzie."

She smiled in spite of her annoyance. It was good to hear her sister's voice.

"In case you missed it I picked up the dress from the dry cleaners and dropped it off at your place."

Kenzie's gaze rested on the garment bag. "I just got home and saw you'd been by. How was the honeymoon?"

Without responding to her question, Jamie forged ahead. "So?" The word hung in the air. When Kenzie didn't answer, she continued, "Are you going to put it on tonight?"

Kenzie leaned against the counter. "Stop pushing, Jamie. I promised you I would, and I will."

Undeterred, Jamie continued, "I'm not trying to be pushy. But the sooner you do, the sooner you might discover what your future holds."

Kenzie snapped, "I'm in charge of my destiny, not Gran's dress." She felt bad for speaking sharply to her sister. "I'm sorry, sis. I'm getting ready to go hiking and won't have time until I get back."

"Okay, well then." Jamie's voice dropped. "I'll let you get back to whatever you were doing."

Kenzie could hear the disappointment in her voice and she felt bad. "I promise I'll try it on soon, and when I get home you can tell me all about the honeymoon, just like we planned. Okay?"

"Have fun and be careful," Jamie said. "I know you're with Robbie, but still, there's a lot of wildlife in the mountains and you're notorious for being accident prone."

With a snort Kenzie said, "We will, and I'll do my best to come back the same way I'm leaving."

The girls said goodbye. Kenzie plucked the dress from the door. Draping it over her arm, she carefully carried it into the bedroom. After laying it on the bed, she sank cross-legged to the floor. She dropped her head in her hands. *I'm afraid to try on a dress that is purportedly enchanted.*

It's not like it's going to magically fly off the bed and dress me, like in a fairy tale.

Shadows crept into the room and Kenzie rose, stiff from sitting in one position as she contemplated trying on the dress. She clicked on a lamp. A soft warm glow illuminated the room. She walked toward the door but stopped mid-step. *If I take it out of the bag, I can tell Jamie I tried it on and she'll stop hounding me.*

With a slow, deliberate motion, she opened the bag. Clutching the dress to her body, she made a half turn to face the full-length mirror. In a hushed, almost reverent voice, she said, "It *is* gorgeous." She moved from side to side, the skirt rustling as the dress seemed to whisper to her.

"What would it hurt?" She glanced at a picture of Gran on her bureau. "I hope it was okay I didn't tell anyone that I saw you at the wedding. I kind of felt like it was our secret." She ran her finger over the frame. "If you were here, I know you'd tell me to face my fear and put the dress on. It's fabric, nothing more, unless..."

She stripped off her T-shirt and yoga pants and tossed them to the floor. She loosened the delicate satin laces in the loops of the gown and stepped into the circle skirt. Slipping her arms through the capped sleeves, she pulled up the bodice. With the laces taut, the fabric molded to her figure. Her blue eyes popped and she did a double take.

In a shaky voice, she whispered, "So that's what Jamie meant. It's like the dress was made for me." Tears sprang to her eyes. "This is insane."

Watching her reflection in the mirror, her heart hammered. A woman wearing the wedding dress was prepared to walk down the aisle. Robbie was waiting at the altar, resplendent in a midnight-black tuxedo with a small thistle in his lapel, his hand open and waiting.

She sucked in a deep, ragged breath. The woman turned so Kenzie could see her face. *She* was the woman in the mirror, ready to make the short walk to accept Robbie's hand.

Shaking, Kenzie slipped the dress from her shoulders and stepped out of the skirt. She placed it on the padded hanger and tucked the hem inside the garment bag. After hanging it in the closet, she shut the door and dropped onto the floor. A range of unfamiliar emotions washed over her. After what the mirror revealed, how would she spend the next four days alone with Robbie?

Before dawn, Kenzie flipped back the covers. Despite seeing Robbie in the mirror, she was excited to get to the mountains. The hike would give her time to sort out what she had seen, maybe it was nothing more than a big coincidence. She padded down the short hallway to the kitchen. Her backpack was laying open on the table. She tossed in a few baggies of trail mix and added a bag of apples.

Satisfied, she began to zip it closed. Halfway around the pack, the zipper got stuck. Flipping on the overhead lights, Kenzie discovered the edge of an envelope lodged in it. Giving it a yank, she was able to get the envelope out without tearing it.

She turned it over, her stomach clenching. It was addressed to her in Gran's handwriting.

Using a knife, she carefully slit it open. Gran's last letter. Just like the letter Jamie got right before they went on their sister-cation to Scotland. *Gran must have snuck it in my bag the same time she did Jamie's.* Carefully unfolding the paper, she perched on a stool.

. . .

My dear Kenzie,

By now you and your sisters know my little secret—I wrote letters to each of you. I hope you don't mind that I snuck into your room so I could slip a wee little note into your backpack as a surprise for you.

I wonder, how did Jamie look in our dress? I'm sure she was radiant. I'm sorry dear lass, I digress. Back to the matter at hand.

Each one of you reminds me of myself when I was a young woman. You're strong willed and stubborn. You're the most like me in temperament, so I understand your reluctance to let go and fall in love.

There are so many stories untold and so much I still wanted to teach you. But time has passed us by. I need for you to understand that marrying your grandfather was the best thing I ever did, and I wouldn't have wanted to miss a single minute of our life together. My cup runneth over when I had a son, and my three sweet grand-daughters were truly beyond my wildest dreams. You are the MacLellan future.

Kenzie, true love is waiting for you. Open your heart and a life-time filled with joy will follow. To take the first step is to wear the dress, look in the mirror and be honest with yourself. Who do you see standing next to you? A man you can love with all your heart, who will stand beside you through good times and bad? He is the one for you.

My darling, I have one more letter to write before the night gives way to the morning light. Tomorrow is our last day together. We will take a hike along the waterfall and drink in the sweet smell of the heather in full bloom. Never stop looking for the surprises nature, and what life has to offer you.

Until we meet again—
All my love, Gran

· · ·

Holding the paper to her chest, Kenzie let the tears of grief mixed with happiness silently slip down her face.

Robbie's truck blocked Kenzie's driveway as he loaded their backpacks. He looked at his watch—six o'clock, the sun peeking from behind the horizon. It was time to leave and Kenzie was locking her front door, right on time.

She jogged over. "I'm ready."

"'Bout time," he teased. He couldn't help but notice her eyes were bloodshot and her face pale. "Kenzie, if you're not feeling well we can postpone."

"No, I'm fine. It was a weird night for sleeping and mountain air will do me good." Changing the subject, she said, "Do you think Cheryl can handle the gym?"

"She's been a member for months. Even though she's only been employed for a short time, she knows how particular you are, so I'd say she can." He glanced at her. "It was really nice of you to give her the job when you found out why she stopped coming."

Kenzie dropped her bag to the floor and lowered the visor to block the bright sun. "Divorce sucks and for her ex to leave her broke stinks. She has a little boy to think about."

Robbie backed out of the drive and headed down the road. Quietly she said, "Thanks for driving."

He grinned. "It's my turn. Remember, you drove last year."

"Can we swing by the drive-thru and get coffee? I ran out of time."

"Sure." He flicked his thumb toward the backseat. "I made breakfast sandwiches. That is, if you're hungry." He looked at her from the corner of his eye. He was certain there was more to her story than a restless night of sleep. Clicking his blinker on, he turned into the coffee shop.

She looked out the window and remained silent. Navigating the drive-thru, he placed an order for two large coffees with cream. He handed one to Kenzie and set the other in the center console. He pulled out onto the road and headed out of town.

Breaking the silence, he said, "I double checked the weather and it looks clear, but the nights are going to be cold. They're expecting a heavy frost, maybe even a dusting of snow."

Kenzie stared out the window. Her voice flat as she responded, "We've camped in the cold before. We'll be fine."

"Kenz…" He hesitated. "Did I do something? It seems like you're ticked off at me."

She squirmed in her seat. "No, really, I'm not upset. I'm trying to purge work from my brain." She flashed him a half-hearted smile. "I'm really looking forward to the trip."

With one hand guiding the steering wheel, Robbie relaxed. "I understand. It's a little like leaving a part of yourself behind. You live for that place."

"Look who's talking." Her voice was tinged with laughter. "You're exactly the same way. When was the last time you took more than a few days off?"

"We have members counting on us."

Kenzie snorted, making him laugh. "That's supposed to be my excuse, not yours."

Robbie blinked hard, wondering exactly where he stood with her. "Wow, I thought we shared the same philosophy when it comes to business."

"We do, but as a minority owner in the gym, you have freedom I don't."

With a slow, disbelieving shake of his head, all he could think to say was, "Ouch."

Kenzie jerked her head and looked at him. "I'm so sorry, I didn't mean that the way it sounded."

"How did you mean it?"

"Oh hell. I'm sorry. I slept like crap last night and I have no idea what I'm saying." She laid her hand on his arm. "Robbie, can you chalk up my snarkiness to being overtired and under caffeinated?"

He looked at her and his lip curled into a small smile. "Yeah, let's start over."

"You're the best." She pointed to the side of the road. "Can you pull over?"

With a sidelong glance to check for other cars, he slowed the truck and stopped on the side on the road.

Kenzie unbuckled her seatbelt and hopped out of the truck, closing the door behind her. Robbie strained to see what she was doing. When curiosity got the best of him, he got out. "Kenzie?"

With a sunny smile, she said, "Good morning, are you ready to go hiking?"

"You're crazy." With a shake of his head, he played along. "I thought you'd never be ready. Do you need help with your stuff?"

"Nope, it's already stowed in the truck." She pulled open the door and hopped inside. "Oh look, you stopped for coffee, you're the best!"

Laughing, Robbie settled in behind the wheel. "Hot with cream, just the way you like it." This woman was nuts, and he was crazy like a squirrel about her.

He dropped the truck in drive and pulled off the gravel shoulder, kicking up stones as they eased back onto the road. "Next stop, New Hampshire."

"Did you bring the map?" Kenzie asked. She was definitely looking more relaxed.

Robbie pointed behind him. "In the side pocket of my pack."

She leaned through the seats and retrieved it. "I brought some of those chocolate bars you like, along with nuts, freeze-dried dinners, tuna pouches, carrot sticks, granola bars and some dried fruit."

"I got the water, camp stove and pup tent ready too."

Kenzie spread the map over the dashboard. "Did you pick a good spot for base camp?"

He pointed to it. "It's circled in blue. It's about a six-mile hike in, and from there we can spend the other two days going in the directions highlighted in orange."

Head bent low, she studied the topographical map. Slowly she said, her excitement building, "The base camp location looks perfect. From there we've got a couple of challenging days and then an easy hike out." She glanced at her watch. "We should get to the park in, what, a couple of hours?"

Robbie nodded, her mood contagious. "That'll put us on the trail right before lunch. I thought we could eat first. It'll give us a good meal in our bellies before we head out. It'll take us around two hours to get to base camp and that will give us plenty of time to set up, maybe do a little scouting and get a fire going before we lose daylight."

"When it comes to hiking you're always so practical. A fire will feel nice, and I brought actual food to cook tonight. A couple of sweet potatoes, chicken breast and some veggies cooked over an open fire." She rubbed her belly. "Yum."

"You remembered my favorite meal. Did you bring something for dessert?"

Her mouth twitched with amusement. "Every meal is

your favorite, and for dessert"—she did a drum roll the dash—"s'mores!"

Robbie chuckled. "I should never have doubted you."

Kenzie's face softened. "Do you remember the first time we went hiking? We had to have been what, twelve or thirteen? It was short but our parents were worried and the dads were waiting for us as we came down the trail just at dusk." Her voice held a touch of nostalgia.

Robbie chuckled. "I think your dad talked mine into checking up on us. You know, you being the girl and all."

"I would have protected you if the need arose," she teased.

Robbie enjoyed the casual sparring as much as Kenzie did. "Are you saying I couldn't have protected you?"

Kenzie smirked. "You hadn't had your growth spurt—you weren't much taller than me and certainly hadn't started to work out yet."

He chuckled. "I guess you're right. Look at how far we've come. This is our what, tenth hiking trip in New Hampshire alone?"

"If you don't count all the day trips we've been on. I couldn't even count how many times we'd get our chores done as quickly as possible so we could take off some place."

The miles clicked by as they relived what was special about each trip.

Robbie slowed and pulled into the paved parking lot. He parked the truck near the trailhead and public restrooms. "We've had a lot of good times together."

"We sure have." Kenzie beamed at him and burst out the door. "I always get excited when we're on the verge of a new adventure."

"Some things never change." He smirked and shut the truck off. "Lunch first and then grab your gear."

~

Kenzie stayed by Robbie's side as they made the trek to base camp. After all the miles spent on trails, they hiked well together. They shared the load of supplies.

"Look." Robbie pointed to a bald eagle perched high in an evergreen.

Kenzie dropped her head back and drank in the sight. "I never get tired of the scenery." They watched as the bird's wings spread, soaring on the wind currents.

"Come on, pokey." Robbie tapped her pole with his. "We're almost there."

Kenzie fell into step. He could feel her looking at him. "Do I have dirt on my face already?" He reached up to wipe his cheek.

"No, I was just thinking we've never brought anyone we've been dating. It's always been just the two of us."

Dark glasses hid his eyes. They didn't betray the worry that constricted his heart. Casually he said, "Are you saying you'd like to invite someone next time?"

"Nope, just an observation." She adjusted her ball cap. Slowly she said, "Why, do you?"

"Nah, I've gotten used to your smelly self on the trail. To break in someone new would just be weird."

Kenzie laughed out loud. A flock of birds rushed up from the trees.

Joking he said, "Hey, you're spooking the wildlife."

"For the record, I've gotten used to your smelly self too." She pointed down the trail. "I think I see our hotel."

They picked up their pace. Robbie deposited his pack on the ground. Someone had kindly left two logs next to what appeared to be a fire pit. He dropped to one and pulled the crisp cold air deep into his lungs, then patted the log and looked at Kenzie. "Join me?"

She followed suit and surveyed their surroundings. "It's beautiful here."

He longed to take her hand, but quickly reminded himself he'd rather have her friendship than lose her all together. After a few minutes, he said, "We should gather firewood and get the tent set up."

"I know, but can I have four more minutes?" she said wistfully.

Grinning, he chuckled. "Five is too ordinary and three's too short."

Shrugging, she said, "You know me so well, Burns."

"I should. From diapers to hikers." He hopped up. "You sit for four minutes and I'll get the fire started."

Kenzie got up and stretched. "I'd rather sit fireside, so I'll help." Looking at him sideways, she laughed, "But you owe me."

CHAPTER 10

K enzie was restless as she moved around camp.
The chicken sizzled in the frying pan and she
turned the potatoes at the edge of the fire. "So
tell me, how are things going with Ally Evans?"

Robbie dropped a few more logs on and sat down,
rubbing his hands together in front of the flames. He
cocked an eyebrow and looked at her. "What made you ask
about her?"

She could still picture Robbie wearing a tux and holding
out his hand to her. She plunked down on the log next to
him. "Just curious. I haven't seen her in a while."

"No. I don't think she'll be back."

Casually she asked, "Why? Was she unhappy with her
training?" Kenzie's heart fluttered.

He studied the orange-red flames. Somberly he said,
"Well, if you must know, you were right. She was looking
for something a little more personal and I turned her
down."

Kenzie chewed her lower lip. "Oh, I'm sorry." She felt
like she was floating, the weight of Ally gone.

"No need. She wasn't my type."

"What is your type? It seems to me you've never dated anyone who shares your interests." She held her breath. Did she really want to know?

Robbie was quiet for a few minutes, then said, "I thought I'd be in a permanent relationship by now. I'd love for her to share my interests, but she doesn't have to like everything I do. But I want a couple of kids. My dad would make a great grandpa." Folding his hands together, he stretched his legs out alongside the fire. "What about you?"

"If I ever took the plunge, I'd want to have kids and he'd have to be comfortable traveling." She lowered her head and watched the flames dance. She shrugged. "But I'm fine on my own."

Robbie took her hand. The warmth of his fingertips rippled straight to her heart. His voice was like a caress as he said, "Don't you want more?"

The fire popped and Kenzie jumped up. Drops of grease sizzled and landed on her bare skin. "Darn it." Tears sprang to her eyes and she waved her hand through the air in an attempt to ease the pain. Tiny blisters appeared where the grease made contact.

Robbie grabbed his canteen and poured cool water over her hand. "Better?"

She nodded. "Would you get the first aid kit from my pack? I've got burn cream."

He hurried to the tent and came back with a tube. "Here, let me."

Kenzie held out her hand. "You don't need to take care of me."

He knelt down and cradled her hand tenderly dabbing the cream on the blistered skin, careful not to pop the bubbles that had formed. "I know."

In a soft voice, she said, "Thanks."

A glint of humor touched his eyes. "You've had a bit of bad luck lately, the cut on your foot and now this." He put the cap on the cream. "Maybe we should spend the next couple of days lounging around the campfire and stay off the trails."

Kenzie's head and eyes snapped. Her anger fell flat when she caught sight of Robbie's face. "You're teasing me again."

"You betcha. You're super-careful out here." He jerked his thumb toward the trail. "I'm not worried and you shouldn't be either."

"I'm not." She glanced at her wrist.

Robbie stood up and pulled the skillet from the fire. He pointed at the plates. "Can you grab the plates?"

She crossed to the makeshift table. Looking back over her shoulder, she said, "Doesn't food trailside always taste better?"

She held out a plate. He took it from her and served up a potato, following it with chicken and a foil pack of vegetables.

She took the plate he offered. "What time do you want to get started in the morning?"

"I was thinking we could get up at first light after a quick breakfast." He grinned, teasing. "I know you can't miss your coffee. I'd like to get off the trail and back at camp before the sun starts to set."

"So, we're doing the lake loop tomorrow?" The fork hovered in midair, waiting for Robbie to answer.

"Yeah, it's about ten miles out and I'd like to shoot some pictures before we head back." A bird cawed as it flew through the darkening sky. They both looked up and sighed in unison.

Kenzie's eyes met his. "And then what's our final day?"

"I know how much you love going to the summit, so if we could head out a little earlier in the morning, we'd be able to have lunch there and then back to base."

For the next several minutes they ate in companionable silence. She adjusted her butt on the unforgiving log. "I'll bet there will be some stunning pictures at both places with the foliage at its peak. The colors are spectacular this year."

"Dinner's good." He tapped the side of his head. "How about our next trip you cook the first night's dinner?"

Chuckling, she said, "You've dragged me to enough cooking classes over the years."

He looked at his plate as he scraped it clean. "Then why haven't you hooked a guy?"

"Why haven't you?" she teased. "You're just as good as I am."

"We've talked about this before. When I'm ready, I'll be ready."

"Hey." Kenzie's voice softened. "I didn't mean to get you all riled up."

Nonchalantly Robbie stood. "You didn't." He gathered up the food pack. "If you're done eating, I'm going to secure this in the bear box away from the tent."

"Yeah, sure." Her eyes followed him, her heart heavy. *All I want is for Robbie to give me just a tiny opening. I don't think I would have seen him in the mirror if he wasn't supposed to be in my life, permanently.*

Kenzie rolled over and rubbed the sleep from her eyes. The cool gray dawn was just beginning to show promise of the day ahead. Streaks of purple materialized on the horizon. Robbie's sleeping bag was a jumbled heap.

She crawled out of the small tent and glanced around. The stainless-steel coffeepot was perking while the small fire licked the bottom. She sniffed the air. "This is living."

Rustling leaves caught her attention as Robbie stepped from the dense brush. She called out, "Good morning. Will you just look at the first blush of the sunrise?"

Robbie followed her gaze to the horizon. His eyes returned to meet hers, and he smiled. "Beautiful."

She frowned. "Did you take a good look?"

"I did. I see the beauty all around me. If you need to use the ladies' room, put a wiggle on it and I'll pour coffee. I can't wait to hit the trail."

Kenzie laced up her boots before leaving for a little privacy. When she returned, Robbie held out an enamel mug and pointed to a thick peanut butter sandwich, complete with dried fruit, and two liter bottles of water waiting for her.

She took the mug and he said, "Dig in."

She grinned, "Aw, you fixed breakfast." She rolled her eyes as she bit into a sandwich. "Yum, crunchy peanut butter. My favorite."

"Can't have you faint from hunger, or me for that matter."

Laughing, she said, "I'm not carrying your butt off the trail."

"What?" he said, clutching his chest in feigned fear. "You'd leave me behind?"

"Well, no, I wouldn't leave you, but getting you down the mountain would present a challenge."

Studying his sandwich, he pretended to pout and said, "I'd carry you off the trail."

"I weigh half what you do, and I'm vertically challenged, remember?"

Smirking, he said, "Your compact stature boosts my self-image as big and strong, a manly man."

Kenzie took a long drink of water. "You'd better start getting some ounces down. You need to be well hydrated, manly man."

He held up his coffee. "I'm going to savor the caffeine first and then H2O." He leaned against a boulder and patted the ground next to him. "Let's witness the official start of the day."

Kenzie dropped down crossed-legged and watched in wonder as the land went from dark gray to shades of deep purple to light lavender. The pale yellow sun peeked over the ridge and washed the face of the mountains, leaving the ridgeline bathed in light and the scattered clouds aglow with a golden hue.

As time slipped by, Kenzie's inner clock unwound. The turmoil she had felt over the last couple months evaporated as the last wisps of morning fog fell away by the sun's rays. She stole a glance at Robbie's face. She was struck by the pure joy he wore. A lone tear slipped down her cheek and she reached for his hand. He squeezed it in return. It was just the two of them and a new day.

Finally, the sun revealed herself in full glory. Kenzie took the last sip of water and slowly rose to her feet pulling her hand away from him. Without words, Robbie followed suit and downed his water. He handed her sandwiches and baggies of granola and dried fruit, along with several more bottles of water.

She shifted her weight from foot to foot. "I'll take point?"

"The trail should be well maintained, so we can hike side by side." Looking cheery, he dropped his head and studied the camera, adjusting a few settings. "In case we see something, I want to be ready."

"Hopefully not a bear." Kenzie flipped open her pack and rummaged around inside. She pulled a can out and attached it to her sternum strap. She glanced at Robbie. "Don't forget your bear spray."

He patted his cargo pocket. "All set." Grabbing their trekking poles, he passed a pair to Kenzie. "I'm ready."

They found their rhythm in the first few steps. Birds were chirping in the trees and a soft cool breeze caressed their cheeks while the sun's rays warmed their shoulders.

"It's a perfect day," Kenzie said. Robbie trekked alongside her, humming off key. She pushed her shades up the bridge of her nose. "Have you ever thought about how many years we'll do this very same thing, our annual fall hike? Hopefully we'll be fortunate enough to go every year until we're too old and decrepit to sleep on the ground."

Smirking, he said, "Well, I'm never going to be too old. My future kids are going to come along and carry my gear."

She bounced on her toes. "Aren't you the optimist today?"

His eyes sparkled with amusement. "Don't you want to be out here when you're wicked old and gray?"

Throwing her hands on her hips, she admonished, "Excuse me, I might get old, but never gray!"

He chuckled. "Sorry, I forgot you do have a few girly tendencies."

As the trail grew steeper and the casual banter ebbed and flowed, teasing going both ways. The sun crept higher in the sky and Robbie stopped to snap photos, some with Kenzie as his model and some pure nature shots.

She paused, watching him point and click. "Don't you have enough pictures of this view yet?"

"You'd think, but when I look back and compare them year on year, there's always subtle differences."

Kenzie took off her glasses, annoyance splashed over her face. "How come you've never shown me?"

Continuing to take pictures he remarked, "Didn't think you'd be interested. You live in the moment, not in the past."

Her smile evaporated. "You've never offered to show me either, so I think we're both at fault here. And looking at pictures isn't exactly living in the past." The sadness that flashed across Robbie's face made Kenzie feel bad. "I don't mean to be touchy. But it bugs me when you assume something and don't ask."

He shrugged. "I'm sorry, Kenz." He took a step toward her and stopped. "By the end of this trip, I hope you're feeling a little more relaxed."

She started hiking and muttered, "I hope you're right."

The cadence of hiking was soothing. Kenzie listened to her body as it moved, and just being in the moment always made her thankful there were places like this close to home. "Today's trail is pretty easy."

His lips twitched. "I figured this would be a good way to get in the groove."

"I don't think I ever really lose it." She paused. "Oh, Robbie," she gushed, "just look at how perfectly the hills slide into the valley. It's like one large scoop came in and hollowed it out." Wonder filled her voice.

Joking he said, "It's called glaciers. I think you took history class. Millions of years ago they moved across the land." He muffled a laugh.

Kenzie could feel his eyes studying her. "I know you think I'm stupid."

"Not at all. I like how you see the world. You're a romantic, with a prickly exterior."

She stopped short. "What do you mean by that?"

"Nothing. Let's keep hiking."

Her voice was sharp. "No, I want to know about this so-called armor you say I have."

"Fine. If you insist." He looked deep into her eyes. The intensity surprised her. "Until recently, you and your sisters felt a meaningful relationship meant you had to compromise your independence. What you failed to understand is there are guys out there"—his arm swept the horizon—"who happen to think a strong, independent woman is sexy as hell and would love you and never try to change you. Jamie figured it out. She discovered Caleb is that kind of a guy."

Her mouth dropped open. Stammering, she said, "I don't know what you're talking about. We don't hang onto our independence like some sort of shield."

His eyebrow shot up. "Don't you?"

For a split second she was at a loss for words. "I don't want to argue with you."

"Me either. You asked, and I gave you my opinion." He brushed a lock of hair from her eyes. "Truce?"

She took his hand and squeezed it. "Truce. Now let's get to the lake. I want to have lunch by the water."

"Lead the way." He ushered her ahead of him with a sweep of his arm.

Kenzie marched up the trail and Robbie's words tumbled around her brain. Did she have it wrong? Jamie had found the secret to a meaningful relationship. She made a mental note to have a long conversation with her sisters. The image of her wearing the wedding dress drifted in her memory. *Is it my turn to find love?*

Around the final twist in the trail, the mountain view

opened up and what appeared to be a never-ending lake appeared before them. The surface sparkled like diamonds as the sun's reflection danced off it.

With childlike abandon, she slipped her backpack off and ran to where the water lapped at the edge of the shoreline. Dipping her hands into the icy cold water, she splashed her face. "Oh, that feels so good." She bent down and picked up a smooth, flat rock, flicking it over the surface. One, two, three, four skips. She jumped up in the air. "Did you see that?"

Robbie's laughter echoed in the valley. He joined her on the shore. "I got it all on camera too."

"I should have known." She challenged, "Care for a little friendly wager?"

His hazel eyes twinkled. "Always."

She tapped her finger to her lower lip and looked amused. "Whoever has the most skips out of six times doesn't have to cook or clean up tonight or tomorrow night."

His eyebrow arched. "Feeling pretty confident you're going to win?"

She put her game face on and then burst out laughing. "Let's just say if my first attempt was any indication, I've got this locked."

"And if it's a tie?" he drawled.

Her nose wrinkled. "Best out of seven?"

"Game on."

They went in different directions, selecting what each considered the perfect rocks for the competition. Kenzie's pockets were weighed down when she met Robbie.

"I've done my first, so feel free to let your rock fly." She folded her arms over her chest and stepped aside to give him plenty of room.

Robbie planted his back foot. Turning the rock over in

his hand and holding it at a slight upward angle, he let it sail across the smooth water.

One, two, three, four times it hopped before sinking beneath the glass-like surface.

Grinning, he said, "We're tied!"

Kenzie sashayed to the edge and tossed a flirtatious look over her shoulder. "Watch and weep." With careful precision, she pulled six flat, smooth stones from her pockets. "Do you mind if I do all but one?"

"Not at all," he said. "Hold on, I want photographic evidence."

Kenzie selected her first stone and rocked back and forth in her stance.

Robbie teased, "No creative counting."

The first rock got three hops, the second sunk, the third hopped twice, the fourth hopped five times, and the final rock skipped four times.

"Your turn." Looking pleased with herself she held out her hand. "I'm going to be the photographer now."

He handed her the camera. "Just point and shoot."

Each rock he threw had the same results, just in a different order than Kenzie. "I guess it all comes down to our final toss."

Robbie took the camera and set it down on his pack. "Ladies first."

Kenzie took a deep breath and then let it sail over the water. She jumped in the air and let out a warrior whoop. "*Six*! Beat that!"

Laughing, he stepped up and winked at her. "Wanna see the perfect rock?"

"No." She pointed to the water. "Stop stalling."

With a flick of his wrist, the rock skipped over the surface, the sun's rays highlighting each hop.

Kenzie counted. "One. Two. Three. Four. Five. Six.

Seven." She whirled around, her mouth gaping. "How did you manage that?"

"Years of practice and the perfect triangular rock." He smirked. "Now that KP duty is settled for the next two nights, let's have lunch. And for the record, I'll take care of packing lunch for tomorrow."

"Aren't you the sweetest guy?" she drawled.

"Actually, I've been told I am." He grinned.

"Wasn't that sunrise amazing? The summit trail is more intense. I'm glad we're saving it for tomorrow." Kenzie babbled on, not really expecting answers to her questions. Robbie had been snapping pictures, which kept slowing them down, and it didn't faze her at all. She loved watching him, totally caught up in the beauty around them. "I wish I had a hobby I was passionate about."

Never missing a step, he said, "What have you always wanted to try?"

"I've never really given it much thought. Time hasn't been on my side." She gave him a sidelong look. "I got good grades in school, played sports and decided on a career in fitness. There hasn't been an opportunity to think about it, much less try anything."

"You should slow down a bit. Now that we have Cheryl, maybe you could take the time to find something you've always wanted to do."

She tugged on the shoulder straps and pointed out what she felt was obvious. "Is your photography more than a mere hobby?"

"Kenz, we're not talking about me, okay?" He adjusted the camera strap around his neck. "Ready to head down?"

She kicked the ground, sending pebbles skittering down the trail. "Yeah."

The descent back to camp was uneventful. As he followed Kenzie, he was reminded that she was so close but still so far away. Was he a fool to be in love with a woman who looked at him as a buddy, a friend? Was there hope something could change their relationship and give him what he longed for?

Letting his mind wander, he thought how one of the nice things about hiking was there was plenty of time for personal reflection.

They were rounding the last bend when camp came into view. Robbie watched as Kenzie sloughed off her backpack, leaving it inside the tent. She grabbed some kindling wood, and made a teepee structure in the fire pit. He loved watching her totally focus on the task at hand.

Stretching out her hands near the growing flames, she said. "That feels good."

"Are you cold?" Robbie leaned in and tugged her wool cap lower on her head.

"Not really, it just feels good." She glanced up at the sky. "No cloud cover tonight, so it's going to be pretty chilly."

"I'm going to gather some more wood if you want to get dinner started." He smirked.

With a slow shake of her head, she grinned. "Somehow I thought you might overlook that you're the rock skipping champion."

"Not a chance." He walked toward the edge of the campsite. "Keep your bear spray close."

She held up a can. "You too."

He patted his pant leg and reassured her, "I'm good."

～

Kenzie perched on the edge of the log and watched the flames dance. Today had been good. Hiking with Robbie was always fun, but there was something different this trip. She couldn't quite put her finger on it, but she felt closer to him than she ever had.

The dress. She closed her eyes and could picture Robbie holding out his hand to her. Did he appear because he had always been a part of her life? There were many unanswered questions and no one to help her figure things out. She wished she could call Gran. *She'd* have the answers. If Kenzie tried to talk to Robbie, he'd think she was crazy.

The sun dipped lower in the sky and Kenzie glanced at her watch. The fire was almost ready to start cooking dinner. After crossing the small clearing to the bear box, she flipped open the top. Taking out what she needed, she heard a rustle in the underbrush.

She paused and patted her pant leg. Remaining calm she looked around. *Where was the bear spray?* Slowly backing up, she reached behind her, and her fingers felt the cool metal of the can. Holding it in front of her, she was ready to pull the trigger. Her heart pounded. The rustling grew faint and she let go of the breath she had been holding. Sinking to the ground, she waited for her heart to return to a steady beat.

A tuneless whistle drifted to her. It was like the finest symphony ever written. Robbie.

She leapt up and raced toward him. He dropped the logs as she jumped into his arms. "There." She pointed. "I think. Was. A. Bear."

He looked all around camp while holding her tight. "Are you hurt?"

"No." Slowly she shook her head. Embarrassed about her overreaction, she said, "It just freaked me out. It was close."

Comforted by his nearness, there was something else. Tenderness swept over her. She felt color flood her cheeks and she loosened her arms. For a fraction of a second, she wanted to claim his mouth with hers.

Wriggling against him, she said in a husky voice, "You can let me go now."

Robbie was slow to release her. "I'm okay," Kenzie said. Too often she was seeking the warmth of his embrace, but was there an underlying reason? It was something she had best figure out. "I'm going to start dinner."

She could feel his eyes on her as she moved about camp, adding a log to the fire and setting up the pot to cook on the flat rock.

Robbie walked the perimeter of camp. "You stay by the fire. I'm going to see if we have any unwanted guests lingering."

Determined to face her fear, she announced, "I'm coming with you." She held up the bear spray she still clutched. Her knuckles were white. "I'm prepared."

He chuckled. "You run faster than me, so I'll be its dinner."

His laughter lightened her heart. "He with the fastest feet doesn't become a Scooby snack."

Robbie grabbed a flashlight and pointed it at the under-brush all around camp. "I'm sure he's gone." He looked at her. "Kenz?"

She glanced up. "Yes?"

"You seem…" He shrugged. "I don't know, distracted. Besides the bear thing, I mean."

Giving him a shaky smile, she assured him, "Really, I'm fine."

He took the can from her hand. "Let me help with dinner."

"Heck no. You're not going to be able to hold that over my head. A bet's a bet."

He grinned, but his eyes were clouded with concern. She threw everything together in the pot and set it near the heat to simmer.

She lay a hand on his arm. "I know that look, Burns, and you know me—I'm fine, really."

He stoked the fire. "We should turn in early tonight. Tomorrow's hike is long."

They sat in companionable silence. Kenzie stirred the soup and checked the veggies for doneness. "We'll enjoy a delicious packaged dinner, relax by the fire and turn in. I know you wanted to leave before daybreak, but let's make sure we catch the sunrise."

"Are you making coffee in the morning?" he teased.

Shaking her head, she laughed. "I'm in charge of dinner. Coffee wasn't part of the bargain."

Robbie chuckled softly. "I've got it covered."

Kenzie pointed to their bowls. "Dinner is served, sir."

His smile caused her pulse to find a new brisk rhythm.

What is that all about? Kenzie watched him dig in the backpack for some crackers, and inwardly she sighed. *I'm growing more confused by the day.*

CHAPTER 11

After another cotton-candy-colored sunrise, the hike to the summit had been intense. Kenzie and Robbie had to focus on their footing. Small boulders littered the trail due to heavy rains during the previous few weeks.

Kenzie flopped on a large, flat boulder, basking in the sun while Robbie walked around snapping pictures. With her eyes closed, the soft whir of the camera soothed her jagged nerves. She couldn't put her finger on what was bothering her; it wasn't about her vision in the mirror for a change.

"Hey, Kenz."

"Hmm?" She kept her eyes closed.

"Ya gotta look at this view."

There was something in his voice that prodded her to open her eyes. She pushed herself to a half-sitting position.

"Come here. The way the sun is hitting the ridge is incredible. I've never seen the tree line look like this."

She carefully stepped across the stone, and with a hand shading her eyes she scanned the view. "It's so peaceful here." It was breathtaking—the sky was a brilliant blue with a few large puffy clouds drifting lazily. The silence embraced them and she felt like they were the only two people in the world. She pointed to a tree that stood out from the rest; it was a brilliant orange amidst the rust and yellow colors. "Did you get that tree over there?"

He pointed the camera in the direction of her arm and clicked. "Got it."

"Now let's have lunch before it's time to head down."

He wagged his finger at her and teased, "Not so fast. I need a couple shots with you."

She held out her hand. "You've got me in enough pictures. Give me the camera and I'll take a few of you."

He moved with unhurried purpose, concentrating on the scenery. "After."

She laughed. "You won't give in for a nanosecond, will you?"

Shaking his head, he chuckled. "Nope, not any more than you give into me."

Kenzie mugged for the camera, posing in a variety of silly poses. She took a step back. "Do you have my good side?" The camera whirred as she moved backwards.

"How about now?" She took another step back, and the rocks began to crumble under her weight. Crushing panic took her breath away. With a strangled scream, she uttered one word: "Robbie!"

She felt his hand clamp around her wrist, and jerked. She landed with a thud against his chest. His arms held her tight as he dragged her away from the edge. Their deep, ragged breaths filled the air.

"Robbie? What? What happened?" She clung to him, not wanting to see anything but his shirt.

"You're safe. Don't worry, I've got you." He kissed the top of her head as he made soft, comforting sounds.

"But? What happened?" She saw where she had been standing, the rock was gone. She took one tentative step toward the edge and stopped. Her voice shaking, she said, "Do you see this?"

He nodded, his face ashen. "You almost went for a ride down the face of the mountain."

She shuddered. "A one-way trip." A sob rushed up from deep inside of her. "You saved me."

"Of course I did." Teasing, but his eyes filled with the horror of what might have been. "And you can repay me by building the fire tonight."

Kenzie looked into Robbie's eyes. She blinked back the tears that threatened to spill down her cheeks. A tentative smile slipped over her lips. "I know what you're trying to do."

"What's that?" His arm was still around her waist.

"Make me forget." She laid a hand over his hammering heart. The beat matched hers.

"And is it working?" His voice was tender.

"It is." She was safe in his arms. Inhaling deeply, she drank in his all-male scent. She tightened her arms around his waist. She looked up. The scruffiness of his beard suited him.

Running her tongue over her lips, she knew without a doubt that she wanted him. At this very moment.

She pulled his mouth to hers, claiming it. She felt him hesitate for a fraction of a second before holding her tighter, lifting her off her feet, kissing her deeper. Caught up in her desire, she was driven to taste him, savor him, devour him.

Robbie started to set her down and she clung to him. Her voice broke with huskiness. "Don't stop."

He groaned, "Kenzie, we can't..." His voice died away.

She took his hand and laid it on her breast. "Touch me," she demanded softly.

He scooped her up in his arms and scanned the summit.

"Over there." Kenzie pointed to a partially hidden area in the tree line.

Within a few strides, he placed her on the ground as if she were a porcelain doll. He knelt next to her. Placing feather-light kisses on her palm, he lifted his head, their eyes connecting. "Are you sure?"

She dragged his mouth to hers. "No talking."

Her teeth nibbled on his lower lip. With quick hands, she relieved him of his jacket and layers of shirts until her hands caressed his skin. She had seen him bare-chested thousands of times, but this was different.

Robbie submitted to her tender touch. She traced the outline of each muscle in his arms, over his six-pack and back up again.

"Care to let me explore?" His simple question filled her with excitement. She shivered as he slipped her jacket off a shoulder, taking his time he laid each layer of clothing in a pile next to them. "Are you cold?"

Words died on her lips. She shook her head.

His finger slipped under a bra strap and followed the lace. With a deft flick of the clasp in between her breasts, they were skin to skin. His gaze warmed her skin, his voice like silk. "You are so beautiful."

His mouth claimed her again, heat rising between them. Her breath was ragged.

"I want to see all of you." He piled his discarded clothes as a pillow for her and laid her back. He untied her hiking boots and tossed them aside. Slipping his finger into the top of her pants, he slowly unbuttoned them and the zipper moved south. He stopped, his eyes fixated on her.

"More," she groaned. Lifting her hips he pulled them off, along with her panties. She sucked in a breath.

He stood, leaving her body cooling. Kicking off his boots and hurriedly discarding his pants, he stood in the crisp air, the sunlight dappled through the trees. She had never seen a man who she wanted more. She raised her arms, beckoning him to her.

He lay with her in the soft grass. Robbie slowly ran a finger down the core of her body. Her entire being filled with desire. His lips followed his fingers to her very center. He lingered there, caressing and teasing. She moaned. His hand cupped her breast while his mouth was busy nibbling every square inch of her body. She arched, giving him access to all of her. Her skin felt on fire where he touched. She had never felt like this before. She wanted—no, she needed more.

Her hands traveled the length of his back and up his sides. Tendons and muscle went taut. She marveled how touching him filled her with tenderness and pure joy. Passion roared in her veins. Pushing him to lay back, she started with her lips on his. Her teeth grazed his earlobe, and from there she slid down his neck to his collarbone in triple slow motion, listening as his breath quickened, and she could feel his heart pound under her body.

Letting go of her inhibitions, her hand moved over his taut abdomen. She hesitated and his hand guided hers. She stroked and teased him to the point of release and then moved her hand away. Before she could imprison his body with hers, he pulled a small packet from his jeans, and slipped it over his maleness.

Setting herself on top, two became one. All senses hummed, their connection intense. Without urgency, they moved together like they had years of experience making love with each other, her breasts crushed against his chest, his hands resting on her hips.

Kenzie needed more of him, her desire driving her to new heights. As if he sensed what she needed, he matched her rhythm. She screamed his name. Her world exploded and her defenses shattered. In this moment she was his, heart, body and soul.

Wrapped in his arms, she melted even farther into him. With one powerful thrust, he gave her all he had. Spent, the couple lay wrapped in the cool air, but a newfound connection kept them warm.

He kissed the top of her head and held her close while his heart returned to something of a normal cadence. If this was a dream, he never wanted to wake up. This was the single, best moment of his life.

She gazed into his eyes. A small smile played over her face. She inched closer and lightly kissed his lips. "You're amazing," she cooed.

He traced the line of her cheek with his fingertip and tilted her chin up. "Together we're amazing."

She sighed. "I feel like an overcooked noodle."

Holding her tenderly, he said, "My favorite kind."

A crash in the underbrush reminded him where they were, and the sky held the promise of rain. "As much as I'd love to hold you like this all day, we need to eat and hit the trail."

She pushed herself back from his body and playfully tugged at his chest hair. "Always practical."

He was reluctant to break this moment, as she closed her eyes. Committing how she felt in his arms to memory.

He grinned. "A hike in the pouring rain isn't fun, but we can continue this later, at camp."

A slow, seductive smile crept over her face. "I like how you think."

Robbie helped her up. They quickly dressed, tying their boots tight. They found a nice large rock to sit on for lunch. Kenzie handed Robbie a bottle of water. "Here."

He took a long drink and looked up to the sky to the ominous dark clouds. "We're burning daylight with a long hike ahead, and it's definitely going to get wet."

They inhaled the sandwiches. She began stuffing her cargo pockets with trail mix and dried fruit for a quick and easy snack on the long hike ahead of them. Kenzie was suddenly self-conscious. "Robbie, are you really okay with what happened?"

He gathered her in his arms. "I'm more than okay." Concern filled his eyes. "Do you regret it?"

She stood on her tiptoes and tenderly kissed his mouth. "I have one regret."

Shock flashed over his face. She kissed him again. "I wish we had done this sooner."

Robbie held her. "It happened at just the right time." He bent his head and his lips claimed hers. His kiss was laced with the promise of things to come.

With a last lingering caress of her cheek, he said, "Ready?"

She squeezed his hand. "The trail's calling."

Picking up their poles, they started the trek down. Kenzie kept looking up at the ominous clouds.

Robbie was behind her, keeping a steady pace. They were halfway back to camp and rounding a blind corner when Kenzie turned and smiled seductively at Robbie.

He yelled. "Kenzie! Watch out!"

Turning, she caught a glimpse of a large rock. It was too late. Her hiking boot struck the edge; she was falling.

Instinctively, she put out her right hand in an attempt to break her fall. She couldn't stop herself from going head over heels. Crushing pain from her left ankle registered before her head connected with the cold, hard ground.

A vise constricted his heart. Kenzie was lying on the ground, not moving.

He moved with the speed of a cheetah. Crouching over her, he gently probed the back of her head. Blood. He ran his fingers over her left arm—all appeared intact. Her right wrist was another story. It was twisted at an odd angle.

Keeping his voice steady, he urged, "Kenzie. Come on, sweetheart, open your eyes."

His blood thundered in his veins. He didn't need to examine her wrist; he could tell from experience and the blooming bruise it was broken. He turned his attention to her legs. Her right leg appeared to be fine, but the left ankle was clearly fractured, the bone not quite protruding from the skin.

"Kenz. Come on, I need for you to flash those crystal blue eyes at me." He continued to cajole her as he fumbled in his pack for something to stanch the flow of blood. Cursing, he slipped a bandana under her head, ever so carefully, and tied it tight.

He dug his cell from his pocket and started to dial. *We need help.* "Son of a…" He shoved it back in his pocket. Inwardly he groaned. *No service.*

He rubbed Kenzie's left hand and couldn't help but notice the chill. "Kenz, come on, honey. Stay with me."

Unsure how much time had passed, Robbie gazed skyward. They didn't have many hours left of daylight.

Kenzie groaned. She attempted to move her right hand and cried out. Her face went white as a sheet. "Robbie?" The panic in her voice tore at his heart.

He squeezed her hand. "I'm right here, Kenz. Don't move."

"What. Happened?" she eked out.

"You tripped." He slipped a hand under her shoulder. "Do you think you can sit up?"

She touched her fingers to her forehead and, feeling the bandana, frowned. "I hit my head?"

He moved closer, hoping his body warmth would transfer to her rapidly chilling skin. "You did, but the bleeding has slowed."

Her eyelids fluttered, as if trying to blink away the fogginess. "What's wrong with my wrist? I can't move it."

"I'm pretty sure you broke it when you fell."

She stammered, "And my foot?" She tried to sit up. "Oh my god, I think I'm going…" Her voice trailed off and her eyes squeezed shut.

He caught her in his arms as she fell back toward the cold, hard ground. "Kenz, listen to me." Holding her carefully, he snapped, "Kenzie!"

She moaned. "Stop shouting, I want to sleep."

"You have to stay awake."

"Robbie." Her voice was barely audible.

"I'm here." He rubbed her good hand, hoping it would be enough to help keep her warm.

"I don't think I can walk." She shivered violently.

He crumbled inside. "I'll carry you."

"But we have miles to go. Can't you call for help?"

"No service. Once we get to camp, I'll make you comfortable and then call rescue."

She clutched the front of his shirt, her voice thick. "Help me sit up?"

"If you start to black out or feel sick, focus on my voice."

Tears sprang to her eyes. "It's gonna hurt, isn't it?"

"I'm afraid so. But I'll be as gentle as possible." He hoped his voice was calming and didn't betray the fear that had settled in the pit of his stomach. He slipped his arm under her shoulders. Her eyes fluttered. "I'm going to take your pack off."

With his free hand, he pulled the straps from her shoulders. Beads of sweat appeared on her forehead and she bit her lip as tears flowed silently down her cheeks.

"It's okay to cry," he said gently, "it's just me."

She grimaced. Her voice was determined. "I can't. Give. In. To. The pain." Each word was filled with fresh tears and a gulp of air.

Holding her in his arms, he knew the trip down was going to be brutal. His internal debate raged—should he take the chance to move her, or leave her to search for cell service, then wait for help?

He waited as the tears slowed. "How are you doing?"

She gritted her teeth. "Just great," she snarled. "I want to stand up."

"I like a girl with a little spunk. Tell me when you're ready."

She took a deep breath. "Now."

Holding her like she would shatter, he set her on her good foot while bearing her full weight.

"Robbie!" she cried as she began to sag to the ground. "Wait!"

He scooped her into his arms. "It's okay, I've got you."

"Can I sit down?"

"How about that rock?" He pointed to a boulder a few

feet down the trail. "Maybe I can do something to support your wrist."

Taking deep, ragged breaths, she nodded.

Robbie strode to the boulder. He set her down, careful to not jostle her wrist or ankle. Kenzie hadn't mentioned the odd angle of her foot and he wasn't going to point it out.

Her eyes were closed. With each exhale, she was counting out loud, drawing out each word. "One. Two. Three."

"That's great. Stay focused. I'm just going to grab our packs and take out what's essential for tonight."

Kenzie kept counting, not responding to what he said. Robbie hurried up the path and grabbed the packs, then rushed back to her. Rummaging inside her pack, he found an ace bandage. He unrolled it and fashioned a sling. He guided her injured wrist through the loop and over her head. "How's that?"

She bit her bottom lip and very softly said, "Okay, I guess." He adjusted it and she gave him a barely there smile. "That's better."

He handed her a bottle of water. "Here, drink something."

"It'd be better if it was a wee shot of Jamieson."

"There's my little Scottish girl." He gently cupped her cheek. "The next part isn't going to be as easy."

"My ankle's bad, isn't it?"

"I'm not going to kid you, sweetheart, it's not good."

Worry creased her brow. "What can we do?"

Doing his best to sound competent, he said, "I can make a splint, put it around your boot and secure it."

Matter of factly, she gestured to her pack. "In the first aid kit there should be some gauze."

He dug down to the bottom and pulled out a knit cap and the kit. He carefully pulled the cap over the bandana. Flipping open the lid, he discovered a splint and a tiny roll of gauze.

"If you bleed through the bandana, the cap will help. But there isn't enough gauze to wrap around your boot."

Through clenched teeth she said, "Duct tape." She took several deeper breaths, in through her nose and out through her mouth.

"Huh?" The flash of confusion had her point to the bag. He dumped the bag upside down and pushed aside a few useless items before holding up a roll of hot pink duct tape. "Pink?'

Her lips formed a thin line, her eyes narrowed. "Do you have a problem with pink?"

He shook his head. "Nope, just surprised is all." Robbie sat on the ground and looked at her foot. "This is going to hurt."

She pointed to a small velvet bag on the ground. "Can I have that, please?"

He watched as she unzipped it. She pulled a locket out and slipped it over her head. "My sisters and I each have one and we take them everywhere." She held it tight in her hand. "This way I can pretend they're with us, holding my hand."

Using the pad of his thumb, he reached up and wiped the tears from her cheeks. "That's really sweet."

She murmured, "Get it over with."

Robbie did his best to work quickly and with as little tugging and pulling as possible. He knew how much pain he was inflicting, but it was necessary to get her ankle stabilized before they went any farther. With the final strip of tape secured, he said, "Done."

"Can I sit here for a couple of minutes before you move

me again?" Her breath was coming in short and shallow bursts.

He rocked back on his heels. "Kenzie, I'm struggling. I think you should stay here, but I don't want to leave you to get help." He rubbed her cold hand between his. "I'm scared I can't keep you warm enough until help arrives."

Kenzie's lower lip trembled. "Don't leave me."

He swallowed hard. "I won't."

Trusting eyes met his. Softly she said, "Robbie, we can make it to camp—I believe in you."

He gently pecked her lips. "If the pain gets to be too much, you need to tell me and we'll take a break, as many as you need." He grabbed his bag. "I need to consolidate our packs."

Worry furrowed her brow. "Are you carrying a bag and me?"

"There are things I have to take." He tossed items in his pack and put hers on the side of the trail. After hoisting it on his back, a rustle deep in the trees made Robbie turn around slowly, and he started singing really loud.

Kenzie groaned, "You're off key again."

He kept singing at very loud volume. "I don't think wildlife is concerned if I'm on key, just letting them know that we're here."

"Are we going to make it back to camp?" Fear filled her voice and her teeth chattered.

He dropped to his knees and took her good hand. "I promise you I'm going to get you safely back to camp and to the hospital."

Her eyes locked on him. She brought his hand to her cheek. "I know you will."

"Now, if you're ready, I'm going to get us out of here."

In a small, soft voice, she asked, "Will you be careful picking me up?"

"I can't promise it will be painless, but I'll do my best."

She closed her eyes, seeming to focus. "Okay."

Robbie made a couple of adjustments to the shoulder straps. "You'll need to put your good arm around my neck when I lean over, but don't help me lift you."

She protested, "I'm dead weight."

"I'll bend my knees." He gave her a small, encouraging smile.

"Always the smart aleck."

He bent over and she slipped her left hand around his neck, holding her breath. "One. Two." Robbie lifted Kenzie in the air with ease.

Through gritted teeth, she croaked, "What happened to three?"

"You're mad because I didn't say three?" he teased.

"I wanted to be prepared."

He snorted. "Always wanting to be in control."

Robbie's fast pace ate up the ground as he bantered with Kenzie, doing his best to keep her mind off the pain. The yards clicked off and she kept up the reasons why lifting with his knees was better for his back, and to be fair, giving the full count let the injured party know what was to come. She kept going back over these two points until he felt the first drop of icy rain.

Kenzie was shivering in his arms. He stated flatly, "You're cold."

"No, I'm fine." Her teeth chattering loudly betrayed her. She grew quiet.

He liked it better when she was argumentative. Her silence drove him down the trail faster. The rain became steady. Kenzie's face was drawn tight and her long dark lashes rested against her alabaster skin. He didn't like the way she looked. "Kenzie, does this mean you're not cooking dinner tonight?"

She didn't answer.

"Kenzie?" he demanded.

Her eyes fluttered open. Tears clouded her blue eyes. "Are we there yet?"

"Almost. Another couple hundred feet."

She closed her eyes again and moaned. "I'm so cold."

"I know, sweetheart, but hang in there. I'm going to get a fire going and you'll be warm soon."

"It's raining." She tried to burrow into his chest.

His lips brushed the top of her hat. "I know, but that's never stopped me before."

Softly she said, "You're good at fire."

"Kenzie," he urged, "look. Camp."

With a catch in her voice, she breathed, "Finally."

Robbie's heart was pounding. His blood roared in his head. With Kenzie and a backpack, it was a heavy load. The worst was behind them, he hoped. "I'm going to set you down next to the fire pit and then get your rain poncho."

"It's in the tent."

"Not to worry, I'll find it."

"You think of everything." She groaned as he placed her on a large rock. "My ankle."

He hastened around and carefully positioned her leg out straight. Scanning camp, he found a small stump. "See that log? I'm going to prop your leg up and I need you to stay put."

"I'm not going anywhere." Robbie placed his hand under her arm, bearing the brunt of her weight as she repositioned herself.

He could feel her grow limp, and before the words *I'm dizzy* could leave her lips, he caught her. "Damn it all."

CHAPTER 12

As if through a fog, Kenzie could hear Robbie, but she couldn't understand what he was saying. It sounded like he was calling her a baby.

She struggled to open her eyelids, but they felt as if they had weights holding them down. Robbie was hovering over her, his brown hair damp and curling, hazel eyes clouded with worry.

"Kenz?" He cradled her in his arms.

Her voice trembled. "What happened? Did I pass out?"

"You did, but not to worry, I caught you."

She looked at her foot wrapped in pink duct tape and her arm held tight to her body with an ace bandage. "I was hoping it was a bad dream."

With a shake of his head, he said, "Afraid not."

"I'm not going to take another tumble into darkness." Her words were razor sharp as she tried to move.

"I see you haven't lost your snarky retorts." His gaze held hers.

"Part of my charm." She winced.

Softly he admonished her, "Try not to wiggle around so much."

"My foot hurts." She wiped away the tears that hovered on her lashes with the back of her good hand. "My head hurts, and for good measure, so does my wrist."

He looked somber. "That's because it's broken, cut and broken. In that order."

"Not that one, the good one." Irritation laced her words. "There's a branch poking me."

Robbie repositioned Kenzie. "I wish you'd get some color in your cheeks. And in my defense, all I wanted to do was make sure you didn't hit your head again. I didn't see the branch."

Her eyes fluttered and ignored his comments. "I have a monster of a headache." She reached up, gingerly touching the bandana, and asked, "Have you looked at it again?"

"Not recently, but you're not bleeding through the hat, so I'm taking that as a very good sign."

Her expression brightened a little. "Any chance I could have some water?"

He grabbed her canteen, twisting off the cap as he handed it to her. "If you are feeling okay, I'm going to call for help and then start a fire."

She looked up at him, her eyes round as saucers. "I'll keep it together." Glancing around the clearing, she said, "It stopped raining."

"Our first break." He visibly shrank. "Sorry, I mean it's a good thing the rain stopped."

"You don't need to tiptoe around me." She gave him a tiny smile. "You're punny."

"Don't you mean funny?"

Giving him a wary smile, she said, "Nope, you're just full of puns, hence punny."

"You must have really hit your head. There will be plenty of time for bad jokes later."

"Now go make a phone call and then a fire." She did her best to stop shivering, but her chattering teeth gave her away. "Can you reverse that, fire first?" She held out her uninjured hand to him and he took it. ""Robbie? You've been great keeping my mind off of everything. Don't stop."

Giving it a squeeze, he crossed his heart. "Just like when we were kids, you can count on me." He let her hand drop back to her lap before building the fire. "You'll be warm in a jiff."

Flames shot up from the fire pit. Kenzie focused on each of Robbie's movements to keep her mind off the throbbing pain in her extremities and the pounding in her head.

"Hi, Dad. There's been an accident and we need help."

Kenzie hung onto each word she could hear.

"It's Kenzie. She has a broken wrist and ankle, and a possible concussion. She fell on the way down the trail."

He was nodding. "I need a rescue team. I left papers on my kitchen table where we set up base camp. Can you call her parents and sisters? I'm sure she'll be transported to the medical center in Littleton."

He looked at Kenzie and dropped his voice, but she heard every word he said. "Dad, tell them to hurry. She's in a lot of pain and the temperatures are dropping."

After saying goodbye, Robbie slipped his phone into his coat pocket. "Dad's got everything covered." He added a couple of logs to the crackling fire. "We're going to need to move you closer."

Clutching her locket with a trembling voice, she whimpered, "Please don't make me."

After striding to the tent, he flipped back the door and pulled out his sleeping bag. He unzipped and wrapped it around her back and shoulders as best he could. Concern filled his eyes. "Does that feel better?"

"It does, but what about you?" She broke out in a cold sweat and her pulse raced. What if something happened to Robbie? They'd really be in a pickle.

He rubbed her shoulder, trying to comfort her. "I'm moving around, so I'll be fine."

She dropped her chin to her chest. "I'm sorry." Fresh tears threatened to fall.

He knelt down and pushed it up. Tenderly he said, "What do you need to be sorry about?"

Her lower lip quivered. "Ruining our trip."

He caressed her cheek and pecked her lips. "You didn't. It'll just give us a new story to talk about for years to come."

"That's one way to look at it." Kenzie wasn't so sure she wanted to revisit this adventure anytime soon.

Grinning he suggested, "How about some freeze-dried dinner?"

She attempted to smile a bit. "That might help warm me from the inside out."

He laughed. "You're expecting me to cook? Did you forget you lost our bet yesterday?"

Kenzie grabbed a small rock lying next to her and hurled it in his direction. "Stop teasing me—can't you see I'm in pain?"

He pretended to duck but her aim missed by at least a foot.

Kenzie's eyes darted from side to side as fear wrapped icy fingers around her heart. "How long do you think it will take for someone to get here?" Clumsily she pulled the sleeping bag tighter. "Robbie, will it be hard for them to find us?"

"I was very specific on the map about where we're camping, how far we were hiking each day—very detailed."

"My hero." She sighed and held out her good hand toward the now roaring fire.

He held up his middle three fingers and stood at attention. "Eagle Scout Robbie Burns, at your service."

As scared as she felt inside, something let go when she watched Robbie do the scout salute. She'd rather be injured in the woods with him than with anyone else on earth. She trusted him with her life.

Robbie smirked and held up a couple of packets. "So how about that soup?"

With all the joking around, Robbie hoped Kenzie would never know how scared he actually felt. His stomach was in knots as he held her in his arms, conserving their body heat but needing the reassurance that her breathing was steady.

The fire burned bright. Time crawled and the night sky was dotted with tiny pinpricks of light. The stars gave him comfort; there wouldn't be rain or snow tonight. He longed to call his dad again, but knew it was just a matter of time until help arrived.

Kenzie moaned and shivered, snuggling closer to Robbie as he pulled the sleeping bag tighter. Time seemed to stop, but watching the moon, he knew the hours were creeping by.

He heard voices in the frigid night air. A deep, commanding voice broke the night. "Kenzie MacLellan, Robbie Burns. Are you here?"

Robbie patted Kenzie's arm. "Kenzie, honey, they're here."

"Huh, what?" She tried to sit up, but he held her close to his side.

"Over here!" he shouted.

Beams of light cut through the deep shadows as four men in dark red jackets with reflector patches stepped into camp. The same deep voice announced, "Mountain Rescue Association."

Kenzie lifted her head, her eyes dull. "I'm Kenzie."

An MRA team member said, "Heard you took a bad fall today."

"One minute I was on two feet, the next I woke up lying on my back with a foot I can't stand on, my head bleeding and a wrist that doesn't bend."

Gear was being set around the open area and Robbie stepped aside, giving the professionals room to work while he kept an eagle eye on the situation. He was relieved they weren't alone anymore. Kenzie was going to be fine.

"Kenzie, I'm Mike. I'm going to check your vitals and take a look at your head and wrist, but we're not going to mess with the splint on your ankle. We'll let the pros handle that at the hospital."

Frantically, she looked around. "Wait, where's Robbie?"

Hearing the panic in her voice, Robbie stepped from the shadows. "I'm here, Kenz."

She stretched out her hand. "Will you stay with me?"

His heart flipped and he took her outstretched hand. "I'm not going anywhere."

"Kenzie?" A different man in a red jacket stood in front of her. "I'm going to take your hat off, but I'd like for you to remain perfectly still while I examine the laceration."

Her grip on Robbie's hand tightened. In a small voice she said, "Okay."

Using scissors, the man cut off the hat and bandana. Robbie thought his headlamp cast a halo on Kenzie's bloodstained hair. "It seems to be shallow. Head wounds always bleed a lot, but you shouldn't need stitches."

"Finally, some good news." Kenzie tried to crack a small smile, then caught sight of a metal stretcher on the ground. "Are you carrying me out?"

"Yes, ma'am," said the man who had examined her head. "Robbie, you're going to want to douse the fire, and if there's anything else either of you need, best grab it."

Robbie reluctantly let go of Kenzie's hand. "I'm going to get my keys and our cell phones. I'll be right back."

He hurried around camp, pouring water on the fire and then shoveling dirt into the pit. The last thing they needed was to start a forest fire. Kicking the remnants, he saw there weren't any embers. After throwing items they'd need into his backpack, he took one last look around. "I'm all set. I can hike up and get the rest."

"You can't come back up here by yourself." Kenzie's voice trembled with fear.

He rushed back to her side. "Shh. We're not going to worry about that tonight."

Mike said, "Kenzie, it's time to get you settled and secured into the stretcher."

With a tiny nod of her head, she looked into Robbie's eyes. "I'm ready."

Robbie took the sleeping bag from her shoulders and tossed it into the tent. Two MSA members stood on either side of her and in unison lifted her up. Very gently, they set her in the stretcher, being careful not to jostle her ankle or wrist.

"Lay back, please."

She did as requested. Straps over her thighs, waist and around her chest held her secure. Her wrist was supported with a sling and the broken ankle was propped up slightly. Someone tucked a shiny blanket around her.

"Kenzie, this is light, so it shouldn't add weight to your wrist or ankle, but it's warm."

She bit her lip. "When does everything stop hurting?"

"After we get you to the hospital. They'll give you something before they cut off your boot."

Her eyes were dull as she grumbled, "I just bought them."

Robbie walked alongside the stretcher, holding her hand as the MSA team's headlamps lit the way.

"Robbie?" Her voice was steady.

He glanced down at her. "Hmm?"

"Do you think this will affect my ability to hike or run?" She held onto his hand tight.

He knew she needed something to cling to. When this was over she'd be good as new. "That'll depend on you. If you do what the doctors say, you'll make a full recovery."

"And let me guess, you're gonna be right there making sure I do?" By the light of the headlamps he could see she gave him a half-hearted smile.

Robbie grinned. "You can count on it."

She snapped, "Don't be annoying," and closed her eyes as the group made swift progress down the trail.

One of the rescue guys asked, "Is she always like this?"

With a shake of his head Robbie said, "You have no idea."

"Hey, can you guys keep it down? I'm trying to snooze."

Kenzie's voice was soft, but Robbie caught Mike's attention on the quiet trek and raised an eyebrow. Mike said, "Kenzie, we don't want you to sleep."

Robbie kept his voice steady. "You don't have to talk, but you can listen and answer occasionally."

She fell silent, rocked by the gentle sway of her stretcher. The trip down the mountain was going smoothly.

"Kenz?" He decided to try a new tactic to keep her from drifting off. Annoy her with questions from time to time.

"Hmm?" She kept her eyes firmly closed.

Robbie applied gentle pressure to her hand, hoping she'd look at him. "How do you feel about finding a new place to hike next year?"

She looked at him through squinted eyes. "This is our favorite mountain. You don't want to come back?"

"This trip has been one for the record books. Do you realize you had three mishaps?"

She turned away from him. "No, I wasn't keeping score."

"You burned your hand, almost fell from the summit and then tripped over the rock. That's three."

Kenzie shuddered and shut her eyes. "I don't want to think about the summit."

Robbie's heart dropped. *Does she regret what happened between us?*

She clasped his hand tighter. "Are you driving me to the hospital?"

A deep male voice out of their line of sight said, "There will be an ambulance waiting for you."

"And Robbie?" Her voice quivered. "He's coming with me?"

Realizing he had been quiet for several moments, he said in a rush, "I'll follow in the truck. Your family should be there when we arrive."

"That kinda screws up their week." Fresh tears dripped from the corners of her eyes into her hair.

Robbie patted her shoulder. "You know they'll have to see for themselves that you're okay."

The trees began to thin and the slope of the ground

leveled out. The parking lot was lit up like a Christmas tree with strobing red and blue lights. The sound of metal grating against the pavement had Robbie look up. Someone was rushing over with a gurney. They secured the stretcher that held Kenzie on top of it.

MSA team members were rattling off words so fast it was making his head spin. Kenzie was pushed into the back of the ambulance.

"Robbie!" Hysteria strangled her throat.

"I'm right here, Kenz." He took her hand.

She visibly relaxed when she saw his face. "Please come with me?"

Tenderly he kissed her forehead, running his fingers down the side of the face. He cupped her chin. "I'm going to follow the ambulance."

"I need you…"

"I'm right behind you and I'm not going to leave you."

She tried to nod, but her head was secured as preventative measure against further injury.

Another person from the rescue team asked, "Ms. MacLellan, we need to go."

Robbie leaned over, his lips brushing hers. "I'll see you at the hospital."

She whispered, "Promise?"

Solemnly he said, "I promise."

CHAPTER 13

Robbie raced to his truck, hitting the key fob to unlock the door. He yanked it open and scrambled inside. His heart shattered to see Kenzie leave in the ambulance.

The MSA team had given him the address and he programmed it into his GPS. He squealed out of the parking lot and was right on the ambulance's tail lights.

The ambulance was picking up speed. He pounded his fist on the steering wheel as the lights disappeared around the corner. He pressed the gas pedal and caught sight of them again. He mumbled, "I'm not losing you."

After what seemed like forever but in reality was less than an hour, the ambulance pulled into the emergency room entrance. Robbie found a parking space, which wasn't difficult in the middle of the night. Racing across the lot, he was waiting for her when the back doors opened.

His eyes found Kenzie's and he gave her a reassuring smile. "Hey there. I told you I'd be here."

She lifted her fingers in a half-hearted wave. The

wheeled legs dropped to the pavement and the doors whooshed open. Kenzie was pushed under the harsh overhead lights. Robbie started to follow her down the hall when a nurse hurried over to him. "Sir, can you come to the admitting desk? We need some information."

Torn between following Kenzie or the nurse, common sense won. He needed her to get the best care possible and that meant he had to do his part. He scanned the large empty waiting room. "Has anyone from Kenzie's family called or are they waiting somewhere else?"

"This is the only entrance that's open, so when they get here, you'll see them." The male nurse ushered him to the desk. "Have a seat."

Robbie perched on the edge of the hard, plastic chair. Running his fingers through his hair, he failed to notice headlights sweep the waiting room windows. He was answering routine questions when someone called his name.

Olivia was rushing toward him with James right behind her. "Robbie, where's Kenzie? Is she okay? What happened?"

Before he could answer, Jamie, Caleb and Grace hurried into the room. Robbie opened his mouth to speak, and then his father and Jo brought up the rear.

With a sob Olivia pleaded, "Tell us what happened."

He took a deep breath, steadying his nerves. Calmly he said, "We were hiking down from the summit and Kenzie turned to say something. Before I could stop her, she tripped over a small boulder. She fell, hit her head, broke her ankle and I'm pretty sure her wrist too. We'll know more after the doctor examines her and takes X-rays."

"When did this happen?" James asked.

"Somewhere around two, maybe three, I think." Robbie ran his hand over his three-day scruff. "It all happened so fast. One minute she was smiling at me and jabbering away, and the next she was on the ground, unconscious."

Olivia grabbed James's arm. "Honey, what if she has more serious injuries and all that jostling her down the mountain made it worse?"

James patted her hand. "Liv, they had to move her. I'm sure if there was a significant risk they would have found another way, maybe a helicopter at first light or something."

"Kenzie's pretty tough—you should be proud of her. I can't even begin to imagine how much pain she had to be in, but other than a few tears and fainting once, she was incredibly strong."

Jamie's chin jutted out. "She's a MacLellan."

"Mr. Burns?" The nurse hovered on the edge of the family's circle around Robbie.

He whirled around. "Is she okay?"

"She's asking for you before they take her to X-ray, and since her agitation is increasing, we thought it best for her to see you. But just for a couple of minutes. You can reassure her that you're still here and that her family has arrived."

Robbie watched as Olivia's face fell. "No, her parents should go in to see her."

Olivia straightened her spine and pulled back her shoulders. "Go. Kenzie is asking for you, and if seeing you helps her, that's all I need."

Robbie hesitated. James pointed to the door. "Go," he urged. "She needs you."

He didn't need to be told again. He followed the nurse through the swinging doors.

"Where's Robbie?" Kenzie's voice was shrill as he rushed to her side.

"Right here, Kenz." He took her hand and squeezed it. "Are you giving everyone a hard time?"

Her lower lip trembled. "I thought you left."

"Are you serious? I told you I wouldn't." His fingers grazed her forehead. "The family's here."

"They are?" She tried to pick her head up off the pillow.

"And my dad and Jo too. Seems like everyone wanted to check up on you."

Her voice wavered. "They're taking me to X-ray, and for the record, it hurt like hell when they cut my boot off."

He chuckled and glanced at her foot. "And I'm sure you told them in no uncertain terms."

With a half shrug she stated, "I tried to be ladylike, but it didn't really work. I let a few colorful words fly."

He gave her a tender smile. "I'm sure they've heard it all before and will again."

A pretty blonde lady wearing bright purple scrubs walked into the examination room. "X-ray's waiting, Kenzie." She assured Robbie, "We won't be long and then you can come back in."

Kenzie clung to his hand. "Tell my parents I love them."

"They know you do." He kissed her cheek. "Now be a good patient and don't yell at anyone."

As the gurney was whisked through the doorway, she called out, "I'll try."

With a heavy heart, he returned to the waiting room. Olivia jumped out of the chair and rushed to Robbie's side. "How is she?"

He rubbed his burning eyes. "They've taken her to X-ray and she's as feisty as ever."

Olivia clasped her hands together. "I'll take feisty. I've always heard medical people would prefer to have patients aware of what's going on than silent." Her legs seemed to give way and she sat down heavily in a chair.

"Did they say how long it would be before we could see her?"

Robbie perched on the edge of a chair opposite from Olivia and James and dropped his head in his hands.

James said, "Darlin', we need to be patient. Poor Robbie has been through quite a lot in the last twelve hours or so. Why don't we give him a few minutes? He looks plumb worn out."

Minutes crawled as Robbie stared at the linoleum floor. How long does it take for X-rays, he wondered? He raised his head. "This is my fault. If I had been quicker, she wouldn't have fallen."

Jamie sat down in the chair next to him and massaged his shoulders. "Accidents happen. I know you would have moved heaven and earth to protect her."

Robbie stared into nothingness. Grace crouched in front of him. He was surrounded by MacLellan women. Her voice was gentle as she took his large hands in her small ones. "How are you doing?"

He leaned back in the chair and rubbed his hand across his gritty eyes. "I'm fine, but it should be me in there, not Kenz."

James got up and paced the open floor space in front of the family. Worry was etched on his face. "Robbie Burns, this might not be the best time or place, but since I'm the father of the woman lying in that hospital bed, I'm going to speak my mind."

Robbie pulled himself up from the chair, all six-foot four, standing eye to eye with James. "Sir?"

"Since you were babes, you've been two peas in a pod. Never far from the other. Your affection for my daughter has only deepened and I see she's a strong-willed lass, but dig down deep and ask yourself one question..." Robbie was totally focused on James. "If the worst had happened today and we lost her, would you regret not telling her she's the only woman you've ever loved?"

"Sir. I, we, I mean…" he stammered.

James held up his hand. "Stop! The good Lord doesn't give us infinite chances to live our life to the fullest. Seize the day and do us all a favor: tell Kenzie you love her."

Robbie was speechless.

James caught sight of the doctor and reached for Olivia's hand. They stood side by side with Jamie, Caleb and Grace while Robbie, his dad—George—and Jo waited to hear the news.

"Mr. and Mrs. MacLellan, I'm Dr. Whitehouse, the emergency room physician taking care of your daughter."

"Doctor." James extended his hand. "How is our daughter?"

"She's stable. I just looked at the films and she's fractured her wrist, but it was a clean break, and there's a minor laceration on her head and she's suffered a mild concussion. However, she'll need to have surgery for her ankle. I'm waiting for the orthopedic surgeon to arrive."

"Will they wait until morning?" James inquired.

"We'll get her ready just in case the surgeon wants to go in right away, but it's not life-threatening, so we may stabilize her and get some fluids in her before operating."

Olivia clung to James and asked, "Doctor, what exactly is wrong with the ankle? Is it very bad?"

"Mrs. MacLellan, your daughter's fracture is pretty straightforward; a few screws and realignment should be all it takes. However, short-term recovery will take about six weeks before she can bear weight, and of course physical therapy is to be expected. Longer term, it may take three to four months before Kenzie returns to normal physical activity."

Grace piped up, "My sister's not going to like that; she's very active."

With a shake of his head Dr. Whitehouse said, "She's going to have to let her body heal for a minimum six weeks. Otherwise she'll never fully recover." His pager went off. "The nurse will take you in to see her."

James said, "Thank you, Doctor."

Before the family could talk about what the doctor had said, a nurse zipped into the waiting room. "If you'd like to come with me, I'll take you back."

The family started down the hall when Olivia looked around. "Robbie, aren't you coming?"

"You go ahead. I'm going back up the mountain to get our gear."

"Nonsense. We're going to see Kenzie together. Jo, George, you're coming with us, and I know for a fact Caleb brought hiking boots. He plans on going with you."

George said, "After we see Kenzie, Jo and I are going to head back to Easton. We'll check in with Cheryl too."

Robbie nodded. "Thanks, Dad. The gym is the last thing on my mind."

George pulled Robbie up from the chair and wrapped his arms around him. "Son, you'll see, Kenzie is going to be right as rain in no time."

Pain medication had Kenzie floating, but it was making her jumpy too. She wiped a sweaty palm on the crisp white bed sheet. A hum of voices drifted toward her and the door burst open. She pushed herself up with one hand.

A sob escaped. "Mom!" *They all came, just for me.*

Tears filled her eyes as her parents, sisters and brother-in-law filed into the room, along with George and Jo. She searched the group until her eyes came to rest on Robbie.

Mom rushed to her side and brushed the tears from Kenzie's cheeks. "Sweetheart, are you in pain?"

She shook her head, grasped her dad's hand and held on tight. "No."

He gave it a reassuring squeeze. "You took quite a tumble, lass."

"I don't remember falling, but when I opened my eyes, Robbie was taking care of me."

Grace carefully perched on the edge of the bed. She took Kenzie's good wrist from Dad and laid her fingertips over the artery. She then examined the soft cast on Kenzie's wrist. "How's your head?"

"I've got a headache." She gave a crooked smile. "But I don't need stitches."

Grace slid off the bed and checked her ankle. "Nicely done."

Kenzie tried to be cool. "You know me—no sense in doing something unless I fully commit."

Jamie spoke softly. "How much pain medication are you on?"

"I'm not sure. I might not need it for long since I'm feeling really good."

Grace's eyebrows shot up, she said, "You do realize it's because you're on meds that you don't feel pain, right?"

She seemed to be floating. "Mom, Dad, did you hear that Robbie had to carry me for miles? And then he started a fire so that I'd be warm while we waited for the guys to show up." Her voice was almost childlike.

"No, we didn't." Mom beamed at Robbie.

Kenzie's eyes were having a hard time focusing. "Robbie held my hand and talked to me the whole time so I wouldn't fall asleep."

"I heard," Mom said, obviously relieved to have her daughter safe.

Kenzie grew somber. "They're going to operate. This time tomorrow I'm going to have some extra hardware in my foot."

Grace interrupted before her mom could speak. "It's to stabilize the bones so they'll knit back together."

"Oh no," she muttered. "That doesn't sound like much fun." Her voice was faint. "Robbie?"

"Right here, Kenz."

"What about our stuff? Are you going to hike back in to get it? It's too much for one person to carry."

Robbie stood at the foot of her bed. "Caleb's going with me after sun up. Between the two of us, we can get everything in one trip."

"Are you coming back here or going home?" Tears hovered in the pools of her blue eyes.

His hand rested on her good foot. "Do you want me to come back?" he said, his voice filled with tenderness.

She nodded. "Just until I'm in my room, if that's okay."

"Wild horses couldn't keep me away."

A sharp rap on the semi-open door ended the discussion. A tall, athletically built man walked into the room. Kenzie looked him over. "Who are you?" she said sharply.

"I'm Dr. Barton, the orthopedic surgeon."

"Kenzie MacLellan."

He smiled. "I guessed as much since you're the one lying in the bed. It's good to see you're alert."

"My sister"—she jabbed a finger in Grace's direction— "the junior doctor informed me it's the painkillers."

He stretched out his hand. "Michael Barton."

Grace shook it. "Grace MacLellan, PA."

He nodded. "Very nice to meet you. I'm assuming you've checked your sister's injuries?"

Grace was interrupted by Kenzie, who was miffed they were talking over her. "Hello. I'm right here. The patient."

"Kenzie," Mom gently admonished her, "let's listen to the doctor."

"Oh, Mom, all I want to know is when are they going to insert my screws so I can go home."

Grace gave Kenzie a benevolent look and said, "Yes, and for the record, she's always argumentative like this."

"Good to know." He laid her chart on the table next to the bed and his gaze met Kenzie's. "Mind if I take a look?"

"You're the doctor." Irked, she looked away. This wasn't the place she had planned to be, and to have to lie in this hospital bed, virtually helpless, was not her cup of coffee. She gritted her teeth, expecting to feel pain as he poked and prodded her wrist and ankle.

"What time did you say this happened?"

Kenzie looked at Robbie. "I don't know, do you?"

"It was about two, maybe three. We had about two more hours to hike and we were trying to beat the rain."

Dr. Barton looked at his watch and made a note in the chart. He gave Kenzie a straight-shooter kind of look. "Well, the good news is I can fix this, and with proper rehab you should fully recover and get back to your normal activities."

"The bad news?" Kenzie pushed the button on her bed to raise her head so she was sitting up straight.

"We're going into surgery as soon as the team arrives. You'll be in the hospital a day or two and then home. You'll need help around the clock. You can't use crutches, and a cane is off the list since you broke the wrist on the opposite side of your ankle."

Controlling her temper Kenzie said, "You have to be kidding me. What about one of those walking casts?"

Dr. Barton stuck his hands into his lab coat. "Eventually

you may move to one, but for the first few weeks, the incision needs to heal and its imperative you stay off your feet."

Kenzie studied her hand in her lap. Looking at the doctor she asked, "What time will I go into the operating room?"

"Within the hour is my best guess."

Her face was grim and she gave a curt nod. "Thank you, Dr. Barton." She wouldn't admit to anyone she was scared.

The doctor looked around the room. "Are there any other questions I can answer?"

At that moment, if a pin dropped in the room it could have been heard loud and clear.

Grace shook his hand. "We appreciate your time. I'm sure you'll check on Kenzie after the surgery?"

"Yes, when I make my rounds later in the day. Will you be here?"

Grace looked at the family crowded in the room. "I'm sure we'll be with her."

"Kenzie, I'll be seeing you soon." Dr. Barton dropped his head to the side. "Mr. and Mrs. MacLellan, don't worry, I'll take very good care of your daughter." He left the room.

A shadow of annoyance crossed Kenzie's face. "Grace, did you need to flirt with my doctor?"

Grace's eyes widened. "What are you talking about?"

"Kenzie!" Mom chided. "The doctor treated Grace as a professional."

Grace smiled. "Kenzie, I want to make sure you get the very best care."

Kenzie opened her mouth and then shut it, leaning her head against the bed she closed her eyes. "I appreciate that, Grace. I'm going to take a snooze."

Robbie and Caleb backed out of Kenzie's room and waited for Olivia and James to join them. Jamie and Grace sat on the bed while Kenzie kept her eyes glued shut and tears slipped from the corners. Her sisters each laid a hand on her leg, attempting to comfort her with their presence.

As Olivia came around the corner, Robbie could hear her say to James, "I'm really worried about her. She is… well, I don't know how to put it into words."

Robbie stepped forward. "Olivia, she's in shock and on painkillers. You know she's always the strong one. It's got to be killing her to be lying flat on her back, everything totally out of her control."

James's voice was low but firm. "This is a bump in the road."

Olivia sat in a chair, her shoulders slumped. "Robbie's right. This isn't a normal occurrence for our daughter. Although she's gotten bumps and bruises and the occasional cut, she's never needed surgery. She must be scared."

"James, I'm going to head out and get our gear." Robbie turned to Caleb. "If you're still game, let's tell the girls. Then we'll be here when Kenzie gets out of surgery."

Caleb asked, "You don't want to go later?"

"I'm gonna go crazy just sitting here waiting. The family's here, and if I'm doing something productive, it will be better for everyone." And he needed to clear his head. Too many thoughts and feelings were at war inside of him.

"Then let's go."

Without waiting for Olivia or James to voice an opinion, Robbie hurried down the hallway with Caleb by his side. He pushed open the door and quietly stepped inside. He hesitated. Asleep, Kenzie looked like an angel—a little bruised, but she took his breath away.

Jamie slipped off the bed, careful not to disturb her

sister. Her arms encircled Caleb's waist and she laid her head on his chest. "You're leaving?"

"Yeah, let's step into the hallway." Caleb's hand slipped into hers as they left the room.

Grace rose from the chair. "I'm going to check on Mom and Dad. Stay with her until I get back, okay?" Laying her hand on his arm, she whispered, "Thank you for everything."

Numb, he nodded, then pulled the chair close to the bed and sat down. As he watched her, he wondered, *Why did this have to happen? We had finally taken steps toward a real relationship.*

"Robbie?" Kenzie's voice was like velvet to his ears. He lifted his eyes to meet hers. "I know what you're thinking."

"You do, huh?" A slow smile appeared.

"If our roles were reversed, we'd still be on the mountain."

"Nope, not at all what I was thinking. You'd have found a way to get help. You're a very smart chickadee."

A smiled tugged at the corners of her mouth. "That's an old nickname. You used to call me that when we were, what, twelve?"

"An oldie but goody." His warm hand covered hers.

"Seriously, I'd rather be in this bed than you. And the third time wasn't the charm."

His brow wrinkled. "Third time?"

"The burn, the summit and then the rock. Three incidents." She shrugged and winced.

"Are you in pain? I'll call the nurse." Worry lines deepened on his forehead.

"No, I'm going to have more than enough pain meds very soon; I can wait."

"You know I can read your every expression," he

admonished. "Don't be a martyr," he urged. "If you need meds, take them."

His thoughts turned to the summit. Holding her in his arms was like a dream. Kissing her and loving her, time had stood still. If only he could turn back the hands of the clock and be making love to her again on the mountain.

She patted his hand. "Stop trying to make things better. I'm going to be fine and before you know it, we'll be planning a spring hike. Besides, it sounds like I'm going to have butt-on-couch time, so I can do some internet surfing for new locations."

"Speaking of hiking, Caleb and I are going to take off. We'll be back by the time you wake up, and I'll stay with you here until you're discharged."

Her smile warmed her eyes. "We started our adventure together and we'll end the same way."

"Something like that." He couldn't tear his eyes away from that beautiful face. "You're tired. Do you want me to bring you anything from your pack?"

"I had a book I haven't read. Would you mind bringing it back? I think it's in the tent."

Nodding, he said, "Sure, anything else?"

Kenzie turned her head slightly from side to side. He leaned over kissing the top of her head, and then his lips grazed hers. "Don't give the doctors and nurses a hard time while I'm gone."

Her eyes grew wide and then dark lashes rested on her pale skin as if she didn't have the strength to keep them open. "I won't." She crossed her hand over her heart. "Promise."

The door opened. Jamie peeked her head inside and asked, "Can we come in?"

Robbie stepped away from the hospital bed, his face flushed. "Sure."

Caleb touched her sock-covered foot. "Kenz, I'll see you later. Jamie's going to stay with you."

"And me too." Grace joined them. "Mom and Dad found out what room she's going to be moved to after surgery, so meet us there. Fourth floor, Room 305."

Caleb lightly kissed Jamie's lips. "I'll check in later."

With a hitch in her voice, Kenzie eked out, "Be careful."

"We will," Caleb said, and waved to the girls as he stepped into the hallway.

Robbie lingered in the door, taking one last look. His heart constricted. He was torn. He needed to clear his head, but he longed to be here, just in case.

"Robbie?"

Softly he asked, "Yeah, Kenz?"

Her crooked smile warmed his heart. "Thanks for being my hero."

"See you on the flip side, chickadee." He waited until her eyes closed before leaving the room.

CHAPTER 14

The ride from the hospital had been quiet, with Robbie and Caleb lost in their own thoughts. Robbie parked in the same spot at the state forest and sat with his hands on the steering wheel, staring out of the windshield. Silent.

At last he said, "Thanks for coming,"

Caleb shrugged. "I thought you could use the company more than the help."

Gruffly Robbie stated, "Help is always good."

"I'm married to a MacLellan. I know what you're feeling better than anyone else."

Robbie understood exactly what Caleb meant. The MacLellan sisters were headstrong, but when one got under your skin they stayed there. Permanently. "Ready to hike?"

With an understanding nod, Caleb said, "Remember, when you need someone to talk to about a certain stubborn brunette, I'm your guy."

The sun had begun to climb into the soft blue sky, slipping over the range to light the trail. Leaves crunched underfoot as the frost had been heavy overnight. They hiked in silence to where the accident happened. After Robbie retrieved Kenzie's pack, they hiked back down the trail.

Without looking at Robbie, Caleb gave a low whistle. "You were lucky the rescue team was able to get Kenzie out. This is some rough terrain."

Robbie shifted from foot to foot. "I gotta be honest, man, I wasn't sure I could keep her warm enough. The pain kept her aware, but I was afraid she'd drift off and lose consciousness. I kept talking to her, basically annoying her."

Caleb gave Robbie a friendly sock to the arm. "She's lucky."

With a slow shake of his head, Robbie's words cracked, "Would it seem unmanly to admit I was scared down to my bones?"

"You're human. You kept your head and protected her. Like I said, she's a lucky girl."

Robbie slowed as the campsite came into view and dropped on the log next to the now cold fire pit. Pulling off his wool cap, he ran a hand over his head. *How can she be lucky going into surgery to fix a broken ankle?*

Frustrated, he kicked a charred log. "I keep replaying everything. I should have kept a closer eye on the trail. I should have *seen* the rock."

Caleb listened while Robbie carried on, blaming himself. In a firm voice he said, "Robbie, stop torturing yourself."

"I just feel…" He held up his hands and dropped them in defeat. "Like I let her down."

"Stop. This isn't making her better and it's twisting you in knots. If Kenzie were sitting here right now, what do you think she'd say?"

He snorted. "She'd tell me to *cowboy up*."

"What on earth? Who's a cowboy?"

"It's a long story, but in a nutshell Kenzie loves watching old cowboy movies. You know, the kind where no matter how badly the cowboy is injured, he saves the day. The hero."

"Ah ha. Guess she should open her eyes and take a good look. She has a red-blooded hero standing in front of her almost every day of the week. Other than the horse." Caleb laughed out loud. "Oh, wait, you have horses too."

With a wry grin, Robbie said, "I guess that means I qualify."

"You know I recognize that look in your eye. I had it myself not too long ago. The longing." Caleb studied his buddy. "How long have you been in love with Kenzie?"

Robbie clenched and unclenched his hands. "A better question would be when have I not loved her."

With a sympathetic nod, Caleb said, "For that long, huh?"

Robbie wrung his hands. "We've shared everything. Homework, high school sports, college and returning to Easton. When she decided to open the gym, she asked me to work with her. At the time, I had hoped she'd see me in a different light, to see where we might go. But instead I've watched her date a few really awful guys, most notably a jerk who ended up cheating on her. After that she swore off men."

Caleb leaned forward and said, "And all this time you lived like a monk?"

"No. I dated, had a couple of short-term relationships. But for me, Kenzie is my true north, and I hoped she would see me as the south magnet—you know, where the two sides pull toward the other."

"Man, it sounds like she does. But if she's anything like

Jamie, that logical and independent streak will keep her from letting go and admitting she loves you too."

He crossed his arms. "Any advice?"

"I'd start thinking this accident and the forced downtime as a golden opportunity. She can't clutter up her day with noise like work and exercising. She'll have time to think."

Robbie brightened. "Yeah, you're right."

"While you moon over my sister-in-law, I'm going to strike camp. I don't want my bride to worry if we're not back in a few hours." Caleb began emptying the bear box of supplies.

Robbie slapped his hands against his legs and got up from the rock-hard log. As he rolled their sleeping bags, he wondered if their new-found physical relationship would show Kenz it wouldn't have been that intense if she didn't have deep feelings for him.

Before long, the two men had everything packed and ready for the return hike. Robbie was anxious to get back to the hospital. As they hit the trail, he asked, "Have you done much hiking?"

Caleb matched Robbie's stride. "A little, but nothing like what you and Kenz do. I've never done several days on a trail. Just the occasional day trip."

"If you ever want to take off on a guy trip and give it a try, let me know. Vermont and New Hampshire have some of the best trails anywhere."

"Good to know." The guys finished the trip each lost in their own thoughts.

The parking lot came into view. After hurriedly storing the gear in the bed of the truck, Robbie popped the locks and checked his cell phone. He had a text from Grace. *Surgery went smoothly, she's in recovery. See you soon.*

He looked up. Caleb was checking his cell. "I got a

message from Grace—Kenzie's doing fine. Did you get a text from Jamie?"

"Yeah, basically says the same thing." His fingers paused over the keys. "I'm going to tell her we'll stop and pick up something to eat, if that's okay with you."

"Yeah." At the mention of food, Robbie's stomach let off a deep grumble. He laughed as the sound made Caleb's head snap up. "Sorry about that, my stomach reminded me I haven't eaten since, well, I'm not sure when."

"Hold that thought. Lemme finish this text." Caleb's cell phone buzzed. "She said there's a sub place near the hospital and she's going to text me their order and the address."

Robbie put the truck in reverse and spun out of the parking lot. All he wanted to do was get back to the hospital as quickly as possible. Hopefully he'd arrive before Kenzie woke up.

Robbie laid his forehead on the steering wheel and took a few deep breaths.

Caleb asked, "Hey, man, you okay?"

"Sure. Just tired." His shoulders slumped with exhaustion.

A sharp rap on the window caught his attention. Jamie was standing outside, rubbing her arms, shifting from foot to foot. Caleb opened his door.

"What are you two doing?" She took the box of grinders from Caleb, turned toward the hospital and then stopped. "Are you coming?"

"Honey, can you give us a minute?"

She looked from Robbie to Caleb, who gave her a shake of his head. She gave a half nod. "I'll meet you upstairs, but don't take too long." She lifted the box a little higher. "I've got the food."

They sat in silence. Finally, Robbie said, "You don't need to stay."

Stating the obvious, Caleb replied, "You're exhausted, and if you get lost between here and Kenzie's room, my wife is not going to be happy with me."

Robbie slowly lifted his head, which felt like a lead weight. "When Kenzie comes home from the hospital, I'm going to lay it on the line, and if she says we don't have a future, I'm leaving Easton. I can't keep living this way. I hope she'll realize we're good for each other."

Caleb looked at Robbie directly. "Leaving sounds a little drastic."

"James was right when he asked me how I'd feel if something serious had happened and I squandered my chance." Robbie peered out the window up toward the fourth floor. *I can't go back to the way things were before we made love, and that's what it was, not just sex.*

"Do what you need to do, but for now let's get upstairs and you can see for yourself she's going to be fine."

"Caleb, sorry I've dwelled on this all day. I've never told anyone how I really feel about her."

Caleb clapped a hand on Robbie's shoulder. "You think you've kept this a secret? You should look in our wedding pictures. Every shot of you and Kenzie together, it's written all over your face. The only person you may have been fooling other than yourself was Kenzie."

Robbie felt totally lost. "What if she doesn't have the same feelings as I do?"

"Accept the relationship for what it is and move on. There's one thing I've discovered being a married man for all of two and a half weeks." He chuckled. "When you find the woman you love, don't give up."

Robbie kicked open the door with his foot. "If I fall asleep over my dinner, save it for me."

Caleb's hearty laugh filled the cab. "You won't. You've been around the MacLellans your whole life, and you know how loud they all are when they're together."

Robbie laughed. "But you forget, one of the loudest voices will be sleeping." Caleb chuckled. Robbie said, "Before we head up, I want to stop in the gift shop and buy some flowers."

Caleb slapped a hand on his back. "Now you're thinking like a man out to win a girl's heart."

Robbie wondered what it would take for Kenzie to listen, really listen, to what he had to say. *Time will tell if I can get through her stubborn side and get her to see how good we are together in every way possible.*

CHAPTER 15

Kenzie struggled to open her eyes. It was as if her lids were glued to the lower lashes, and why did she leave the television on so loud? It hurt her head. Through closed eyes she could tell the room was filled with bright overhead lights. Her heart raced. For a split second she thought she was having a nightmare, and then the memory of the fall and Robbie holding her in his arms came flooding back. She was in the hospital.

She concentrated and forced her eyes open. Through the haze she could see her mom's concerned face hovering over her. "Sweetheart. Open your eyes, honey."

Kenzie groaned, "Got any toothpicks?"

"What do you need them for?"

"To hold my eyelids up."

She closed her eyes and slipped into the comfortable, pain-free darkness.

Kenzie could feel a cool hand holding her wrist. She slowly opened her eyes to an older woman checking the IV line.

"You're awake." The woman's smile was kind. "You just missed your family. I told them to go into the lounge and that you were resting comfortably."

"Thank you," Kenzie croaked. She ran her tongue over her dry lips. "Any chance I could have some water? My mouth is so dry."

"I'll be right back." Sneakers squeaked across the linoleum floor.

Kenzie looked toward the foot of the bed where her ankle was suspended in a sling; she assumed it was to avoid swelling. Her toes were covered with a loose-fitting sock. She then looked at her right wrist, in a cast propped up on a pillow. Her hand that was attached to the IV line was free. She reached up and gingerly touched the bandage on her head.

"Here you go." Robbie came in with an insulated cup and a bouquet of flowers. *Thank heavens he's back.*

He held a straw to her lips and Kenzie took a sip. "That's good." She reached out and drank a little more. He set it on the bedside table within reach of her good hand.

She rested back on the pillows, her eyebrow arched. "What happened to the nurse?"

"I saw her coming out of your room and asked how you were doing. She said you asked for water and I volunteered to bring it in I wanted spend a little time with my favorite person." He placed the flowers on the table and looked up and down her body. "Are you in pain?"

Kenzie shook her head. "Not really. I hate lying around."

He flashed a comforting smile. "It's a good thing you're in shape; it'll help in your recovery."

"Did anyone tell you how the surgery went?" She squirmed in attempt to get more comfortable.

"From what your nurse said, it was just as expected. Dr. Barton will be around a little later and you can ask him for yourself." Robbie straightened the covers, careful not to bump her foot or wrist. "Can I get you anything else?"

She was struggling to keep her eyes open. "How long has the family been in the waiting room?"

He took her hand and caressed her palm. "About ten minutes, I think. Would you like me to get them?"

Kenzie closed her eyes. "Not yet. Give me fifteen. They've been waiting all day and they deserve some time to..." Her voice faded away.

"That I can do." Robbie settled in the chair next to the bed, fingers entwined with hers. "If you need anything, I'm here."

Kenzie gave up the fight. "Thanks," she murmured before drifting off.

A hum of voices brought Kenzie up from the depths of drug-induced sleep. Willing her eyes open, she discovered her room was wall-to-wall people. Her insides melted. She was lucky to be surrounded by people who loved her so much to drop everything to be with her.

"Mom." Kenzie's voice was barely above a whisper.

Mom perched on the edge of the bed, careful not to cause movement. "Hi, Kenz. How are you feeling?"

"Pretty good, but I'm sure the painkillers have some-thing to do with it." The corners of her mouth turned upward. "Did you get outside at all today?"

"No, I didn't want to leave you." Mom smoothed Kenzie's hair down.

Robbie stirred. He was dozing in the chair, but slowly came around while Kenzie was whispering to her mom. He yawned and then smiled. "Hey, chickadee."

"Hi. Have you been here the whole time?"

Robbie shook his head. "Remember, Caleb and I hiked to base camp. To get our stuff."

Confused, she asked, "Our backpacks were on the trail?"

"Yeah." He never broke their eye connection.

She shook her head. "I don't remember. Why didn't we bring everything with us?"

"That would have been tough, since you came down in a stretcher in the dark."

Her voice was soft. "Oh." The word was hanging in the air.

"We made good time."

She laughed a little. "Must be those long legs." Looking toward the bedside table, she frowned and asked, "Can you push that closer?"

Robbie positioned the table over her lap. Kenzie reached for the cup and straw. He picked it up and held it to her lips. She sipped, then laid her head against the pillow. "I'm starving—any idea when they'll let me eat?"

Right on cue, Grace came into the room holding a tray, grinning. "Did I hear you might be hungry?"

Robbie pushed a button on the side of the bed and the head rose to a sitting position. Kenzie eagerly awaited Grace setting the tray down. "What did you bring me?"

Grace pulled off the food warmers. "Looks like chicken broth and Jell-O, and some apple juice."

Kenzie wrinkled her nose. "That isn't going to fill me up."

"Sissy, it's a start. They're not going to give you

anything solid until you can keep this down. You've just come out of anesthesia."

Kenzie struggled to reposition herself and leaned closer to the table. Inwardly she groaned; this wasn't going to be pretty, being a righty and all. Using her left hand, she picked up the spoon and fumbled with it until she felt confident. She studied the family, all six sets of eyes watching as the spoon hovered over the broth. Joking she said, "I'm not sharing, so stop staring at me."

Caleb laughed. "I'm not going to tell you what we had, so you feel free to slurp it up."

Jamie playfully smacked her husband's arm. "Stop teasing her."

Grace, being the ever-vigilant medical professional, watched as Kenzie discarded the spoon and picked up the cup of broth. After drinking that down, she broke the Jell-O into chunks and stabbed them with a fork, and drank the small cup of apple juice.

"How's your belly?" Mom asked.

"Less empty." She perked up. "Grace, do you think you could round up some crackers and peanut butter?"

Grace removed the tray to the other side of the room. Briskly she said, "Let's give this some time to digest, and if you don't have any problems, I'll see what I can do."

A knock at the door interrupted what was to be Kenzie's comeback.

"Dr. Barton, join the party."

The doctor walked into the room and asked, "How are you feeling, Kenzie?"

He picked up her medical chart and scanned the notes taking in the now empty dinner tray. Finally, he looked at his patient again.

Noting the serious expression on his face, she said,

"Pretty good, considering. I don't have any pain. Grace got me something to eat and I've been drinking water."

Dr. Barton stepped in front of Mom. "Excuse me." He checked the bandage on Kenzie's head. "Any dizziness or nausea?" His questions were direct.

"No."

He walked to the foot of the bed and carefully removed the sock from her toes. "Any numbness or tingling?" He inspected their color.

"No, but they're getting cold now that you took the sock off." She laughed to soften her response. Grace took the sock and slipped it over Kenzie's toes with a firm but gentle touch.

He then carefully picked up her fingers, looking at her nails. "Are your fingers stiff?"

"A little bit."

He looked around the room and pointed to a pillow on the window ledge. "Grace, would you hand that to me, please?"

He held up the cast and slid an extra pillow on top of the stack. "Try to keep your wrist above your heart for the next several days."

"I will." Cautiously she asked, "Is there anything else I need to do?"

He paused as he was making a note. "You'll need to keep your ankle up as well."

Kenzie nodded. "Will I be able to get up and use the bathroom?"

"It's going to be a little tricky. We're going to have to show you how to use a knee walker."

Frowning, she said, "What the heck is that?"

"The physical therapist will be in tomorrow morning to work with you, but you're going to place your knee in the seat and scoot around, very carefully. It will be a bit unstable and stairs are out of the question, but at least you'll be able to get up and use the bathroom," he stated. "With help, of course."

"I'm going to need a babysitter?" Kenzie snapped.

"You'll need to either stay with family or have someone stay with you. But we can talk about it when you're ready to go home."

"And will that be tomorrow?" she challenged.

Dr. Barton consulted the chart and avoided looking at his patient. "More likely the day after." He looked at Grace. "Would you be able to stay with her?"

Robbie stepped forwarded and stated, "I'll be living with her."

Kenzie's head swiveled. Her mouth dropped open. "You're doing what?"

"I'm going to be staying with you at night and when I'm not at the gym."

Mom smiled. "That is so sweet of you, Robbie. If you stay overnight, we can take the days. It's perfect!" She fussed over the pillows, taking care with Kenzie's wrist.

Jamie grinned. "We'll work out meals too."

Caleb said, "I'll cook dinner and lunches every day, then all Robbie has to fix is breakfast."

Jamie held up a legal pad. "Let's start making a list for when you come home."

Kenzie couldn't help but give a sleepy grin. "Leave it to you to have a pad. But can we do it tomorrow? I'm really tired."

Mom's voice was filled with concern. "Kenz, do you want us to leave so you can sleep?"

Her eyes fluttered. "I plan on sleeping through the night. Why don't you find a motel? If I need something, I can text you." She looked around. "Do I have my phone?"

Robbie handed it to her. "Fully charged."

Mom was straightening her blankets and fussing over her. "I don't want to leave you. What if you need something?"

"Mom. I'll be fine, there are nurses around the clock. If I need anything, I have this little button." She picked up the cable on the bed. "I'll just push it and poof, instant help."

Mom looked at Dad. "James, what do you think?"

"Liv, I'd love a shower and to sleep in a bed. We can come back first thing tomorrow." He heaved himself from the chair. "It will be better than sleeping in this unforgiving chair."

"Are you sure?" Worry filled Mom's eyes.

"You're all off the hook." Kenzie looked at each person around the perimeter of the room.

Forcefully, Grace said, "Mom, you and Dad go ahead. I'm staying with Kenzie tonight."

"I'll be with Kenzie. You can go with your parents." Robbie sat down in the chair Dad had just vacated.

"Robbie, don't be silly, go with them," Kenzie half-pleaded. "I'll be fine, really."

"We're not going to argue about this. I'm staying here." He stretched his legs out and said, "Now close your eyes and drift off to dreamland."

Kenzie threw up her good hand. "I give up, you all go ahead." She flicked her thumb at Robbie. "Text him the name and address of the motel. If I get him to change his mind, he'll meet you there."

Mom leaned over and kissed Kenzie's forehead. "Sleep well." Dad did the same. Jamie and Caleb tweaked her good foot.

Grace hesitated. "Robbie, why don't you go along? I'm happy to stay with Kenzie."

Robbie stood up and took Grace gently by the shoulders. He turned her to face the door and whispered in her ear. Grace took one final look at Kenzie. "See you tomorrow, sis."

Kenzie watched as she left and said to Robbie, "What were you two whispering?"

"Only that I promised to watch over you and if anything happened I'd shoot a group text."

"Robbie, I really appreciate everything you've done, but this is really above and beyond."

"I'm going to ask you one question." His voice was soft and tender. He took her good hand and brushed her forehead with his lips. "If it was me lying in that bed, where would you be?"

Kenzie looked deeply into his golden hazel eyes. "Message received."

CHAPTER 16

R obbie watched Kenzie fall into what he hoped was a dreamless sleep. As the dark of night gave way to dawn, he began to drift off, smiling to himself. His last thoughts were, *she's my girl, but why hasn't she said anything about the summit? Oh my God, does she even remember?* With a shake of his head he reminded himself they hadn't exactly had any alone time with the entire family hanging around.

Her whisper broke through the fog of sleep. "Robbie?"

He bolted up. "What's wrong?" The room was filled with a soft morning glow.

Still whispering, she said, "Nothing. I'm surprised to see you're still here."

He leaned over the bed. "Where did you think I'd be?"

A smile crept over her face. "Honestly, I was hoping you'd come to your senses and gone to the hotel." She reached for his hand. "You're running on empty."

In a husky voice, he said, "I'm right where I want to be, with you."

"I want to go home." In an unusual display of vulnerability, she started to cry.

He interlaced his fingers with hers, unconsciously caressing them. "I don't think that's in the cards today. Remember, according to Grace and your doctor, there are several things you need to do first."

"Yeah, I know." She sniffed, her eyes downcast. "Be able to navigate on that scooter thing and get into the bathroom."

"Kenz, give yourself a break," he said softly. "It's been less than twenty-four hours since you had surgery."

A new face popped through the door. "Good morning, Kenzie. I'm Annette. your nurse for today." She efficiently checked Kenzie's vitals and nodded. "Breakfast will be in shortly and if you need something, ring."

Kenzie waited until they were alone before asking, "Have you checked in with Cheryl?"

Robbie leaned back in the chair and folded his arms over his midsection. "She said to stop worrying, she has it under control."

"When we get home, you need to go down and make sure everything is running smoothly."

"You"—he pointed at her foot—"need to relax."

She frowned and said, "Easy for you to say—you're not the one with your leg dangling in the air."

"Here we are," Annette chirped as she came in carrying a breakfast tray. "I just saw your physical therapist and she'll be in soon."

Kenzie brightened. "One step closer to going home."

Annette laughed. "Dr. Barton will be in to see you later."

"Will I go home today?" Hope filled her face.

She laughed again. "More than likely tomorrow."

Kenzie picked up the large plate cover. "Scrambled eggs

and toast." She licked her lips. "I'm starving." She peeked under the lid on a shallow bowl. "Oatmeal." Using a steady hand, she dipped the spoon in and held it out to Robbie. "Want some?"

He shook his head. "I'll run down to the cafeteria after your parents get here."

"Why don't you head home today?" She scraped the bowl clean, then picked up a fork. "I've got a handle on this silverware thing." With eggs midway to her lips, she said, "I think my parents might want to drive me home."

Robbie frowned. "I'll think about it."

"Good morning, you two." Olivia sailed into the room.

Kenzie's eyes lit up. "Mom! Where's the rest of the fam?"

"Your sisters and Caleb stopped to get Robbie some coffee and breakfast, and Dad dropped me off at the door before parking the car, he'll be up soon." She bussed Robbie's cheek before kissing the top of Kenzie's head. "How did you sleep?"

"Like a rock. I don't have any pain, and after breakfast the therapist is going to show me how to use the knee walker."

Mom's eyes grew wide. "Are you ready for that?"

"Only one way to find out. Besides, I have to be able to get around a little bit on my own."

Mom's brow furrowed. "You've always been so stubborn."

Kenzie gave a short snort. "Apple and tree, Mom," she gave a weak grin towards her father, "and Dad."

Laughing, Mom straightened her blankets. "Have you finished eating?"

Kenzie drained the small glass of juice and grabbed the banana off the tray. "That'll hold me for now."

Grace and Jamie burst into the room with balloons,

followed by James. Grace picked up her chart and scanned it. "Robbie, has our patient been giving you a hard time?"

Grinning, he said, "Not too bad." He winked at Kenzie.

Jamie tossed a bag in his direction and Caleb walked in carrying two cardboard trays filled with insulated paper cups. Kenzie brightened. "By any chance did you bring one for me too?"

While Caleb held a straight face, his eyes betrayed him. Teasing, he said, "You're not the hero of the moment."

"That's the criteria for getting coffee and whatever is in that bag?" Kenzie's blue eyes sparkled.

"You're feeling more like yourself despite the two broken limbs holding." Robbie reached out and took a foam cup. He pulled off the lid and, inhaling, closed his eyes. "Kenzie, this smells *so* good."

She demanded in good humor, "Stop teasing and fork one over before I get out of this bed and kick some booty."

Caleb hooted. "I'd like to see that, but your sister would kill me if you even made an attempt." He handed her a cup. "Enjoy."

Kenzie wrapped her good hand around it and very carefully attempted to make her fingers on the broken hand pry off the top.

Olivia reached out to take the cup as Kenzie struggled. "Let me help."

She gritted her teeth and sucked in a breath, ignoring the throbbing pain in her fingers radiating up her arm. "I can do it myself."

Olivia withdrew her hand as if the coffee burned her. Robbie saw the hurt look come and go on her face.

Grace said, "Mom, can you go to the nurses' station and find out how long before they're getting Kenzie up?"

Olivia hurried from the room with James right behind her. When they were out of ear shot, Grace took the coffee from Kenzie and set it on the table. "What is wrong with you?" Keeping her voice low, she admonished, "Do you need to be so stubborn? Mom was trying to help you. She dropped everything to get here as fast as she could."

"I don't want to be a burden on anyone," Kenzie looked from Grace to Jamie.

Grace continued, "No one has ever thought you're a burden. We're all just trying to do everything we can to help you recover."

Kenzie's eyes grew huge. Tears welled up. "But…" *Why was she being so sappy?*

Jamie stepped in between her sisters. "Girls, that's enough."

Blinking the tears away, Kenzie sniffed, "I'm the one who got hurt."

"Understood, but our parents have been worried sick, and you being Miss Independent isn't going to cut it. In the coming weeks you're going to need to let us help you." She waved her hand around the room. "All of us."

With a sob, Grace raced out the door. "Where's she going?" Kenzie asked. "Grace?" With eyes wide, she said, "I don't understand why she's so upset." She pulled at her blankets.

Robbie's steady gaze held hers and his voice softened. "You're always the strong one and seeing you laying in that bed is hard on Grace. On all of us."

Kenzie looked out the window. In a quiet voice, she said, "I'll be fine."

"Kenzie." Jamie's voice was edgy. It was obvious she was worried about Kenzie.

"What do you want from me? I'm flat on my back, and I hate it."

Jamie dropped onto the bed, careful not to jostle Kenzie's

wrist or leg. "We get it. You're a woman who hates having to rely on anyone. But sometimes we get knocked on our butts for a reason. Maybe for the first time in a long time, you've been given a chance to take stock of the people in your life."

Kenzie's chin jutted out and her gaze roamed from face to face. "Caleb?"

"Well…" He shrugged. "If that was me lying there, I'd feel the same way and I'd hope someone would remind me that I'm pretty fortunate to have an amazing family."

Kenzie chewed on her bottom lip, her wheels turning. "Can you see if Mom and Dad are in the hallway, and Gracie too?"

Jamie ducked out the door and came back with Mom and Dad, and Grace brought up the rear. Kenzie noticed Mom's eyes were red and puffy.

She took a deep breath. "It has been brought to my attention that I've been doing my usual *I can do everything myself* thing, and I'd like to apologize. I'm going to try to not give anyone a reason to worry about me." She held out her hand to Mom. "I'm sorry, Mom."

Mom took a step closer to the bed and grasped her hand. "Sweetheart, it's fine. Let me mother you just a wee bit. I promise I won't become a full-sized helicopter."

"Will you make me your world-famous banana bread with chocolate chips?"

Mom laughed and wiped a tear from her eye. "I think I can manage a loaf or two."

Jamie got off the bed just as a new face entered. "Hello, I am Anna, your physical therapist today."

Kenzie was surprised to see a tiny woman, short and slender, with long dark hair and a thick European accent standing in the doorway. Next to her appeared to be a little scooter.

"Good morning. Are you the key to my escape?" Kenzie's smile grew wide. "Can I get out of bed now?"

"Let me get a nurse to help and then we'll see how it goes."

Robbie stepped forward. "I'll help." He stuck out his hand. "Robbie Burns."

Anna beamed at Robbie and gave his hand a firm shake. "You're a lucky young lady to have such a supportive husband; it will most certainly help in your recovery."

Before Kenzie could correct her, Robbie said, "That's if she listens."

Anna stepped into the room. "Can I ask everyone but Robbie to leave, please?"

A worried look lingered on Mom's brow. "Are you sure you won't need more help?"

"It would be better if the three of us work on this. You can wait in the hallway."

The room slowly emptied and Anna waited until everyone was gone. She closed the door. "I brought a pair of socks with non-slip soles."

"I'll put them on her," Robbie said. Anna passed dark blue fuzzy socks to him. "Anna, why don't you tell Kenzie what to expect?"

"Well, I'm going to have you place your wrist in a sling for support. Then we are going to swing your legs over the side of bed. I'll want to see if you can bend your leg and place your knee on scooter. No worries, it will be locked in place. If it's too painful, I have back-up plan."

Kenzie nodded as Anna adjusted the sock on her good foot and checked to make sure her toes were covered on the other. She sat up as Anna draped a black sling over her neck and helped position her arm inside. Anna held on to her good arm. "How does that feel? Comfortable?"

"I guess so." Kenzie tugged on the fabric. "Is it supposed to be this tight?"

"To provide good support, yes." Picking up the cord, she depressed a button to lower the bed. "We're going to move in triple slow motion. Robbie, why don't you go ahead and pull the covers back so Kenzie doesn't get tangled?"

He quickly moved to the side of the bed and said, "Are you ready for me to take your leg from the sling?"

Taking a deep breath and holding it, Kenzie nodded. Robbie gently supported the ankle as she scooted her way to the edge of the bed.

Anna was on her right side, Robbie on her left. "Whenever you're ready, I want you to put your good foot on floor. Robbie will support the cast and when you tell us, we will help you up."

Kenzie held her elbow close to her side and tried to slide her foot over the floor. Satisfied the grippers were doing their job, she put her good hand on the bed rail and said, "Let's give this a try."

With a *humpf* and using the bed and Anna for support, Kenzie rose to a standing position, thankful Robbie was there to hold her up. "How am I going to put my knee on the scooter?"

"Reach out for the handle and pull it back toward you. It will slide just a bit."

Kenzie did as she was told, and with one hand holding it securely, she hopped forward. Her ankle began to throb with each movement. She bent her leg at the knee, determined it was going to work. Beads of sweat popped out on her forehead.

"Breathe, Kenzie," Anna encouraged her. "You're almost there."

Nausea overtook her. "It hurts!" she groaned.

Robbie held her tight. "Okay, back to sitting on the edge of the bed."

"It's okay, Kenzie. I have a backup plan." Anna made sure Kenzie was sitting firmly on the bed. "I'll be right back."

Kenzie took several deep ragged breaths. "Do you think this means I won't be able to go home?"

Before Robbie could answer, they heard, "Here we go." Anna pushed a wheelchair into the room. Her eastern European accent was distinctive. She said, "I thought a scooter might be too much at the moment considering you have a broken wrist too, but there is no reason why you can't get around in a wheelchair. With help you can get up and move around, just to keep your blood flowing."

Kenzie's face fell. "Does this mean I'm going to have to stay in the hospital?"

"Not at all. With a bit of instruction, you will be able to go home."

Robbie said, "How about you try getting in? If nothing else you can tour the hallway."

Kenzie looked up at Anna. "Will I be able to use the restroom?"

With a big smile, Anna said, "Of course, it's part of our lesson for this morning."

Robbie said, "Anna, do you mind waiting outside the door for a few minutes?"

"Um," Kenzie hesitated. "Robbie, maybe Anna can help me."

He chuckled, "Sure thing, but are you ready to get into the chair?"

She nodded, determined. Using her good foot, she scooched herself to the very edge of the bed.

"Being in such good physical condition will help you

recover more quickly." Anna slipped her hand under Kenzie's armpit. "Ready?"

"Robbie?"

"We're ready when you are."

Kenzie heaved herself forward and up on one foot. Robbie slipped one arm around her waist. "Don't put any weight on your toes," he whispered in her ear. "I won't let go."

Anna waited until Kenzie seemed to be steady. "You're going to lean on me and then pivot so your butt is lined up with the seat."

Nodding, she followed Anna's lead. She inched around, facing the bed.

"The chair's locked so you can sit down."

As Kenzie lowered herself, Robbie dropped to one knee, and gently held up her leg and positioned the foot brace under it.

Anna asked, "How do you feel, Kenzie?"

She exhaled. "Not bad."

"Good. I'll help you navigate the restroom now?"

Using her good foot, Kenzie pushed the chair backward to the bathroom door. Robbie clicked on the light. "All set."

Kenzie grabbed the arm of the chair with her good hand. Tucking her elbow tight in the sling, she tried to heave herself upwards. It slid into the door.

Anna pointed at the side of the chair. "Kenzie, flip that lever to keep wheels from moving."

"Good to know." Kenzie gave it a try and discovered it did in fact click easily into place. "Now I'm ready."

Without waiting for Anna, Robbie slid a firm hand between her sling and body.

Kenzie was surprised at how Robbie jumped right in. She gripped the arm and rose to a standing position on her own power. "Now what?"

Anna said, "If I support you, can you grab the wall and hop, very carefully?"

"Why can't I have a crutch for this?"

Robbie chuckled. "And how are you going to hang onto it?"

"Squeeze it under my arm. At least it would give me an extra limb."

"We can try. Hold on just one moment." Anna dashed out and right back in. She tucked it between Kenzie's body and the arm on the broken ankle side. "Now squeeze tight and remember, don't use it to support all your weight. It's just for extra stability."

At a snail's pace, Kenzie moved forward and rested her hand on the wall while keeping the crutch locked in place. "Look at me. I'm upright."

Robbie cautioned, "Don't get cocky. Can you grab the bar?"

Moving inch by inch, Kenzie grasped it and stared at her reflection in the mirror. "I look like I've been dragged through hell and back."

Anna laughed a little and said, "It's not that bad."

Kenzie looked at Anna's reflection. "Robbie, you need to wait outside, and any chance you could close the door?" She saw a concerned look flit over the therapist's face. "Anna, I promise, if I need help, you'll be the first to know."

"All right, I compromise—halfway?" Anna pulled the door partially closed.

"I'm going to have to get used to less privacy, aren't I?"

In her clipped accent, Anna said, "For short while, yes."

Kenzie was sitting in the chair as Robbie pushed her down the hallway. Mom and Dad grinned.

"Where are the others?" Kenzie turned in the chair.

"They went for a walk," Mom said.

Plotting? Kenzie wondered. She flipped the lever to apply the brake. "So, this is how I keep the chair from moving around, and I can get myself up and navigate into the bathroom."

Dad chuckled. "Mom and I were talking about the situation, and we're going to stay at your place for the time being, instead of Robbie. He can concentrate on running the gym."

Kenzie opened and closed her mouth. "Sounds good." She hated feeling totally dependent on everyone.

He grinned broadly. "See, Liv, I told you she'd come to her senses once she got on her feet."

Kenzie's parents couldn't see Robbie shake his head and point to his chest. She shrugged and sighed. "It is harder than I thought to get around. But Anna assures me it will get easier."

"Kenzie, would you like to get back into bed now?" Robbie held onto the back of the chair.

"Not yet. It feels good to be sitting upright and looking at a new view, albeit a hallway. But at least it's different."

Anna was walking past them and said, "When you're ready to get back into bed, a nurse can help."

Gratefully she said, "Thank you, Anna. You've been very helpful."

"You're welcome. I see you tomorrow."

Kenzie's face fell.

"We need to double check before I sign off on your ability to move around, but really, it will be your doctor who determines your status."

Nodding, Kenzie watched Anna stop at the nurse's desk. She made a few notes in a chart and disappeared.

Kenzie yawned. "Can we do a loop before I lie down?"

Dad walked to the back of the wheelchair and teased, "Buckle up, lass."

They were coming around the corner when Jamie, Caleb and Grace stepped off the elevator. Grace's eyes popped. "What happened to the scooter?"

"It seems high pain levels can cause one to think about tossing their cookies, so until I have less pain, this will be my mode of transportation." There was no way she was going to confess how intolerable the pain really was. She could get through this—the worst of it would be behind her soon.

Dad stopped at her room. "Here we are."

Jamie held the door open wide and Dad navigated the chair next to the bed. Robbie had the blankets pulled back. Mom said, "I'll get a nurse."

"Wait. Mom?"

She knelt beside the wheelchair. "What do you need, Kenzie?"

"Since I need help when I get home, maybe it would be easier to try now."

Grace smiled at Kenzie. "Mom, come around here and put your hand between Kenzie's side and arm. Be careful not to jostle the cast."

Mom did as Grace instructed.

"Dad, when Kenzie stands, can you pull the chair away? And Kenz, pivot on your good foot and sit on the edge of the bed."

Solemnly, she nodded. "Will do."

Robbie stood in front of Kenzie. "I'm right here, so if you get lightheaded, just say the word."

Kenzie pushed herself to stand and swayed slightly.

Robbie held out his hands, ready to move in an instant. With a shake of her head, beads of sweat appeared. Her voice shaky, she said, "I'm ready to sit down." She sank to the bed. "I'm exhausted."

Grace laughed. "That would be the lingering effects of your super-duper painkillers." Supporting Kenzie's leg, she said, "Let's get you comfy."

Amid groans, Kenzie held her leg aloft and, using her good foot and hand, managed to squirm into place. Mom tucked the blanket around Kenzie as best she could and Grace settled her ankle back in the sling.

Kenzie took a long drink of water and, with a small smile, said, "I better not drink too much. I don't want to have to get up any time soon."

Grace opened her mouth to speak, and Kenzie narrowed her eyes. "I'm not using a bed pan."

Dad chuckled, "That's my girl, feisty as ever."

Kenzie lay back and closed her eyes, taking shallow breaths to push away the pain seeping in. She needed to clear her mind. She also needed to talk to her best friend. He had been a rock through everything.

Trying to replay the last few days was like trying to hold sand in her hand. Parts kept slipping away. It was odd, he had been acting overprotective of her with everyone. But there was one very important detail she did remember. She made up her mind they needed to talk about it. "Hey, if you all don't mind, would you give me and Robbie a few minutes alone?"

Caleb jerked his head towards the hallway. Jamie and the family filed out of the room, with Grace closing the door.

"Have a seat." Kenzie patted the edge of the bed.

He raised an eyebrow. "Do you need something?"

"No, but you do?"

Confused Robbie cocked his head. "Huh?"

She looked at her hand in her lap. Softly she said, "An apology."

With a slow shake of his head, he said, "Nah, you have nothing to apologize for."

"Yes, I do." Robbie started to interrupt, and Kenzie laid a finger on his lips. "Please let me do the talking."

He remained quiet, his eyes locked on hers.

"Over the last three days, you've been so sweet to me, taking care of my burned finger, catching me before I fell off the summit and then carrying me back to camp, and keeping me warm." She swallowed hard and decided to hold off on addressing the very intimate moments with him. "Despite everything that happened, not once did I feel scared. I just knew it was going to be okay."

"You're one tough chickadee and you'd have…"

She wanted to smooth away the dark shadows under his eyes; she knew the lack of sleep was because of her. "Shh, remember, I'm doing the talking. You'll get your turn." She continued, "When we got to the hospital, I don't know what happened to me. But cranky me came out full force. And for that I have no excuse. So, I'm sorry."

She paused. How did she talk about them making love? In a snap decision she decided that topic was better left until they were back home.

Her mouth went dry, so Kenzie took a sip of water. "I'd like to ask a favor. It's not that I don't want you here, but I'm worried about the gym. Would you go home and check on things? I don't trust anyone but you with the real workings of the business."

His shoulders slumped and his eyes clouded. "If you really want me to go back to Easton, then I will. But I do plan on spending nights at your house so your parents can have a breather, if you'll let me."

"You'll need to convince Mom, but the door is always open."

He winked. "Your mom loves me, so that's easy."

"Oh, and one more thing. Convince my sisters and Caleb to go with you. There's no reason everyone I'm related to has to hang out. It's bad enough Mom and Dad will be staying."

Robbie tweaked her nose. "I'll talk to them, but only if you're sure."

She smiled and patted his hand. "I'm positive."

"I'll leave you with two helicopters instead of six."

"Now this is why you've always been my best friend." She squeezed his hand. "Thanks."

"See you in Easton, chickadee."

With a small wave, she said, "See you at home, Robbie."

Robbie wandered into the hall and, seeing the MacLellans at one end, he stopped and looked out a window. *Does she remember we made love? Has she forgotten about it? Or worse, is she pretending she doesn't remember? Maybe she thinks we made a horrible mistake. Do I talk to her or wait for Kenzie to talk to me?*

Feeling at a loss, he ambled down the hall to talk to the MacLellans and then make the long, lonely drive home. This was definitely not what he had in mind, but her parents driving Kenzie home was for the best.

CHAPTER 17

K enzie had the most tantalizing dream last night about her and Robbie being close, *very* close. She smiled remembering how amazing it felt to come alive under each caress and kiss they shared.

Pushing the memory aside momentarily, she perked up as she noticed the highway sign. Easton. "I'll be glad to get home. I'm getting cramps in my leg."

Mom half-turned in the passenger seat. Concerned she asked, "Do you need Dad to stop so you can stretch?"

Kenzie glanced out the window, barely able to contain her joy. "No, we're almost home." Sighing she said, "The sky is so blue and the foliage is still going strong, but it still feels like I've been gone forever."

"You've been through a lot both physically and emotionally." Mom's smile shone with relief and happiness. "But now you're on the road to recovery."

"Do you know if Grace or Jamie had time to stop at the grocery store? I know the fridge was pretty empty when I left."

"I'm not sure who did what, but Jamie sent a text and said the condo was ready."

Her forehead wrinkled. "What does that mean?"

"Robbie and Caleb moved a recliner from our house into the living room so you can have your foot elevated. Grace mentioned the couch was too low and you might fall if you tried to get up by yourself."

A smirk flashed across Kenzie's face. "You all know me so well." She saw her condo complex up ahead. Gleefully she said "Finally!"

Dad put the car in park and Mom wagged a finger at Kenzie. "Stay put, I'm going to get the door."

Kenzie muttered, "Like I have a choice." She drummed her fingers on the seat and studied the front walkway. Dad opened the hatch and unloaded the wheelchair. "Hey, Dad? How am I going to get up the steps?"

He closed the hatch and opened the car door. "Mom called Robbie and Caleb; they're on their way."

In disbelief she asked, "Are they going to carry me, chair and all, in the house?"

He chuckled. "I believe that's their plan."

She peered out the window and saw Robbie's truck pulling in with Caleb right behind him.

"Hey, you look better than the last time I saw you." Robbie was grinning from ear to ear. He leaned in and planted a kiss on her cheek.

The tenderness in his eyes caught her off guard. "It's only been two days."

"Give me a break," he teased, "the last time we talked, you kicked me out along with your sisters and Caleb."

She bantered, "Really? You were much better off here than hanging around the hospital."

He smirked. "Just saying."

Caleb leaned into the car and smiled. For her ears only, he said, "Don't be teasing him. He's been lost without you around."

Her eyes popped open. She protested, "It's the way we talk to each other."

"Maybe it's time you cut him a little slack," he suggested.

I didn't think about what Robbie must have gone through these last few days. Her expression softened.

Robbie knelt down next to Kenzie. "I'm picking you up. Don't help me, and if something hurts, let me know."

She nodded. Caleb hovered in the other door and said, "I'm going to support your leg."

She bit her lower lip and nodded again. "Okay." She had a feeling this was going to hurt like hell.

Robbie said, "Now put your arm around my neck and I'm going to ease you over the seat and out the door. Whatever you do, don't put any pressure on your foot."

With a catch in her voice, Kenzie said, "Hold on a sec. I need to adjust my sling, it's twisted."

Robbie said, "I can fix it." Gently he smoothed the strap, and Kenzie held her wrist up until he was done, marveling at his tender touch.

She blinked back a tear and, pretending it was from the pain, said "I'm due for a pain pill in a half hour, so everything is starting to throb."

"Not to worry. I'll be very careful."

His manner comforted Kenzie as she slid her good hand around his neck, clutching his fleece. Through gritted teeth, she said, "Go ahead." She sucked in a breath and held it.

Caleb held her cast off the seat as Robbie pulled her against to his chest. Tucking his arm under her knees, he lifted her smoothly and with great care.

Kenzie felt like she was a delicate piece of fine crystal. Although she had pinpricks of pain in her foot and wrist, and despite the circumstances it was nice to be this close to him.

Robbie took a step toward the chair and changed direction. She asked, "What are you doing?"

Quietly, he said, "You're comfortable—why jostle you and risk more pain?" His strode up the sidewalk and he carried her through the door. He hesitated and then took the last steps to the recliner. "Is this okay, or do you want to lie down in bed?"

She didn't want him to put her down, at least not yet. She squeaked, "The chair's good."

Mom rushed in behind them and pulled the lever to lift the footrest. Robbie lowered Kenzie to the chair, holding her steady. After positioning her ankle on the pillow, Mom had a smaller pillow for her wrist. He carefully set her down.

Kenzie grimaced and fought back the tears. The pain went from a two to eight in moments. She held her breath until she was settled in the chair, and then she exhaled.

"Mom." Her voice shook. "Can I have my pain pills now?"

"Honey, it's not quite time." Mom looked at Robbie. "What do you think?"

Robbie glanced at her ashen face. "Olivia," he said, "I think it's a good idea. Especially since she's been bounced around during the drive home. But if you're really worried, call Grace."

Kenzie concentrated on taking deep breaths, trying to block out the mini debate.

Mom hesitated, then hurried into the kitchen and came back with a glass of water and the pill bottle. Kenzie tossed two pills into her mouth, took a long drink and threw her head back. She closed her eyes and waited. *Too bad pain relief isn't instant.*

Mom flitted around the chair. "Sweetheart, are you warm enough?"

Keeping her voice even, she winced in pain, "I'm okay, Mom." She leaned deeper into the chair. Within moments she was drifting off.

Kenzie's eyes fluttered open. Robbie was reclining on the sofa sipping a mug of something that smelled an awful lot like coffee. Groggy, she mumbled, "Hey, you're still here."

"Yeah, I wanted to make sure you were okay. Good snooze?" he drawled.

"Not bad. A side effect of painkillers"—she gave him a lopsided grin—"they make me very sleepy."

Kenzie tried to readjust the pillow under her foot, and Robbie was at her side in a flash. "Hold on there, let me help."

She groaned and tried to use her good hand to pick up her leg. "I can do it. I just need to bend my knee, my leg's getting stiff."

"Do you want to stand?" He held out his hands.

She grinned. "Any chance you can help me down the hall?"

He hesitated a half beat. "I can get you to the door, but I really don't think I should help you in the bathroom."

"I think I can manage," she said, her voice full of confidence. "Is Mom still here?"

"Yeah, your dad went to the pharmacy and your mom is baking."

She brightened. "I wonder if she's making cookies." She sniffed the air. Chuckling he volunteered to find out.

Kenzie fidgeted in the chair. He really was an amazing guy. In the midst of her drug-induced sleep, he'd slipped into her dreams again, smiling like they shared a secret.

"Sweetie?" Mom came around the corner with a dish-towel on her shoulder, wiping her hands on an apron. "Do you need something?"

Kenzie grinned. "I hear you're baking."

Confirming, Kenzie's suspicion, she said, "Brownies with nuts."

"And chocolate chips too?" Kenz asked hopefully.

Mom laughed. "Well, of course. Is there any other way to make double fudge brownies?"

Robbie asked wistfully, "Is there milk?"

Mom cracked a smile. "Of course, and a full pot of coffee."

He did a fist pump in the air. "Now we're talking."

"Hello, before you get too excited, I need to get up." Kenzie pointed down the hallway. "Remember?" She cocked her head to one side.

Mom tossed her apron on the coffee table. "I'll go first, and Robbie," she announced, "you'll help Kenzie creep down the hall?"

"I'm on it." He turned and studied Kenzie's situation. "Should I carry you? It might be easier than trying to stand up from the chair."

With a trace of indignation, Kenzie said, "I'm going to walk. I can hop on my good foot if you wrap your arm around my waist and support me."

Mildly irritated he said, "On one condition."

Kenzie held up her hand. "Let me guess. If I feel any pain, I'll tell you so you can throw me over your shoulder like a sack of potatoes?" she said, failing to stifle a smirk.

He wagged his finger. "It's either that or you have to use the wheelchair."

She made the sign of a cross over her heart and mocked, "Promise."

Robbie bent over and slipped an arm around her back and under her legs. "On three?"

She took a deep breath and held it. He straightened and took a step away from the chair. She clung to his neck and stammered, "It's going to hurt."

"If it does, I'm right here." Robbie was doing his best to reassure her. He didn't bother to count, he lifted her as they talked. She noticed but was relieved to have it over with.

"Set me down, please." With her right foot firmly on the ground, she locked her knee. Robbie was glued to her left side, his arm around her waist and holding her left hand.

"Whenever you're ready..."

Leaning heavily into Robbie, she did a tiny hop and teetered. His arm tightened around her waist. "I've got you."

Determined, she took another hop. He took a miniscule step. At a snail's pace, she hopped down the hall, ignoring the pain, toward her goal, the open door. What felt like a lifetime later, she hopped through the bathroom door.

Robbie reminded her, "I'm right here."

Mom closed the door. Kenzie clutched the vanity and let the tears course down her face.

With a sharp rap on the door, Mom called out, "Honey, are you in pain?"

With a loud sniffle, she said, "No. I'm fine."

"Are you crying?" Mom asked through the door.

"Nope, I'm fine, really, Mom."

Wiping the tears from her face, she looked in the mirror. *He never let go, not once. He held onto me the whole way down the hall. Could he really be in love with me? Why else would he be so sweet and attentive? What if I don't love him that way? I don't want to hurt him. Worse, I don't want to lose him.*

CHAPTER 18

S omeone was shaking her shoulder. Grace's voice penetrated the fog. "Kenzie. Wake. Up!"

She dismissed the concern she heard in Grace's voice and grumbled, "You don't need to shout."

"I've been trying to wake you for over five minutes." She picked up Kenzie's wrist and laid her fingers on her pulse. "Excuse me for getting worried. I've set up a dinner tray for you and everyone is going to eat in here."

Glancing around, alarmed, Kenzie said, "What?" She pushed herself upright. "I've got white carpet."

"Relax." Grace placed her hand on the arm of the chair and teased, "You have my word we won't resort to a food fight."

A relaxed smile spread across Kenzie's face. "Did you see Mom made brownies?"

Grinning, Grace glanced over her shoulder. Kenzie looked around and said, "She's not hovering."

Grace held up two fingers and rubbed her mid-section.

Kenzie's mouth fell open. "How'd you get two? She been guarding them like a lioness with cubs."

"I have my ways." She winked. "I confess Robbie distracted her while I snuck two off the plate." From her jacket pocket she pulled out a rumpled napkin, glanced over her shoulder again and handed it to Kenzie.

Her eyes widened. "You're going to share?"

"You'd do the same for me if I was sidelined," she said confidently.

"You're loving this, aren't you?"

"Who, me?" Grace smirked.

"I'm not going to be in this cast forever and you're not as fast on your feet as I am, so you might want to think about not teasing me." Kenzie loved the easy banter.

Grace clapped her hands and laughed loudly. "And you're saying what?"

Kenzie crossed her good arm over her chest and lifted her chin. Doing her best to keep a straight face, she said, "I know how we can settle this."

Grace sat on the arm of the sofa. "Do tell." Her face split into a grin.

"After I get cleared, we'll run a 5K."

"I seem to recall there's one every year around St. Patrick's Day." Grace stuck out her hand. "I'm game."

Kenzie's mouth curved into a smile and she held up her good hand. "You're on."

Robbie walked in as the deal was sealed. "What are you two hatching now?"

"Grace and I are going to run in the Racin' the Shamrocks."

His mouth dropped open. "Let me get this straight. Grace is going to run a race?"

With a snap of her head, Kenzie replied, "Yup. Care to join us?"

He stroked his five o'clock shadow. Thoughtfully he asked, "What are the stakes?"

Grace twirled a lock of hair around her finger. "I thought it was for bragging rights, but having something tangible might make it a little more interesting," she mused.

Jamie and Caleb walked in carrying overflowing dinner plates. "What are you guys talking about?" Jamie asked.

Robbie said, "A little sisterly competition is brewing."

Jamie set her plate down and rubbed her hands together, grinning. "Count me in."

"Do you want to hear what your sisters have planned first?" Caleb asked.

Robbie looked at Caleb. "You might want in too. There's a race in March, and so far, Kenz, Grace and I are entering. How about you two?"

"Oh, that sounds like fun." Jamie perched on the arm of Kenzie's recliner. "Do you think you'll be ready?"

"Hell yeah!" She shifted in the chair. "What do you say the person with the best time gets dinner cooked for them for a week by the losers?"

Grace's worry lines popped out on her forehead. "We don't have to win the entire race, just beat the rest of us?"

Kenzie nodded. "Right, this is just between the family."

"And you think you're going to be able to come back from this accident to win?" Grace asked her.

With overwhelming confidence, she said, "I do."

Grace looked around the group. "Is everyone in?"

Kenzie extended her hand, palm down. "Who's with me?"

Robbie put his hand on top. Jamie, Caleb and Grace followed.

"There's no backing out, you know." Kenzie grinned broadly.

Grace said, "Don't you worry about us, Kenz, but there

is one caveat. If your doctor doesn't clear you, the bet is delayed until you're ready."

She nodded and grinned again. "Don't worry, I'll be ready."

Robbie's eyebrow arched. "If you're sure, we'll seal it with our slogan."

Caleb teased. "You have a slogan?"

Jamie giggled and said, "As kids, whenever we made a bet, we'd say *Wee Scots*."

Robbie said, "We're all first-generation Americans, but Scottish in our DNA. My dad is from the Lowlands and the MacLellans are from the Highlands."

Caleb chuckled as Jamie gave him a playful shove. "Cut us some slack, we were kids."

Caleb threw one arm around his bride. "You do realize you've grown up, right? And I'm Irish."

Grace informed him in no uncertain terms, "A slogan is forever, and besides, you married a Scottish lass, so you're an honorary Scot now."

Robbie reminded the group, "Dinner's getting cold, so on three?"

Kenzie said, "One."

Jamie said, "Two."

Grace finished, "Three."

In unison, they shouted, "*Wee Scots!*"

Mom and Dad came rushing in. "What are you all up to now?"

"Nothing to worry about, Mom," Kenzie reassured her parents. "We're just making plans for when I'm back on my feet again."

Mom smiled and set a dinner plate next to Kenzie's chair. "I gave you extra salad, dear, since I happen to know that you snuck another brownie."

Kenzie's eyes grew wide. "Grace!"

She held up the palms of her hands. "Don't blame me. I didn't squeal."

"A mother has eyes in the back of her head. Eat your veggies and I'll see about dessert." Mom headed back into the kitchen.

Kenzie called after her, "Do we have ice cream?"

Mom's laughter was music to Kenzie's ears. "Eat your dinner and we'll talk."

Robbie handed Kenzie a fork and pulled the tray closer to the recliner. "Can I get you anything?"

"No, thank you."

He sat close, watching her as she crunched on salad. He was relieved she seemed to be doing better, considering her limitations. Her eyes held an intensity that reminded him how she looked on the summit before they…

"Robbie, what's going on at the gym? Has it been busy?" Kenzie's voice broke through his daydream.

"Well, Cheryl has everything running like a fine-tuned machine. The place is spotless and she's signed up a few new members. I asked her to contact the people who take classes to let them know we're going to have a schedule adjustment for the next few months."

Between bites, Kenzie said, "I can help from here. It'll give me something to do besides sit on my butt."

He said, "I'll have Cheryl email you a copy of her ideas and you can take a look." He set his plate aside. "So, your home schedule for the next couple of weeks will consist of your parents here during the day. I talked them into letting Grace and me stay here at night until you can get around by yourself. Jamie and Caleb are cooking dinners and will breeze in and out to keep you company."

"Huh. That's quite a plan. I'm not going to have any alone time?" A flash of annoyance crossed her face. She looked from Grace to Robbie.

Grace wiped her mouth with a napkin. "Don't blame Robbie. We all agree. For the next few weeks, you'll have someone with you all the time, just to be safe."

"When will I get a walking cast?"

In a practiced medical tone Grace said, "After Dr. Barton checks the incision and it's healing, more than likely he'll give you a boot and you'll be able to get around a little easier and even take a shower—with help, of course, because of your wrist."

A sour expression flashed across Kenzie's face. "Aren't you full of happy news."

"With everything you've got going on" —Grace frowned and made a circle in the air with her finger —"ankle surgery and a fractured wrist, it's going to take time."

Kenzie's shoulders slumped. Robbie reached out and massaged one. He said in an upbeat tone, "On the positive side, you'll have plenty of time to get through the stack of books you've been wanting to read."

Her voice was flat as she said, "Just what I wanted to hear."

Robbie suggested with enthusiasm, "And we can watch all the movies you said you wanted to see."

"Whatever." She gave a dismissive wave with her good hand and deftly changed the subject. "Caleb, dinner's delicious—pasta is one of my favorites."

His face lit up. "A little bird told me what would whet your appetite."

Kenzie wiggled her toes and started to scooch forward.

"Wow, where do you think you're going?" Robbie asked.

"My foot's really cold and my sock is on the floor somewhere."

Robbie knelt down and retrieved the sock from under the chair. Gently he slipped it over her toes. "Does it hurt?"

Kenzie shook her head. "No, just cold." Her voice trailed off. "Thanks." She ran a hand through her short-cropped hair and wrinkled her nose. "Any chance I can wash my hair tonight? I haven't been able to since before we went hiking."

"How about we do it in the morning?" Mom said.

Kenzie's head dropped, dejected. Thankfully Robbie diverted conversation. "Have you decided if you want to sleep in bed or in the recliner?"

Softly she said, "I would love to sleep in my own bed. I'll be spending a lot of time in the recliner for the next couple of weeks."

Grace paused as she picked up a dirty dish. "I bought a couple of nightgowns for you. They'll come down to your knees and will be easy to get on over your wrist. Putting on PJ pants will be next to impossible."

"Did you think of everything, squirt?" Kenzie teased.

"I tried." Grace glanced at her watch. "How's your pain level?"

"It's creeping up, but I'd like to hold off until after dessert. They make me nauseous." She made a funny face, causing Robbie to chuckle.

"Hey, Caleb, any chance you could help me out?" Robbie asked, moving across the room to the television.

Kenzie's eyes narrowed and she asked, "And what are you up to now?"

Robbie wore a sheepish grin. "You'll be able to see the TV from your recliner, but from the couch I'll have to crick my neck. If we move things around a little bit, it'll work for both of us."

"Wouldn't it be easier if you moved the armchair and footstool next to my chair? You can leave the TV tray in between us."

"I didn't think of that." He was looking pretty pleased with himself. "Caleb, you heard the lady. Let's do it before she changes her mind."

Caleb flashed a wide grin. He slid the chair into place while Robbie adjusted the footstool. He sat down and stretched out his legs. "Not bad."

"Don't get too comfy, Burns." A mischievous look played over Kenzie's face.

He chuckled. "Too late, I'm thinking with a few minor adjustments your living room will actually look lived in."

Her voice was frosty. "For your information, I like my living room *and* my condo just the way it is. Tidy and all mine."

For a split second, Robbie could see the two of them sitting side by side on a cold winter night, cozy on the couch watching an old movie. He sighed heavily. Hopefully they were one step closer than they were a week ago.

Once Kenzie was better, Robbie was going to find a way to broach the topic of their very intimate encounter on the mountain.

Kenzie clumsily crossed her good arm, trying to look stern. "And what, pray tell, are you grinning about, Burns?"

He replied without hesitation, "Just thinking about what comes next, MacLellan."

CHAPTER 19

K enzie lay wide awake. The semi-darkness enveloped her like a comfortable old blanket. Her foot was propped up and draped with a light-weight covering. With her good hand, she tugged the hem of the nightgown down over her thighs. A soft snoring sound drifted through the open door; Robbie was sawing wood on the couch. Though she'd never admit it out loud, she was comforted knowing he was a few steps away.

She punched her pillows and lifted her wrist to reposition the cast. She wasn't in physical pain, but her heart was heavy.

What's wrong with me? I've got a wonderful family and I'm lying here feeling sorry for myself.

"Kenzie?" Grace hovered in the doorway, the hallway lamp casting a soft glow around her. "Everything okay?"

"I'm sorry—did I wake you?" Kenzie pushed herself to a half sitting position.

"No. I was thirsty and heard you moving around, so I thought I'd check in."

"I'm just a little keyed up. Go back to bed and get some rest."

Grace padded into the room and perched on the edge of the bed. Folding her robe around her legs, she said gently, "Do you want to talk?"

In a hushed voice, to avoid waking up Robbie, Kenzie said, "I wouldn't have any idea where to begin."

"What are you feeling right at this very minute?"

"Grateful, relief, happy, sad and maybe a little angry."

"Why are you sad?" Kenzie could hear the concern in Grace's voice.

In a rush she said, "Everyone's had to rearrange their lives because I need help. There's not much I can do for myself, not even wash my hair."

"Sis, we're family. Besides, it's temporary."

Through a soft sigh Kenzie asked, "So why is Robbie snoring on my couch?"

"It's simple. He cares about you."

Kenz smiled in the darkness. "He was sweet the night of Jamie's wedding, when I cut my foot. He wanted to take care of me." She shivered remembering what it felt like when he carried her in his arms.

Fussing over her, Grace tucked the blankets around Kenzie. "Have you thought maybe the universe is trying to give you a nudge?"

"To tell me what?" Confusion seemed to cloud her usual clear thinking.

"Sissy, only you can figure that out." Grace took Kenzie's good hand.

The dark surrounded the sisters as they sat quietly. Kenzie's voice cracked. She confessed, "I tried it on."

A sharp intake of breath was followed by, "I assume you mean the wedding dress."

Kenzie snapped, "Is there something else I should have tried?"

"I'm going to ignore your sarcasm and ask, when?"

Regretting her response, quietly she said, "The night before we went hiking."

"Did it fit?"

Kenzie sighed wistfully. "Like a dream. Remember when Jamie said it felt like the dress was made for her? That is exactly how I felt, and it was overwhelming to look in the mirror and see me as a bride."

Slowly Grace asked, "And did...you see anyone else?"

Kenzie nodded and turned away from her sister. "I saw a man waiting at the end of a long, flower-strewn aisle."

Grace asked, "It was Robbie, wasn't it?"

If Grace could have seen Kenzie's face, she would have seen a shocked expression. "How did you guess?"

Grace snickered. "You've been acting weird, even for you."

"Stop teasing," Kenzie grumbled, "and be serious for two minutes."

"Kenz, why are you wound tight as a tick? It was just a vision, and you can make of it what you want."

"Sorry. I've never thought of Robbie as husband material."

"I know that. But you have to admit there's a force pushing you into close quarters, and if you want my advice, think about what Gran would say to you." Grace kissed her sister's cheek. "I'm going to bed. I'll see you before I leave for work."

"Thanks, Gracie. You've given me a lot to think about."

Grace left the room as quietly as she came, leaving Kenzie with her whirling thoughts. After watching another hour come and go on the clock, she resorted to an old relaxation trick she learned in camp; erasing numbers in descending order from a blackboard, succumbing to a deep restorative sleep.

In the early morning hours, the sun was weakly peeking through the slats on the blinds. Kenzie inwardly groaned. Oh, shoot. She needed to use the bathroom. She draped her sling over her neck, easing her wrist inside.

Yelling, "Grace? Robbie?" she waited for less than a minute. The house was quiet as a church.

She flipped the blankets off and eased her good foot to rest on the cool, hard floor. With her good hand supporting her bum leg, she swung it off the bed, being careful not to bear any weight on her toes. Grabbing the edge of the nightstand, she took tiny one-legged hops to the dresser, along the wall she finally reached the bathroom door.

She slumped heavily against the wooden frame. With sweat forming under her armpits, she gritted her teeth and held her broken wrist close to her body. Her toes hovered mere inches from the floor. Eyeing the distance between where she stood and to the vanity, she said, "A few more hops."

Pulling herself upright with her right knee bent, she took a single hop. The toes on her left foot grazed the floor and searing pain radiated up her leg.

She cried out, "Son of a…!"

"Whoa." Robbie came up behind her and slipped his arm around her waist. "Lean on me."

Kenzie resolved not to cry and tried to pull away. Surprised she said, "You're sweaty and gross."

"I went for a run but it's nice to see you too." He inched her forward. "I guess you couldn't wait a couple of minutes for help?"

"I called for you or Grace, but neither of you answered and nature demanded action."

With a glint in his eye, he said, "I gathered."

Kenzie leaned against the vanity and Robbie supported her non-injured arm. "Wait and I'll get Grace."

He took one step when Kenzie shook her head. "I can take it from here."

His brow furrowed. "Really?"

She heard the doubt in his voice. "I almost made it in here; I think I can manage a couple more hops."

"You're a stubborn girl, Kenz." He stepped through the doorway and hovered. "I'll be right out here. Call if you need me."

She waited for the door to close. She'd never admit how much pain she was in because she didn't want to hear him say *I told you so*.

Through the door, she shouted, "I'm brushing my teeth too!"

Robbie leaned against the wall. His heart hammered in his chest. What if she had fallen? She might go right back to the hospital. Tomorrow he'd skip his run.

He heard the shower water turn off in the main bath and peered out of Kenzie's bedroom door. No Grace. The sink water was running in Kenzie's bath. He lingered. He would get Kenzie in the wheelchair and into the living room, then tell Grace what had almost happened.

"Robbie?" Kenzie's voice cracked.

"Coming."

He hurried through the bedroom and opened the bathroom door. Kenzie's face was deathly pale. He scooped her up in his arms. "I've got you."

She groaned. "My little adventure took more out of me than I anticipated. Any chance you can put me in the recliner?"

Just as he was walking past the main bathroom, Grace stepped out, wearing a thick terrycloth robe, her curly hair dripping. Her eyebrow shot up. "What's going on here?"

Kenzie's chin thrust upwards. "Nature called. Robbie came in just as I was almost in the bathroom and now it seems he's carrying me into the living room."

Grace's blue eyes darkened, her hand flying to her mouth. "Kenz, I'm *so* sorry. I thought I could get a quick shower in before you woke up. I never thought…" Her voice trailed off.

Kenzie said, "It was going fine until I hit my toes on the floor."

"Where were you?" Grace said pointedly to Robbie.

"I went for a run. After this, I'm thinking we should coordinate our schedules."

With a quick nod, Grace asked, "Kenzie, do you want to get dressed before Mom and Dad get here?"

Her face lit up. "Yeah, it'll be better than staying in this nightgown all day. I wouldn't want to stress Mom out by worrying about hitting my ankle or wrist." She glanced up at Robbie. "Can we reverse direction?"

Grace started to towel-dry her hair. "Give me two minutes and I'll be in to help you."

"Take your time." With a touch of melancholy in her voice, she said, "Unfortunately I'm not going anywhere."

Robbie's eyes locked on the deep blue pools just inches from his as he carried her down the hallway. "Are you in pain?"

She shrugged. "A little."

"How about some juice and your pills?"

"You don't need to baby me." Her eyes brightened. "But if you really want to do something nice—well, besides getting me painkillers—can you brew a pot of strong coffee?"

Reluctant to let go, Robbie carefully set her on the edge of the bed. Her smile warmed his heart. "I can whip up some eggs for breakfast."

"I'm good with coffee and juice."

He gently reminded her, "Protein is good for healing broken bones."

Grace rushed into the room oblivious to the conversation going on between them. "Baggy sweatpants, a T-shirt and fleece?"

Kenzie wiggled her toes and frowned. "Don't forget socks. My feet are freezing."

Robbie said, "I'm going to whip up breakfast. Grace, can I interest you in some eggs?"

"Yes, please!" She pulled open the top drawer and grabbed a pair of thick wool socks and a sports bra. "Toast too?" she asked hopefully.

He did a mock salute. "You got it."

He left the girls talking about the merits of Kenzie's attire, causing him to chuckle. He had never been in such close proximity to the MacLellan sisters this early in the day.

He knew this condo as well as his own apartment. He started the coffee and filled a tall glass with orange juice. Consulting the pill bottle, he shook out two and placed them next to the glass. Finally, he whipped up eggs, spinach and cheese. Just the way Kenzie liked them.

"Shoot. I forgot the toast." He popped slices into the toaster. He took out three plates, coffee mugs and then forks and a knife.

Hovering in the doorway in her wheel chair Kenzie said, "Wow, look at you, Mr. Domestic."

Looking pleasantly surprised he asked, "How did you get in the chair?"

Kenzie flipped her thumb over her shoulder and

winked. "Seems Grace has many hidden talents. She knows how to get me from the bed to the wheelchair effortlessly."

"Why don't you get settled in the other room? I'll deliver breakfast."

Grace leaned against the door jamb. "This is something I, for one, could get used to."

Kenzie smirked. "Don't. I'll be back on my feet in no time, and Robbie will be cooking breakfast at his place and you'll be eating cold cereal in your apartment."

Grace pushed Kenzie to the recliner chair and locked the wheels, muttering good-naturedly, "Spoil sport."

Robbie smiled as he listened to the girl's banter while he scooped up eggs and added the toast. Grace wandered into the kitchen and surveyed the counters. With a tsk tsk, she said, "You might be a good cook, but you sure can make a mess."

"What do you mean?" he protested. "It's not that bad."

She pointed to the plops of egg mixture and droplets of coffee. "You'd better clean up before Mom gets here."

With a snappy retort, he laughed, "She loves me."

Kenzie shouted from the living room, "Not that much!"

Robbie called back, "I can hear you." He handed Grace two coffee mugs and he balanced three plates as they joined Kenzie. "No worries. I'll clean up after we eat. I hate eating cold eggs."

CHAPTER 20

Kenzie fidgeted in the recliner, mindlessly flipping channels on the television settling on a show about new cookware. The last two weeks had crawled. She read the last of the books from her to-be-read pile to pass the time. But that too had dwindled to nothing. The only bright spot had been her doctor appointment. Her incision was healing right on schedule. She still couldn't bear weight, but it was progress.

She clicked off the mind-numbing show. "If I watch one more hour of television, I'm going to lose what's left of my mind."

Mom popped into the room. "Did you say something, Kenz?"

She rolled her eyes. "Sitting on my butt is driving me buggy. How do people do this day after day after day?" She groaned. "I am dying to get out of this house before I become a blob permanently attached to this stupid chair."

Mom laughed. "I wondered how long it would take you before you started to go stir crazy."

"What am I going to do? I've read every book in the house. Robbie and I have been watching all the movies on my back list."

"Let's go for a drive and swing by the gym," Mom suggested.

Her eyes widened. "When do we leave?" With her good leg, Kenzie started to push the recliner to a sitting position.

"Hold on there. I'm going to need some help getting you into the car, let me call Dad and see if he can run over."

Tapping her fingers on the arm of the chair, Kenzie asked, "How long do you think it will take him to get here?"

"Thirty minutes, maybe less?"

Her wheels started turning. "Mom, would you mind grabbing me a sneaker? And there's an oversized sweater in the bottom drawer of my tall dresser."

"Sure. Why don't you call Robbie and let him know we're stopping in?"

Kenzie picked up her cell and paused. "It'll be good to see Cheryl too." Frowning she said, "Robbie said everything was running smooth as silk." She sulked. "But I want to see for myself."

"And you will." Mom hurried from the room and Kenzie heard dresser drawers opening and closing. She came back into the living room carrying one sneaker and a heavy fisherman-knit sweater.

Kenzie held the sleeve up to inspect it. "Do you think it will fit over my cast?"

Mom looked skeptical. "I'm not sure, honey. It looks a little narrow."

With a burst of frustration, she demanded, "What am I going to wear?"

"I'll ask Dad to bring over one of his heavy jackets. It should be roomier."

Dejected, Kenzie said, "I hope so."

Mom's cell phone rang. She dashed into the kitchen to answer it.

Kenzie picked up her cell and with the fingertips of her casted hand typed a quick text to Robbie. *On my way to the gym. See you soon.*

Her phone buzzed. *We'll be waiting.*

Kenzie heard the front door bang. *Wow, that was fast.* Dad was whistling as he breezed into the kitchen. "I came right away. Is Kenzie ready?"

She could hear Mom say, "Go ask her. She's in the other room."

Dad came in grinning from ear to ear. "I hear you want to escape?"

"That's an understatement." Kenzie scooted forward on the chair.

"How can I help?"

She pointed to her wheelchair. "If you drag that over and then lock the wheels, I can get up, easy peasy."

Dad did as she asked. "It doesn't look like it'll be safe." His hand was shaking. "Your mom is so much better with all this stuff."

Kenzie noticed her dad seemed to be nervous. Softly she asked, "Is that why you're not hanging around a lot?"

"Lass…" His head drooped. "I'm not proud of it, but it has never been easy for me to see my girls sick or hurt. Mom is much better at this nurturing stuff."

"Dad, you don't have to do anything. It would be nice to have your company from time to time. Your stories are certainly much more captivating than television."

He gave her a smile and said, "Duly noted." He locked the wheels. "Do you need a hand?"

"If you can just stand there in case I get wobbly, that'd be great." Kenzie saw the flash of worry cross his face. "Don't worry, Dad, I'm so much better at this than I was."

She did a one-eighty while hanging onto the arm of the chair. Taking a last look to make sure she was lined up butt to seat, she carefully dropped down.

Dad helped her slide her wrist cast into the fleece and then hurried around in front and put the footrest down for her ankle. Kenzie placed her good foot down on the other one.

"Mom! We're ready." She suspected Mom was deliberately giving them time together.

Dad pushed her to the front door and Mom appeared from the laundry room. "I needed to turn off the dryer before we left." She rushed to open the door. "After you."

Kenzie's mouth formed an O. Surprised she asked, "Who built the ramp? And when did it happen? I never heard a sound."

"Robbie and George installed it a few days ago. You don't need to worry, it's temporary."

She felt her face slide into a smile. "That was so sweet of George, and of course Robbie."

Dad maneuvered the wheelchair down the ramp to the car. "Front or back?"

"Back, so I can prop my leg up." Kenzie reversed her process to get into the car. She flashed him a huge smile. "Thanks, Dad, for helping me escape."

Kenzie peered out the back window. "Can we drive around one more time before we go to the gym?"

Mom turned in her seat. "What's so special about cruising town?"

Kenzie's face glowed. "I've missed it." She slid the window down and took in a lungful of cool, crisp air. "There's nothing like the smell of Vermont in autumn."

Dad caught her eye in the rearview mirror. "Aye, a hometown is a special place."

Kenzie waved to the mailman who was on the corner. "Hey, Matt."

He called out, "Good to see you, Kenzie!"

Dad turned down Main Street and there was an orange cone in the middle of a parking space. He slowed the car and came to a stop. Mom jumped out to move it to the sidewalk.

"I'm sure Robbie thought it'd be easier for you to get out in front of the building." Mom opened the back door while Dad set the wheelchair up and locked the wheels. Using her good hand and foot, Kenzie slid herself out the open door.

She looked at her Mom. "I'm getting quicker each time."

Mom held out her hand. "Easy."

Putting her good foot on the ground and holding her cast aloft, Kenzie grabbed her mom's hand and heaved herself upright. Grunting, she hopped to the sidewalk and Mom held tight. She grinned. "Well, I'm definitely faster, but not fast." She plopped heavily in the seat.

Mom unlocked the wheels and Dad held open the door to Kenzie's home away from home. Her heart constricted. It felt good to be back.

She drank in the sights and sounds of her gym. "Cheryl," she called out, and waved.

Cheryl hurried from behind the desk and bent over, hugging Kenzie. Her face lit up. "Boss! It's good to see you."

"It's good to be seen." Kenzie looked around. Casually she asked, "Where's Robbie?"

"He's in a personal training session." Looking at her watch, Cheryl said, "He should be done in five minutes. He thought you were coming later."

"Dad knew I was anxious to escape." Kenzie relaxed. "Tell me, how's everything? I know you got thrown into the job without much training."

Cheryl leaned against the desk. "No worries. You had everything so well organized it was easy to step in. I've been cleaning like it was home, everyone's friendly and understanding if it takes me longer to do something."

Kenzie's head bobbed. "Good to know you've settled in so well."

Laughter drifting from the weight room caused Kenzie to look over. Her blood slowed. Ally Evans was draped over Robbie like a wet blanket. Standing on her tiptoes, she placed a lingering kiss on his cheek. She then reached up to wipe away the imprint of her burgundy lipstick. Kenzie didn't want to keep staring, but it was like watching a car wreck, mesmerizing and heartbreaking in the same moment.

Dad coughed. Robbie took a step back, his face scarlet. "You can see Cheryl about setting up your next appointment."

Ally's lower lip jutted out. She drawled, "Can't you help me?"

His head jerked toward the lobby. "I need to talk to Kenzie."

Her head swiveled in Kenzie's direction and a smile crept across her face. "Kenzie, I was sorry to hear about your accident." She gazed at Robbie, clearly besotted. "You were lucky you had a big strong man with you."

Bile rose in Kenzie's throat. She clutched the arm of her chair. Through gritted teeth, she said, "It was too bad our annual fall hike was cut short."

"Well, maybe you can go next year. Unless of course either of you has *other* plans." She strolled the short distance to the desk and tapped her nails on the counter. "Cheryl, would you please pen me in for Thursday at five, with Robbie?"

"Sure thing." Cheryl hit a few keys on the keyboard. "You're all set, and just as a reminder your membership is up for renewal next week."

Ally fluttered her fingers in Robbie's direction. "Ta-ta for now."

He responded in a curt, formal tone, "See you Thursday."

After the door closed, a chill fell over the small group.

"Kenz, I didn't..."

Interrupting him, she said tersely, "I gathered that." She jerked a thumb at the retreating woman. "I thought she was done with personal sessions."

He held up the palms of his hands toward the ceiling. "She stopped in last week and we discussed what she wanted to accomplish with her fitness routine. After that, she decided to have three more and then she's on her own. Should I have turned her down?"

Sharply she asked, "Mom, could you and Dad run down the street and pick up some biscuits for dinner?" Kenzie was confident Mom could read between the lines.

She heard Mom say, "James, walk with me."

They left the gym and Cheryl looked from Kenzie to Robbie. "I'm going to tidy up the woman's locker room." She hurried from the room without a backward glance.

Kenzie's lips were in a thin, hard line. "What is going on between you two?" she demanded.

"She's a client, nothing more, nothing less."

Anger knotted in her stomach. "Have you started to make it a habit of letting your clients kiss you?"

Robbie clenched his fist. "You're kidding, right?"

She could hear the frostiness in her tone. "Do you deny she was falling all over you?"

"You saw everything and know exactly what happened. *She* kissed me, not the other way around, and you know I'm not attracted to her in the least."

Hurt stabbed her heart. "You could have fooled me."

Frustrated, he said, "Do you want me to cancel her next appointment and refund her last three prepaid fees?"

With temper spiking, she said, "What I want is for you to be professional, especially in my absence."

"I am extremely professional. I've never crossed a line with any client and I certainly don't intend on starting with Ally Evans. If you haven't noticed, she's not my type."

She thought *she* was his type, but instead of speaking her mind, she plowed ahead. "From what I recall, she is exactly the type of woman you date. One who falls at your feet when you come into a room."

His eyes grew dark, his temper rising. "That's laughable."

Her voice was harsh. "I'm not laughing."

"Kenzie…" With an uncomfortable cough, he said, "I think your pain meds have skewed your thinking."

"Ha." Her voice echoed in the lobby.

"Really, that's all you have to say?" Robbie's voice ratcheted up.

"Since you seem to be distracted by *other* things, I'm going to let you off the hook. You don't need to stay at my place tonight. Grace has been wanting to hang out. It'll give you time to figure out what's next for you."

"What are you talking about? I don't need to figure out anything. I thought we both knew what was coming next."

"I guess we see things very differently." She looked at her hands. Her throat constricted. "I'm tired."

"Kenzie," he pleaded, "we need to talk about why you're really upset with me."

She wanted to run from the lobby but had to settle for saying, "You don't need to stay with me anymore and we'll talk tomorrow. I just want to go home."

"But...?" Robbie's question hung heavy in the air. Stony silence and a hard look had him say, "I'll get your Mom."

He pushed open the glass door and walked out. Cheryl peeked her head into the lobby and walked over to Kenzie. "It might be none of my business, but you're right—she's chasing him. But Robbie's been nothing but professional. Don't hold him responsible for her actions."

Kenzie wiped a lone tear from her cheek. "I appreciate what you're saying, but that's not how it looked to me."

"It's the truth." Cheryl stuck out her pinky. A small smile crept across Kenzie's face and she held up her pinky. They joined fingers. Cheryl smiled, "Pinky promise."

"Thanks, Cheryl," she said grimly.

Robbie scratched his head. What the heck had just happened in there? He couldn't wait for Kenzie to come into the gym, and within a few minutes harsh accusations were flying. He wanted to pull her into his arms and tell her she was the only woman for him. After what had happened between them in New Hampshire, she had his heart and soul for all eternity. What held him back? Fear of Kenzie saying she didn't have *those* kinds of feelings for him? Or worse that she would say she making love with him was a huge mistake?

He felt sick. How was he going to ever reach her if every time he worked with Ally she accused him of lacking professionalism? She needed to apologize—he had done nothing wrong and it wasn't up to him to come crawling back, looking for forgiveness. Not this time.

CHAPTER 21

F our days. Four long and tortuous days. Kenzie called Robbie, but other than talking about work, there was zero personal conversation between them.

Mom picked up the tray of dirty dishes next to Kenzie's chair. She paused and said, "If you apologized, things would go back to normal."

She looked at Mom with sorrow-filled eyes. "I don't know what came over me, seeing Ally kissing him and hanging all over him."

"Jealousy, perhaps?"

Kenzie's head snapped back. "Huh? I don't know what you're talking about. I'm not jealous of her."

"It's an open secret. Robbie has been crushing on you since you were eight or nine years old. I know you asked him to think about what is next for his future. Maybe you should take your own advice."

Kenzie shifted uncomfortably in the chair, but not from her injuries. Mom had hit a nerve. "I don't know what you're talking about."

Mom's eyes grew wide. "You might be able to fool yourself, but you can't fool your mother."

Kenzie flipped on the television, effectively ending the conversation. "I'm tired."

Mom left the room, leaving her alone with her thoughts. She pulled her phone from her fleece pocket. Hitting a few buttons, she waited for Jamie to pick up.

"Hello, Jamie Sullivan."

"Hey, Mac, any chance you could swing by after work?"

"Kenz, are you okay?"

She sighed. "Physically, yes. Mentally, I'm not so sure."

Jamie paused. "I can be over around four and I'll make dinner."

"Aren't you having dinner with Caleb?"

With a small laugh, she said, "He'll survive."

"I'll shoot Grace a text and ask her to pick up takeout." Kenzie felt her heart lighten. "Time with my sisters is just what I need."

Jamie replied without hesitation, "What are sisters for?"

She smiled into the phone. "Thanks, Jamie. See you later."

Mom came in carrying a glass of water. Kenzie was staring out the window. "Did I hear you talking?"

"It was Jamie. She's stopping over tonight."

"That sounds nice, sweetheart. You girls haven't had sister time since before Jamie's wedding."

Kenzie's smile grew. "It will be a nice change of pace. Sitting around is driving me buggy and I can't start physical therapy until I get both casts off. I have another four weeks of doing nothing."

"Dr. Barton did say you could go into work. What about taking a few hours at the front desk? That would break up the day," Mom suggested.

"It's a pain for you or Dad to drive me down."

Mom patted her hand and reassured her, "If it would put a smile on your face, it'd be worth it. Seeing Robbie might help too."

Kenzie barked, "Ya know, I'm tired of everyone sticking up for Robbie. I wasn't the one sucking face with a client."

Mom withdrew her hand. "Kenzie, you've got to be kidding."

With her voice growing in volume, Kenzie exclaimed, "I can't believe you're taking his side." She knew she was blowing this out of proportion, and she wished she could go for a run and burn off the anger that burned her gut.

Mom argued, "I'm taking your side. But I'm trying to point out is there are two sides to every story and your perspective may be a bit *skewed*." She set the glass on the side table with a thud and stalked from the room without another word.

Kenzie squeezed her eyes shut. The memory of Ally kissing Robbie made her see red. Before she could open them, she flashed back to the summit and Robbie holding her close and Kenzie initiating that mind-blowing kiss.

Her eyes popped open as if she could really see for the first time. With sudden clarity, she knew she had to stop fooling herself. Their relationship had changed dramatically on that summit.

Sitting in the middle of her condo, she knew the simple truth: she was head over heels in love with Robbie.

She closed her eyes again and replayed Robbie carrying her back to camp. The pain had been overwhelming, but she felt safe. No, it was more than that—she was loved. Could she really be jealous over a client or could she blame it on her pain medication? She had to face it, the latter wasn't an issue, as she was taking non-aspirin pain relief during the day and something mild to sleep at night.

She was out of her comfort zone with this topic. She'd never been jealous of anyone.

Her sisters would know exactly what to do. She laid her head back on the chair. With deep faith in her sisters, she believed with all her heart everything would be fine.

Mom closed her book and set it aside. "What time will your sisters get here?"

Kenzie glanced at the clock and grinned. "They should be walking in the door any minute."

Casually Mom said, "As soon as they do, I'm going to take off."

"Mom, stay, have a glass of wine with us."

Mom's eyebrow shot up. "Should you be drinking?"

"I sent Grace a text and asked. She said since I was off the pain killers I could have a wine spritzer, which consists primarily of club soda and a splash of wine." She crossed her fingers over her heart. "I promise. You know the junior doctor will make me toe the line."

Mom frowned. "You really shouldn't call her that. It took her years to become a physician's assistant and her patients respect her."

Kenzie's eyes grew wide. "I didn't mean any offense—it just sounds better than a PA. You know, throwing the word doctor into the sentence."

Mom wore her serious parent look. "I know for a fact it hurts Grace's feelings."

Kenzie's face fell. "It does? Why didn't she ever say anything?"

"She looks up to you. There are some things we put up with from the people we love, but don't necessarily like."

She hung her head. "I've been pretty self-absorbed if I didn't notice."

"You've been focused on other things." Mom rose from the couch and picked up her book. She leaned over and kissed the top of Kenzie's head. "I'm going to let you girls enjoy yourselves, talk about boys or anything else that might come up."

"Hey, Mom?"

"What, kiddo?"

Being completely sincere, Kenzie asked, "Am I really a lousy sister?"

Mom messed her hair. Softly she reminded her, "Not at all. You tend to be tough on the people you love. I think it's your way of challenging everyone to be their very best. Don't forget people are living the way it makes them happy."

Kenzie protested, "But Grace would have made an amazing doctor. I thought if she became a PA, she was settling."

With a half-smile, Mom said, "She's happy and doing what she loves."

"Why do I get the feeling you're trying to tell me something more?"

The front door banged and they heard, "Hello."

Mom patted her cheek. "Please think about what I said."

Sheepishly Kenzie nodded. "Thanks, Mom."

Jamie burst into the living room, arms heavy with bags. "I come bearing food. My sweet husband, made us dinner."

Kenzie looked around. "Where's Grace? I thought she was here too."

"She was right behind me." Jamie dropped the insulated cooler bags on the floor. "Be right back."

As she disappeared into the front hall, Kenzie could

hear a murmur of voices. She dropped the recliner's footrest and scooched on her butt, curiosity propelling her forward. Who on earth were they talking to? Before she could get to her feet, the front door banged and her sisters were coming down the hall.

"Hey, Kenz, how are you doing today?" Grace held a bottle of red wine in one hand and a huge bouquet of flowers in the other.

Kenzie's face split into a wide grin. "You didn't need to bring me flowers."

Grace shook her head and beamed. "I didn't. Robbie dropped them off."

Her heart skipped. "Where is he?" She started to get up anxious to see him.

"He said he couldn't stay." She set the vase on the coffee table and pulled a card from her pocket. "Here you go."

Kenzie sat back in the chair. *KENZIE* was scrawled on the envelope in Robbie's bold handwriting.

Mom said, "How about I help you unpack and get dinner reheated, and we'll let your sister read her card?"

Jamie and Grace followed their mom's lead and backed out of the room.

Kenzie turned the card over in her hand. Her eyes drank in the beauty of the wildflower bouquet. He knew her so well—no fussy flowers, just deep rich colors and fragrance.

Sliding her nail under the flap, she eased open the envelope. She pulled out a photo. Her mouthed formed an O. It was Kenzie and Robbie mugging for the camera with the White Mountains in the background. Her heart thudded in her chest. She unfolded the paper.

Dear Kenzie,

I'm sorry we argued. I promise you, I've treated every person that comes into the gym with respect and professionalism. I've told Ally that moving forward, I can't work with her as things must remain friendly but nothing more. Which has brought me to a decision I should have made long ago.

I don't think we should work together anymore. I'm going to wait until you're back on your feet and then I'll move to Burlington. We'll still be the best of friends. I firmly believe this change will be what is best for both of us.

Love always,
Robbie

Her mouth dropped open and her hand flew to her lips. Tears formed, but they didn't fall. He was leaving her.

A heartbreaking sob came from the depth of her heart, and she screamed. "NO!"

"Kenzie." Grace rushed in and knelt in front of her. "What happened?"

Unable to find the words, Kenzie thrust the card into her hands.

Grace scanned it and passed it to Jamie, then took her hand. "Do you want to talk about it?"

Kenzie swallowed the lump in her throat. "There's nothing to talk about. You read the note—he's leaving me."

Grace said, "You could change his mind. Tell him how you feel."

"That's the problem!" Kenzie cried. "What if what I think is love is really gratitude and friendship?"

"Who are you trying to kid?" Jamie handed the card to Mom and perched on the edge of the recliner. "Do you really think what you feel is nothing more than friendship?"

Kenzie shrugged. Her voice cracked. "How does anyone

ever really know? I don't want to make a mistake and end up hurting Robbie or me." She wiped the tears from her face. "This sucks!" she cried. "I've spent more time crying in the last few months than I have in the last ten years. And why? Ever since Gran's wedding dress showed up, I've been in a tailspin."

She looked at her sisters and mom. "I can't think about this anymore. If he wants to leave, let him. I'm fine on my own. I can hire a new trainer and I've got Cheryl. And you read the note. We'll still be friends. Who knows, maybe by this time next year we'll have gone on our annual hiking trip and everything will be back to normal." She prattled on, her smile tight, "Grace, will you fix some adult beverages? And Mom, stay. We're going to hang out and eat some delicious food."

Mom said, "I'm going to leave and I will talk with you"—she pointed to Jamie and Grace—"tomorrow and I will see you"—she pointed to Kenzie—"in the morning."

Grace said, "I don't have to be to work until nine, so no need to rush over early."

Mom gave each girl a hug and said, "Enjoy your evening." She cupped Kenzie's cheek. "I'm sorry about Robbie."

Tears filled her eyes. She blinked them away and waited for the front door to close. "Do you think taking care of me has been too much for Mom?"

Jamie gave her sister a sweet smile. "Are you kidding? Having the chance to fuss over one of us is helping her adjust to retirement, and Dad loves being around. You know that."

Kenzie's face dropped. "I feel bad. I thought they'd want to get back to Scotland before the holidays."

Jamie said, "Nah, and miss Thanksgiving and Christmas

with us? Mom said they're going sometime in March and spend the spring there, maybe into summer."

Relief filled Kenzie's eyes. "I'm glad they'll be here for the foreseeable future. It wouldn't be the holidays without them."

Grace hopped up from the floor. "I'm going to get our wine and see if your hubby packed any appetizers in one of those bags."

Kenzie patted her belly. "Without working out and wearing sweatpants all the time, I'd better be careful or I see a diet in my future."

Grace cautioned, "Kenz, now is not the time to start any kind of a diet."

Kenzie started to have a quick retort and it died on her lips. "Thanks, sis, for your concern."

Grace blinked. "No snappy comment for the junior doc?"

Kenzie dipped her head. "I happen to know, from first-hand experience, that you're brilliant and I should listen to your advice more often." Teasing she said, "I hear people actually pay you for it and I can get it for free."

Grace's face flushed from the compliment. "Well, thanks, Kenz. I appreciate the vote of confidence."

She walked around the corner and Jamie poked Kenzie. "What's gotten into you?"

"Mom made some good points about how everyone needs to follow their heart and be happy. Grace is damn good at what she does, and even if I felt she should have become a doctor, she's happy and living her dream, that's all that matters."

Jamie pursed her lips. "I'm impressed."

"And for the record, count me in for stripping hideous old wallpaper at your new place once I get back on my feet."

"Your support and elbow grease are most definitely appreciated. Besides, at some point my cottage is going to be too small for us."

Kenzie perked up. "Are you going to be making an announcement?"

Grace walked in. "Who's saying what?" She handed Kenzie a wine glass with pale pink liquid with lots of bubbles floating up from the bottom. Then she handed a glass to Jamie. "To the Mac sisters."

They clinked glasses. Grace looked at her sisters. "What did I miss?"

Kenzie tilted her head up to wink at her. "I'm not sure, but Jamie might be getting ready to make an announcement about the next generation of Scots, mixed with a wee bit of Irish?"

Grace went to grab Jamie's wineglass. She laughed and pulled it out of reach. "Not yet, but Caleb and I are talking about starting a family. We'll have enough bedrooms at the new house for a small army."

Grace grinned. "Will you tell us first, before you even tell Caleb?"

"Uh, no. That particular information starts with a husband first and then sisters and parents." Jamie grinned. "But have no fear, there will still be stuff you'll hear before Caleb."

Grace sank into the sofa cushions. "I can't believe how much things have changed in a little less than a year. Gran died, we got the dress and the journals. Jamie got married, Kenzie got hurt and the man she loves is moving away and I'm still stuck in the same place."

Jamie crossed the room and sat down next to Grace. "That leads me to a question I have for you."

Grace's eyes grew wide. "You can't give me the dress. Kenzie has to keep it indefinitely."

Snorting, Kenzie threw her head back, "You see how well that's working out for me."

Jamie gave Kenzie a look that had her fall silent. "Caleb and I have a tentative date to move into the new house. We're targeting April 1st."

Grace smiled. "Sure, I'll help you move."

With a laugh and a shake of her head, Jamie said, "That's not what I was going to ask, but I'll take you up on it."

Grace's forehead wrinkled and eyes narrowed. "Okay, well, how can I help?"

"It's not what you can do for me, it's what I want to do for you."

"I'm confused." She gave Kenzie a quizzical look.

Jamie drawled, "A while back you mentioned wanting to buy your own place and get out of apartment living, but you didn't know when you'd have enough in your house fund and you don't want to touch the money Gran left you."

"Are you offering me a loan?" Grace waved a hand at Jamie. "I'm not taking a penny from you or anyone."

Jamie laid a comforting hand on her arm. "I wasn't going to offer you cash, and if you'd stop interrupting me, I could tell you."

Color flushed to her cheeks. "Sorry. You have the floor."

Jamie grinned and winked at Kenzie "Well, that is kind of the point."

Kenzie suggested, "You'd better stop dragging this out."

"Kenzie, what do you know that I don't?"

She pointed at Jamie and pretended to zip her lips.

Jamie smiled broadly. "If you're interested, you can rent my cottage with the option to buy, and all the rent will go toward the down payment."

Grace hopped up and grabbed Jamie, hugging her tight

and squealing, "Are you serious? You want to sell me your house?"

Jamie's eyes gleamed. "I do. You'd have a home of your own and I'd know you bought something that was in good repair."

"Always the big sister, but what about Kenzie?" She plopped on the arm of the chair. "Do you want to buy the cottage?"

Kenzie shook her head. "I love condo living. Someone takes care of the outside, all I have to do is maintain the interior."

Grace's face lit up. "Are you sure?"

"I'm sure." Kenzie smiled. "And I'll help move you in too."

"Then I accept." Grace flung her arms around Jamie, dancing around all the while hugging her sister tight. "I can't believe you're doing this for me." Grace was singing over and over, "I'm gonna be a homeowner."

"There's your answer, Jamie." Kenzie laughed.

Jamie chuckled. Grace squeezed her tight. "Thanks, sis, you really are one of the best sisters a girl could have."

"Just one?" Jamie teased.

"I have the best sisters ever." Grace bent over and hugged Kenzie. "Thank you for not wanting the cottage."

Kenzie laughed out loud. "You are most welcome, kiddo." She held up her wine spritzer. "Let's make a toast to new beginnings."

Jamie and Grace clinked glasses with Kenzie. They sat back on the couch, and Jamie looked at Kenzie. "It's time we talk about what was on your mind when you called."

Kenzie took a small sip. "It doesn't matter now."

"Yes, it does. Fess up," Jamie demanded in a gentle but firm voice.

She scowled. "Robbie's note makes everything irrelevant."

"How you're feeling makes it important," Grace urged.

Kenzie ran her finger around the edge of the wineglass.

Jamie said, "Stop stalling, Kenz, and spill it."

"All right, the other day Mom and Dad drove me down to the gym and I saw Ally Evans, falling all over Robbie and she kissed his cheek. We got into this big fight after she left, and I accused him of being unprofessional."

Grace winced. "Jeez, that doesn't sound good."

Sarcasm laced Kenzie's voice. "Wait, it gets better. I was so mad at him I said some things I regret. Like he should figure out what he wants for his future. I'm sure that's what pushed him away."

Grace leaned forward. "Is that what you wanted, for him to leave Easton?"

With a shake of her head, Kenzie blinked back a tear. "No, of course not."

"So, you got jealous and instead of acting like a rational person, you lashed out at him." Jamie pointed out, "Seems like that backfired."

Kenzie looked around. "There's more. This kind of goes back to the wedding. Heck, maybe long before that. But really at the wedding I had this weird feeling in the pit of my stomach when I saw Robbie, all dressed up in his suit." She sighed dreamily. "He looked drop-dead gorgeous."

Grace concluded, "Is that the first time you really saw him as a tall, lean, loveable hunk?"

She nodded. "He's always been, well, Robbie. I've seen him filthy on a hiking trail and dressed for work, but rarely in a suit, and I'd be lying if I said it didn't stop me dead in my tracks."

Jamie settled into the sofa cushions. "Tell us what happened on your hiking trip."

"What do you mean? I never said anything happened."

Jamie continued, "It's just a guess from the way you've been acting and asking us to come over tonight. I drew my own conclusions."

"Well, if you must know the whole trip kind of blurs together, but the first night out, I burned my hand and he put salve on it. The next day was wonderful—we had a blast." She handed Grace the photo. "Our last day, right after we took this picture, the ledge started to break away. If he hadn't caught me, I wouldn't be sitting here."

"What aren't you saying, Kenz?" Grace demanded, while her and Jamie's eyes were locked on Kenzie.

"All that adrenaline pumping and him holding me close...I kissed him and I didn't stop there."

In unison, her sisters shouted, "YES!"

Kenzie's face grew warm, her eyes all dewy. "It was wonderful and magical. So different but yet familiar at the same time." She sipped her wine, stalling. "Afterwards"— she felt her face go hot—"you know, we made our way back down to camp. I fell, and from there the rest is history."

"He carried you, kept you warm and safe until help arrived," Grace finished for her.

"What are you're leaving out?" Jamie studied her sister carefully.

Kenzie licked her lips. "Well, you know, we got *close*. We haven't talked about it and now he's leaving. Maybe it didn't mean anything to him."

"Kenzie, do you think it's possible Robbie thinks *you* regret it?"

She hung her head. "I dunno, maybe."

Grace took her hand. "And you're starting to figure out that you're in love with him."

Exasperated, Kenzie said, "That's just it. How am I

supposed to figure out anything if he's not even in the same town?"

"It's pretty simple, Kenzie," Grace said softly. "Ask him to stay. Tell him you need to talk to him."

In an instant, Kenzie made a decision. "He's made up his mind, so I'm going to just continue on with my life and he'll find a new one in Burlington."

Jamie shook her head. "Don't make a rash decision you may live to regret."

Trying to keep the hurt out of her words, Kenzie said, "Don't worry about me, Jamie. I'll be just fine. Nothing has changed. Not really."

CHAPTER 22

A fter swinging her cast over the edge of the bed, she carefully set it on the floor. If today went well, she'd have a walking cast. The last six weeks had been like molasses going uphill in winter, but at least during her last appointment the wrist cast was removed. Tomorrow she was starting physical therapy for her wrist.

Maneuvering the knee scooter closer to the bed, she set her knee on the pad, hanging the cast off the end. She inched her way toward the bathroom and mumbled, "Who would have thought I'd get good at using this handy-dandy scooter?"

Grace popped her head around the doorjamb. "Morning, Kenz. Need any help?"

She smirked. "Nope, I've got this. You know, you can start staying at your place anytime."

"I will if you get your walking cast." She pointed to the scooter. "You make me nervous the way you whip around on that thing."

Kenzie chuckled. "It's better than the wheelchair. That was like being in prison."

"It'll be a nice Thanksgiving if you're walking, for all of us."

Kenzie hovered in the bathroom doorway. "Do you think the doc will let me drive?"

"He'll check your wrist, and since you're starting PT tomorrow, I'm sure he'll release you to drive short distances."

"I just want to drive around town. Being chauffeured has gotten *very* old."

Grace wandered down the hall. Kenzie could hear her snickering. "You're not an easy patient either."

"I heard that!"

More laughter answered her.

"Wow, the doctor today, physical therapy tomorrow and then Thanksgiving. It's going to be a busy week." Brushing her teeth, she remembered what else would happen today. Her heart ached. As much as she wanted to get the walking cast, it would mean Robbie was one day closer to walking out of her life.

Jamie and Grace were right—she loved him with all her heart, but it was too late. She wasn't about to confess her feelings now when he had made his choice. It was a small consolation they'd still be friends. *I want the chance for more, but I'm terrified to ask for it. What if he has moved on with Ally?*

She ran a comb through her hair, added a bit of gel, and applied moisturizer to her face and a special cream under her eyes. With a final swish of mascara, it was time to get dressed for the trip back to Laconia. Looking at her reflection in the mirror, she mused, "It wasn't that long ago Jamie was badgering me to wear just a touch of makeup. Who says a girl can't change?"

Kenzie sauntered out of the hospital with a cane in her left hand and a walking cast on her foot. She waited with Mom while Dad went to get the car.

"You have no idea how good it feels to be standing upright, taking a deep breath of cold air that goes to the very tips of my toes." She twirled her right wrist and prattled on, "And look at this, pain-free, just a tad stiff. But otherwise I'm doing pretty darn good, and who knows, if I do really well in four weeks, I might be able to start riding an exercise bike and build up my endurance to run."

A look of concern flashed across Mom's face. "Don't push yourself too hard, Kenzie. You don't want to have a setback."

"My sisters signed up to do the race in March and I'm going to be right by their side. I won't be fast, but I'll be running."

Casually Mom asked, "Is Robbie going to run with you?"

Kenzie's eyes grew misty while her jaw jutted out. Curtly she said, "I have no idea. It's totally up to him."

"I wish you two would patch things up."

"We're cool, Mom." She gave her a one arm hug. "Stop fretting." She took a halting step forward. "Here's Dad."

He opened the driver's door. Coming around to the passenger side, he held both doors open while Kenzie slid into the back Mom climbed in the front.

Flashing a grin to her dad, she said, "You are such a gentleman."

"Aye, nothing wrong with good manners." He closed the door. "How about we stop for a bit of lunch?" he asked.

"That's a great idea, and then I can head right to work and show off my new cane to everyone." She straightened her shoulders and plastered on a smile in spite of the sadness she felt when she thought of Robbie.

Dad eased onto the road. "There's a diner up ahead. How does that sound?"

"Sure." Kenzie slung her handbag over her head. "It feels good to not have to worry about getting around with the scooter or wheelchair."

Mom's voice held a warning tone. "You need to be careful, Kenzie. We want you to enjoy Thanksgiving pain-free."

"Are Jamie and Caleb hosting at the new house?"

Mom glanced over her shoulder. With a laugh she said, "Oh, I guess you haven't heard. They decided to gut the kitchen along with the bathrooms. They like the old-fashioned look, but you know your sister, she'll recreate it with new."

Kenzie smiled. "I'm sure it will be beautiful when they're done. She has great taste and that extends to her husband."

"It's nice when a heart finds its soul mate."

"Are you speaking from personal experience?" Kenzie teased.

Mom blushed. "Your dad and I did get lucky, finding each other and recognizing it before it slipped away."

Although Mom didn't mean anything, her words stung. Hadn't Kenzie let love pass her by?

Dad parked the car. "They have really good burgers and fries."

"If we're doing burgers, you know what that means." Kenzie grinned. "Chocolate milkshakes all around."

Taking it slow, Kenzie hobbled down the front steps, momentarily reliving the memory when she came home from the hospital as Robbie carried her in the house. Shivering from the frosty air, she took small steps toward her car. She opened the door and cautiously sat down. She flung her bag on the passenger seat and took a deep breath. That took forever. "I'll never take independence for granted again."

She slowly backed out of her drive. After the short trip, Kenzie pulled behind the building, parking in her usual spot. She tucked her cell phone into her jacket pocket.

The back door flung open and Cheryl was waiting for Kenzie. Her heart sank. She had hoped Robbie would be waiting for her.

She pushed open the door and grabbed her cane. As she held it firmly, the hard plastic of her walking cast made contact with pavement. One cautious step and then another.

"Hi, Cheryl, it's good to see you." Kenzie smiled and looked down at the uneven ground.

Cheryl beamed. "It's really good to see you. It's just not the same when you're not here."

Kenzie glanced up. "It's nice to know when I'm out of sight, I'm not out of mind."

"Are you kidding?" Cheryl laughed.

Kenzie stepped into the front lobby and gasped. A crowd of people were shouting *welcome home!* and balloons and crepe paper ribbons were draped from every doorjamb. A banner stretched over the front windows: *Welcome back, Kenzie!*

Tears welled up in her eyes her heart lodged in her throat. "Oh, you guys! You didn't need to do this."

Jamie and Grace, along with her parents, Caleb, his brother Steve and his fiancee Yvette, and lots of gym members filled the lobby to capacity.

Robbie stood behind the desk, grinning. "Kenz, we couldn't let your first real day back go unnoticed."

She hugged each person and said, "Thank you, everyone. This is just, well, unexpected, and I'm speechless."

Robbie stepped from behind the desk holding a huge vanilla-frosted cake. "That's okay, you don't have to talk. We've got cake."

People started milling about, the noise growing as the party got underway. Kenzie lost count of the number of times she was told her spin class was the one thing Robbie just couldn't do justice. He was too easy on everyone, and when would she be able to get back in the seat?

Her eyes followed Robbie as he mingled with the members and her family, smiling and laughing just like always. Did she dare hope? Maybe he wasn't going to leave.

As the crowd thinned, Cheryl went into clean-up mode and the cake was eaten, with one piece for Kenzie to take home. Her family went their separate ways, and other than a few people working out, Robbie and Kenzie were the only people in the lobby.

Robbie asked, "It went well at the doctor's?"

Kenzie nodded, suddenly feeling shy. "It did. A few more weeks with this boot and then I can start PT for the foot and maybe even get back on an exercise bike. I told Dr. Barton I plan on running the St. Paddy's Day race."

Robbie raised an eyebrow. "Really?"

She chewed her lower lip. "I won't be back to my normal gait, but it feels good to have a goal."

He nodded, agreeing, "Something to work toward."

Her gaze roamed over the space. "The place looks great. Thanks for keeping everything running smoothly. I know it was a lot to take on."

He shrugged. "Not a problem. Cheryl has the daily logs up to date."

"That's good." Kenzie hesitated. "Robbie, I wanted to say…"

"Wait, before you say anything, I want you to know my last day will be December 31st."

Kenzie felt like she'd been hit with a two-by-four. She stumbled back and took a shaky breath. "Oh, well, okay," she stammered. "I should be able to hold class by then."

"I've written down the names of a couple of people who will be able to replace me."

"I appreciate that." She looked at the floor. She wanted to tell him he was irreplaceable, but the words died on her lips.

He continued, his voice steady, "I've left their numbers on the desk. You can set up interviews when you're ready."

She nodded. Quietly she asked, "You've taken care of everything for me—what about for you? Do you have a new job and a place to live?"

"Yeah, I'm moving in between Christmas and New Year's, and I start at the new place on the second."

"All right, well then, um, let's plan a little going away party with everyone before Christmas, as it sounds like you're going to be pretty busy the last week of the year." She felt like pieces of her heart were breaking off leaving her with deep, gaping wounds.

A forced smile flitted across his face. "Sure, that'll be fun, but if it's easier we can just get together for drinks with everyone someplace in town."

"No, I'm hosting. After all, it's the least I can do for my best friend." She had to fight the overwhelming urge to throw her arms around his neck and pull his lips to hers. Her voice thick with unshed tears, she cried, "Wait. Can't we go back to the way things were between us?"

His hazel eyes were unreadable. "Give it some time,

Kenzie." He leaned down and pecked her cheek. "Before you know it, we'll be just fine."

Robbie turned and walked out the back door, closing it firmly behind him.

Standing alone in the middle of the empty lobby, she whispered, "Now what do I do?"

CHAPTER 23

Kenzie had researched physical therapy for the wrist. She wasn't sure why she needed to go— most rehab was stretching and could be done at home. Dr. Barton had been insistent she have one or two sessions to learn the correct method before beginning the process. It was imperative she regain full functionality, quickly. She had clients to train.

Much to her chagrin she had a temporary handicapped plate and pulled into a designated spot near the front entrance at the medical center. Her face lit up. Grace was waiting outside the double glass doors with an umbrella.

She hurried to the car. "You made it." She held an umbrella over Kenzie as she slid out of the car and took one tentative step. She stumbled.

Grace thrust a firm hand under her arm. "Take your time."

Annoyed, she said, "I'm so clumsy with this darn cane and boot, and I'm scared to use my hand for anything."

"That's perfectly normal," Grace soothed. "You haven't

been able to use it in weeks, but after today you'll have more confidence."

The girls made slow progress to the door. As it swung open automatically, they stepped into the vestibule. Grace shook the umbrella and closed it. "We're going to take a left and it's the fourth door on the right."

They started down the hallway, one slow, halting step at a time. Kenzie said, "Dr. Barton wanted me to see the sports medicine therapist. I'm assuming I'll see him for the ankle too."

"How many visits do you have for your wrist?"

"Two. I think it's more to help me get ready to lift weights. He knows I'm anxious to get started." She glanced at Grace as if challenging her.

Grace snorted. "You can't cut yourself any slack, can you?"

"You're forgetting I'm down a personal trainer at the end of the year."

Grace's face fell. "Robbie's really leaving?"

"Yeah. I've come to the decision I'm not going to try and stop him," she stated.

Shaking her head at Kenzie with obvious disappointment, "I don't get you."

Concentrating on putting one foot in front of the other, Kenzie finally stated, "I pushed him away one too many times. Instead I'm going to focus on getting back to work and train for our race."

Grace opened her mouth to speak and instead pointed to a chair. "I'll check you in."

Kenzie took an empty seat. Curious, she asked, "Don't you have patients?"

"I want to make sure you get off on the right foot." Grace grinned. "Sorry, poor joke."

Kenzie shook her finger and laughed. "When are you

going to start training? You've got a little more than three months."

"I'm sure you have my training planned down to the minute."

Kenzie's quick retort died on her lips when she noticed Ally Evans walking toward her.

"Hi, Kenzie." She smiled. "I'm going to be working with you today."

Stunned, with a withering look directed to Grace, she asked, "Did you forget to tell me something?"

"Is there a problem, Kenzie?" Ally questioned.

Grace slipped away, saying they'd talk later. Kenzie rose to her feet, pulling herself up to her full height of five feet. The other woman slim and confident, stood in front of her. "Not at all. I didn't have any idea you are a therapist."

Ally's smile was tight. "My specialty is helping athletes rehab and you certainly qualify—you're in fantastic shape."

"I was." Kenzie hobbled down the hall with Ally. Inside she was seething. She'd like to walk out the door or demand an appointment with someone else. But she'd get through this session if it would get her one step closer to getting back in fighting form.

Ally was talking, and Kenzie caught some of what she was saying, "I promise if you do the exercises exactly as I prescribe, you'll be back in the swing of things in no time."

"My doctor said I'd only need one or two sessions for the wrist."

Ally nodded. "That's right, but once the boot comes off, we'll be working together three times a week."

Inwardly, Kenzie groaned. "How many weeks?"

"I predict four, but if needed, we'll get more visits approved from the doc." Ally stopped at a door and stepped to one side. "Why don't we get started?"

Kenzie admired that she was all business. If Ally was the way to getting back in shape, she'd bite the bullet.

She had Kenzie sit down and provided her with a stool to prop her ankle. "Are you still keeping your leg elevated?" She looked at Kenzie pointedly.

"As much as practical."

Her voice was clipped and efficient. "You may need to do that for several months, even when you are out of the boot. Ankle surgery can be a tough recovery, more so if you're very active."

Slowly nodding, Kenzie replied, "Good to know."

Ally guided her through a series of stretches for her wrist. Kenzie listened intently. She was surprised by Ally's patience as she went through each exercise.

Ally's smile was encouraging. "You did fantastic. I'm going to give you a copy of the exercises. I'd like you to do them in the morning and at night, but no more than twice a day." She cautioned. "If you feel pain, stop immediately."

Kenzie set her boot on the floor and stood, steadying herself as she studied the room. The walls were covered with posters of anatomy of bones, muscles and tendons.

"Here you go." Ally handed her the papers. "If you'd like to hold off on another wrist appointment, that's fine. I'm confident you can do this part of the rehab on your own."

"When do you think I can start using light hand weights?" Kenzie tucked the papers into an inner jacket pocket.

"Only you can be the judge of when you're ready, but I think next week you can start with soup cans and increase slowly." Ally reminded her, "Listen to your body."

Kenzie protested, "I use heavier weights."

"You did," Ally stated matter-of-factly, "but don't add

undue stress to a healing fracture. Go slow. If you don't, you'll end up sliding backward."

"So, like I could start today with the cans?"

Ally laughed. "I guess you just missed it when I said give stretching a few days to limber things up and then yes, you can start."

Kenzie hesitated. "Thanks for today. I wasn't sure what to expect, but for the first time in weeks, I feel like I'm starting to be me again."

"If you're ready to try weights the next time I'm in the gym, I can check your form."

Looking away, Kenzie said, "No, that's okay, I wouldn't want to bother you."

"I offered, you didn't ask." Ally smiled warmly. "Besides, if I help you get back in shape, you'll be holding spin class again, and I hear it's not to be missed."

Kenzie relaxed and beamed. "I'll save you a seat in my first class, on me."

Ally drawled, "I have another patient. If you need something, feel free to make an appointment. I'm pretty sure you've got this under control and as soon as you're ready to get that ankle back in shape, call." She turned toward the door.

"Ally?"

She stopped mid-step. "Yes, Kenzie?"

"There's a race in mid-March my sisters and I entered. Grace and Jamie are going for their first 5k, and I want to do the half marathon. Do you think I'll be ready?"

"Wow." Her eyes grew wide. "That's ambitious and it's hard for me to say. Most of it will depend on when the doctor releases you for therapy and how much swelling and pain you have as you recover."

Kenzie's chin drooped. "If I'm hearing you right, there's a chance I won't be ready?"

Bobbing her head up and down, she confirmed Kenzie's fear. "Potentially, but again, most of this recovery is in your hands."

"Well then, this patient is determined to be in the race, and when I cross the finish line, I'll feel like I've conquered the biggest hurdle in my life."

Ally flashed an encouraging smile. "That's a great attitude. I'll do all I can to help."

Kenzie took Ally's smile as a positive sign. She saw Grace hurrying down the hallway with a smile. "Hey, Kenz, how did it go?"

"Really good." Despite the boot, she had pep in her step.

Ally turned and greeted her next patient as the girls walked toward the exit. Nonchalantly Kenzie said, "I may have misjudged Ally."

Grace gave her a sideways glance. "Interesting."

Kenzie shrugged. "She was encouraging and offered to help me with hand weights in a few days or so. She's not at all what I thought."

"Good to know. Maybe you only thought you saw something between her and Robbie?" Grace gave her a soft shoulder bump.

"Oh, no!" Kenzie's eyes popped. "I saw her kiss Robbie's cheek and I think she wanted to date him, but I should cut her some slack. She's new to town and he is a really nice man and"—she sighed—"*so* easy on the eyes."

Grace joked, "And she had no way to know about the two of you either."

"True."

"Oh, look, it's stopped raining." Grace stepped outside.

Kenzie pulled her car keys from her pocket. "I think I'm going to stop off at the gym for a few hours and then go home."

"Is Mom still hovering?"

"Only to help with laundry and cleaning. I'm going to send her and Dad away for a long weekend once I am fully independent again."

"You mentioned that, and I think it's sweet." Grace held open the car door as Kenzie got in.

She secured her seatbelt and started the car. "If you want to swing by after work, feel free."

Grace said, "I'll pick up a pizza and salad."

"Sounds good. See you tonight."

She hovered next to the door, "Have fun at the gym, but promise you'll pace yourself."

Kenzie gave her a mock salute. "Promise."

She found herself smiling on the short drive to the gym. She was anxious to spend a few minutes with Robbie.

His truck was parked in his usual spot. She hobbled to the back door and eased it open. The sound of weight machines clanging was music to her ears. Rounding the corner, she saw Robbie sitting behind the front desk.

"Hey, how was PT?" His smile warmed her soul.

"Excellent! You'll never guess who's my therapist." Without waiting for a response, she rambled on, "Ally, and surprisingly she's very knowledgeable."

"Huh. She never said she would be working with you, but I would guess that's due to privacy laws or something."

Chatting with Robbie was easy, but Kenzie's stomach clenched. She longed to say she was sorry about everything and ask him to stay; he was being friendly but distant. Moving to an easier subject, she casually asked, "Have we been busy today?"

"The usual crowd. Typical for this time of year until New Year's. Then there's the onslaught of people wanting to get in shape for their resolutions."

At the mention of New Year's, Kenzie's mouth went dry.

Robbie pushed the chair back from the desk. "Here, have a seat and I'll check on the folks in the cardio room."

She watched him hurry from the room. Each step widened the distance between them until Kenzie felt as if it was a never-ending chasm.

CHAPTER 24

Kenzie gripped the steering wheel, her knuckles white. She stared at her parents' house. Thanksgiving had always been her favorite holiday and the Burns family had been coming for years. But this year it would be hard to see Robbie and know this would more than likely be the last one they spent together.

With a heavy heart, she opened the car door and stepped into a pile of wet slush.

"Great." Gently shaking the boot, she looked around. The rest of the driveway was clear except the exact spot she chose to park. *This is not the way I'd like to start the day.*

A vehicle pulled in behind her car and she knew before she saw him—Robbie. A smile spread across her face and lit up her eyes. "Hey you."

He stepped from the truck and flashed an easy grin. "Hey, Kenz. It's good to see you." He pulled a bag from the passenger seat. "I brought rolls and butter."

"Your usual." she teased. "Come on in. I'm sure Mom wants to pop them in the oven before dinner. Where's your dad and Jo?"

"Right behind me."

As if on cue, Jo's truck pulled up the drive. She hopped out. "Happy Thanksgiving, Kenz."

"Did you bring your appetite, Jo?"

Before she could answer, George got out of the passenger side balancing a pie in each hand. "Kenzie!" he exclaimed.

"George, it's good to see you."

He kissed her cheek. "How's the foot doing?"

"A little cold at the moment, but healing nicely. I should be out of this contraption soon."

They walked side by side to the kitchen door "That is good news," he said.

Robbie held it open. "After you."

Kenzie and the Burns clan walked into the chaos of the family rushing between the kitchen and dining room. Mom stopped what she was doing to take the pies from George and asked Robbie to set his bag on the counter.

Kenzie kissed her cheek. "Happy Turkey Day, Mom. Can I borrow a sock? I stepped in slush."

Dad rushed out of the kitchen carrying a handful of forks. "I'll get it, Olivia. Kenz, take a seat in the living room. Caleb and Steve are watching the game."

Wow, he was a whirlwind, she thought. She was happy to join the Sullivan brothers and get some space from a certain guy.

Caleb hopped up when he saw her. "Hey, Kenz, the game's on."

"As long as Mom lets us hide out, I'm game." She laughed at her pun. "I'm surprised you're not in the kitchen."

"I prepped some vegetables at our place and they're in the oven."

"And Mom let you? She must be going soft. She's very attached to her traditions."

Caleb chuckled. "It's my charm, and I *am* her favorite son-in-law."

Steve laughed. "You know us, we're good with the ladies."

"You two? You're kidding. First of all, Caleb, you're her only son-in-law, and Steve, you were so hung up on Yvette, Caleb had to wait in the wings while you made up your mind to rekindle the romance with her before he could date Jamie."

Caleb beamed. "It turned out okay—I married the love of my life and Steve is engaged to his."

Dad walked in carrying one sock. "Here you go, lass."

"Thanks, Dad." She patted his cheek.

"Did I hear you talking about your ladies?"

"You did," Caleb said. "I'm not even sure how we got on the subject."

Jamie poked her head in. "Mom said dinner's ready."

Kenzie tossed her wet sock under the end table and pulled the dry one on. She hurried into the dining room. She wanted to get a good seat on the opposite side from Robbie. She stopped in the archway and cringed. Robbie was sitting in the chair next to her usual seat. Grace was sitting in the only potential spot. It seemed all chairs were spoken for.

He looked up. If he noticed the look of dismay on her face, he didn't react.

She slipped into her chair. Robbie whispered for her ears only, "Is this okay?" He pointed to their chairs.

"Yeah. Sure." Her heart thudded. "After all, not everything has to change."

Mom carried in the turkey platter and set it down in front of Dad. "Dear, will you carve the beast?"

He picked up a large knife and fork and paused. "Who wants white meat?"

Kenzie felt as if she'd held her breath during the entire meal. Conversation flowed among everyone but her and Robbie. She wasn't sure if everyone noticed but she had. Clutching the steering wheel, she dropped her forehead to rest on her hands and took several deep breaths. She didn't cry, not because there weren't tears ready to course down her face, but because it wouldn't change anything.

"What's the point?" Turning on the headlights, she dropped the car into gear.

She made the drive to her condo after taking a long route via Robbie's apartment. His truck was parked in the lot. In a few short weeks... She wouldn't let her thoughts go there.

After parking her car, she slowly walked up the shoveled path and turned the key in the lock. Opening the door silence greeted her. Mechanically she placed her keys in the bowl and shrugged out of her jacket. Hanging it on the hook, she dropped her shoulder bag on the bench. She stepped forward in the darkened hallway.

I never noticed how empty my place is. Or my life.

Thinking better of wandering in the dark, she clicked on the lamp. A soft glow filled the small space. She wandered into the living room and clicked on another lamp, then walked into every room, filling the condo with light. Tonight, for the first time, being alone was gut-wrenchingly lonely.

She hurried down the hall. Locating her cell phone, she dialed.

"Hi, Grace, want to come spend the night? There's clean sheets on the bed in the spare room."

The next few weeks, Kenzie's routine of work and home didn't vary, with the exception of the hours she spent at the gym increased. Loneliness had become her constant companion.

Kenzie looked up from the computer. Cheryl was wiping down the counter. "Cheryl, I have a doctor's appointment tomorrow. Can you cover the desk? Robbie will be here if you need something."

"Sure thing. Are you losing the boot?"

Kenzie leaned back in the chair and stretched. "I hope so. I'm itching to start training for the race."

Unable to keep the surprise from her voice, Cheryl asked, "Your sisters are running, right?"

She brightened. "Caleb and Steve too, and Jo's considering it, and Yvette and our parents will be the cheering section."

Cheryl sat down her concern evident all over her face. Kenzie was touched. "It might not be my place to ask, but do you really think you'll be able to run thirteen miles?"

With a careless shrug, Kenzie said, "I'm going to try. I'm hedging my bets and made an appointment with Ally to start PT."

"That's the power of positive thinking." Cheryl smiled. "It must have been hard to be on the sidelines with everything going on."

With a crooked grin she said, "You have no idea. Exercise is my stress reliever. Coming here every day reminds me I'll be back in the groove soon."

"Mine is chocolate," Cheryl laughed. "When do you think you're going to be doing spin again?"

"I'm hoping in a few weeks, but that might be aggressive."

Cheryl looked around the room. Dropping her voice, she said, "Do you think you can convince Robbie to stay?"

Kenzie's face fell. "It's too late."

"That's too bad. Clients love him. Are you going to post a notice he's leaving?"

Surprised she hadn't thought of that, Kenzie asked, "Do you think I should?"

Bobbing her head sympathetically, Cheryl said, "I do. He's been a fixture around here since you opened. You're like two peas in a pod."

Kenzie frowned. "It seems like our peas got shelled."

"I'm really sorry. You know Ally means nothing to him."

Keeping all expression from her face, she said, "I appreciate that, but we missed our chance."

"It's not over unless you want it to be over." Cheryl's smile fell away. "Believe me, I speak from experience. Once upon a time, I fell in love with the most wonderful man. He was so much like Robbie, kind and generous, and I took him for granted, thinking he would wait for me. Sadly, I got hooked up with Ollie's father and he turned out to be the wrong guy."

Curious, Kenzie asked, "What about the nice guy?"

"He moved on."

"I'm sorry Cheryl." *Just like Robbie, moving away.*

Cheryl shrugged one shoulder. "Who knows what's going to happen next? I spent five years with a man who didn't love me or want to spend time with our child. If I'm lucky enough to get another chance, I'm not going to squander it." She laid a hand on Kenzie's arm. "Don't make the same mistake I did."

"Thanks, Cheryl, but it takes two to make a relationship work."

Robbie strolled into the lobby. "Ladies, I'm going to the coffee shop. Can I get you something?"

Cheryl rubbed her hands together. "Oh, rumor has it they're serving up sugar cookies and hot cocoa. I know we probably shouldn't have treats here, but..."

Kenzie laughed. "Since you're doing the fly, I'll buy. Make that two cocoas and see if you can get a small tray of cookies."

"Be back shortly."

With a wide grin and a knowing wink, Cheryl said, "Who are you trying to kid? The air sizzles between you. Every time you walk into a room his eyes follow you and you do the same thing with him. And then the way you finish each other's sentences, well I've never seen two people more in sync with each other."

Kenzie's chin jutted out. "I don't know what you're talking about. We're just friends, nothing more." Standing, she announced, "I'm going to stretch my legs."

Cheryl called, "Wait, Kenzie! I'm sorry if I overstepped my place."

Kenzie's gaze softened. "You're a good friend, and around here we speak our minds. Kind but true is our motto."

Cheryl threw her arms around Kenzie. "I got lucky when I wandered into this town."

The front door opened and a blast of artic air rushed in. Robbie was carrying a cardboard tray with three covered paper cups and a small plate balanced on the top, covered with foil.

Kenzie looked up. "That was quick."

"I called in the order ahead of time." He grinned. "I knew once I mentioned cookies, you were all in."

Cheryl gave her a little nudge in his direction. "Kenzie, this is one sweet guy."

Kenzie peeked under the foil. "They look delicious." She took one off the plate and nibbled. Closing her eyes, she said, "You have to try one. They're so buttery."

Robbie placed the trays on the counter. "Save one for me. I have a client."

Using her cool-as-a-cucumber voice, Kenzie said, "I didn't see anyone on the schedule."

"Last-minute appointment. Ally's coming by. This is our last session together."

"Oh." Kenzie took one of the mugs and drew back the plastic tab on the lid. She took a sip. Fanning her mouth, she cried, "Hot."

The door opened and Ally breezed in. "Hey, everyone." Her gaze drifted to Robbie. "Hi, are you ready?"

"Give me a minute." Robbie headed toward the back office.

Ally caught the look on Kenzie's face. "Did I interrupt something?"

"No, we're just enjoying a festive coffee break." She held up the tray. "Would you like one?"

Ally shook her head and looked at Cheryl. "Thanks for getting me in today."

"My pleasure." Cheryl hurried from the room.

Ally's gaze took in the room, looking for Robbie, Kenzie guessed. "How's your wrist?"

Kenzie twirled it in a 360-degree spin. "Good. I'm using five-pound weights and on Sunday I'm going to try ten."

Robbie walked in, rubbing his chin. "I hate to interrupt, but are you ready?"

"Right behind you." Ally flashed a smile at Kenzie. "Remember, take it easy. Any pain, stop."

With a cock of her head, Kenzie said, "Yes, ma'am. Don't worry, I'll be fine."

Why was it every time Ally was around, she felt herself go green? This was ridiculous. Robbie didn't look at Ally the way Kenzie knew she looked at him.

She slumped in the chair and studied a blank screen. *This is going to get harder before it gets easier.*

CHAPTER 25

Kenzie reviewed the list on the kitchen counter one last time. Robbie's going away party was going to be epic.

She strolled around her living room, finally free of the boot, straightening throw pillows and double-checking she hadn't forgotten the extra napkins placed strategically around the room. Her Christmas tree sparkled in the corner, adorned with her special ornaments, including every one Robbie had given her.

Glancing at her reflection in the sliding door, she saw her earlobes were bare. She walked into her bedroom and flipped on the overhead lights. Her closet door was ajar. She pushed it closed but it popped open.

"What the heck?" She pulled the door back only to discover Gran's wedding dress was caught between the jamb and door. "That's odd." She tucked it back in the closet and firmly closed it. The image of her wearing the dress and Robbie holding out his hand to her came back in a rush. Her heart constricted, reminding herself it was just a dream.

The doorbell ringing and then a sharp knock pulled her back to the present. Despite the awkward gait, she pulled the door open just as Jo's knuckles were poised to strike again. "Hey, what took you so long?"

Kenzie pointed to her foot and cane. "I'm still at a turtle pace."

She stepped to one side and Jo entered, followed by a throng of people. Jamie, Caleb and Grace were the last in the group. Grace gave Kenzie a fierce hug. "You look beautiful."

Kenzie squeezed her harder, relieved to have her sisters with her tonight. She said, "Steve and Yvette are on their way and Mom and Dad will be here soon. They're swinging by to pick up George."

"The party's starting to rock." With the cold air to her back, Kenzie's gaze roamed the room. "I don't see the guest of honor."

"Here I am." A deep male voice hovered next to her ear, his warm breath caused goose bumps to race down her arms.

She turned and slipped her arm around his waist. Holding him close, she teased, "I thought you got lost."

"I could find you in my sleep," he drawled.

She hesitated, unsure how to respond. "Please come inside before we heat up the outdoors." Realizing how that could be taken, she could feel the pink rise in her cheeks.

His grin broadened. "That might be fun."

Being this close to Kenzie was going to destroy him. He hadn't wanted to come tonight, knowing their lives were on the cusp of change. Over the last few weeks he had tried to keep his distance, but he longed for her to ask him to stay. If she had, his resolve would have crumbled. His life wouldn't be stuffed in boxes waiting for the journey across the state.

He was here to etch her into his memory, to drink in her subtle and oh so Kenzie perfume, sweet and full of life. He wondered, watching her navigate the room— couldn't she feel the love oozing from the depths of his soul or was she prepared to give him a hug and kiss and watch him drive away? He had so many questions and no answers.

She walked by, carrying an empty plate. He followed her into the kitchen. Withdrawing a wrapped square box from behind his back, he handed it to her. "This is for you." His fingers grazed across her face as he hands her the box.

"I have something for you too," she stuttered, and turned.

His hand grasped hers. "You can give it to me later."

She gazed into his eyes. Did she have something to say? She looked away, breaking their connection.

"After the party." He knew she would open it alone. Tucked inside there were two handcrafted items: one a hiking boot ornament, and the other a diamond necklace designed to look like a maple leaf. He hoped when she wore it she'd be reminded of all their special moments.

Her lashes fluttered. With quiet confidence, she said, "We'll open them together."

Laying his lips lightly on hers, he murmured, "Merry Christmas, Kenzie."

She blinked away the tears hovering in her crystal-blue eyes. They would be forever in his dreams.

Breaking contact, he pulled open the fridge door, "Is there beer?"

She cleared her throat and with a sad smile said, "Your favorite and plenty of it."

He chuckled. "I won't be tying one on, but by the looks of this crowd, you'll have plenty of takers."

He melted into the partygoers, guests clapping him on the back and wishing him well. He found Caleb and Jamie by the appetizers. He picked up a slice of salami and chomped down. "Hey, guys. How's it going?"

Caleb gave him a quizzical look. "Not bad, and you?"

"Fine." He selected an olive. "Thanks for helping Kenzie. This was way too much work for her given she's still recovering."

"It's what we do." Jamie pecked Caleb's cheek and slipped away.

"Let's get some air." Caleb slid open the deck door and waited for Robbie to follow him.

He was grateful to get outside. All his friends and family were trying to send him off with good wishes and he felt like a fraud.

He brought the beer bottle to his lips. The two men drank in companionable silence.

Caleb asked, "Are you packed?"

"Yeah, other than some last-minute stuff."

"That's good." Caleb peeled a corner off the label on the bottle. Not looking at Robbie he asked, "Do you still think leaving is the right thing?"

Robbie leaned on the railing and looked away. Glumly he answered, "No. But I don't have a choice."

"Man, we always have a choice. It's what we do with it," Caleb argued.

"Kenz confuses me. She says she doesn't have *those* kinds of feelings for me. But when we kiss ah hell..." He ran his hand through his hair.

"You're willing to lose her?"

Frustrated, he slammed his fist down. "Don't you get it? She was never mine."

Caleb shook his head. "You should open your eyes and then look in the mirror. You're both being idiots. And if you want my opinion…"

Half shouting, Robbie said, "Who says I do?"

A flash of anger shone on Caleb's face. "Well, you're gonna get it. Any man would be lucky to share their life with a MacLellan. Turn around and walk in that house, take her in your arms and kiss her until she's breathless. Tell her how you feel. Damn it, fight for her! You'll never find another girl like her."

Robbie's voice filled with anguish. "Don't you think I know that? From the time we were kids, she's been my sunshine. When I was a skinny runt, Kenzie was my best friend; when I grew into the nerdy jock, she was by my side. She was my study buddy. When I spout random history jokes, who laughs? Kenzie. She challenges me to be my best every day."

Caleb clamped a hand on his shoulder. "I'm going to ask you one more time. Why are you leaving?"

Robbie hung his head. "I have no idea. What else can I do? I love her." With a shrug, he said, "Who knows, maybe absence will help her see me in a different light."

With a sympathetic look, Caleb said, "Don't be a stranger."

Robbie raised his head. "Do me a favor—look after her."

Kenzie wondered when Caleb and Robbie were going to come in from the cold. She started toward the slider. As she reached for the handle, Jamie stopped her. "Give him some space."

"Is Robbie okay?"

"He's having a tough night."

Her heart quickened. "Did something happen?"

Sharply Jamie said, "Did you hit your head harder than we thought on that mountain?"

Kenzie's mouth hung open. "*What* are you talking about?"

"This is his going away party. He's leaving his job, home, friends and his family. All because you are both too stubborn to take a chance on love."

She glanced at Robbie through the glass and whispered, "I'm terrified." Her mouth felt like sawdust. "What if..." Her voice trailed off. She couldn't vocalize her innermost fear, what if she told him how she felt and he broke her heart. She couldn't bear having her heart ripped from her chest. It was easier to let him go.

"Who isn't when it comes to love? Sis, I love you, but you're blowing this big time."

Kenzie's face fell. "I thought he would talk to me especially as it's less than two weeks away. But he keeps himself busy at work, disappears as soon as he can, and I haven't had the chance to talk to him alone."

"Is your car in the shop?"

Puzzled she said, "No. Why?"

Jamie pretended to slap the palm of her hand against her forehead. "Did you forget the way to his apartment?"

Kenzie could feel her temper starting to spike. "The road goes both ways."

Exasperated, Jamie said, "It does, but someone has to make the first move."

"He made his move—out of town. That says it all." Her face burned.

"Kenzie."

She held up her hand. "I love you, but I can't talk about this anymore. What's done is done."

"Kenz…" Jamie pleaded.

She plastered a smile on her face and turned to talk to a guest. She was sorry to be rude to her sister, but she was coming unglued.

The rest of the evening was a blur. After the partygoers called it a night, Grace and Jamie were tidying the kitchen when Kenzie came in limping.

"When did Mom and Dad leave?" Jamie asked.

"About an hour ago. They said for me to tell you brunch is at eleven tomorrow." Kenzie got a bottle of water from the fridge and looked around. "Where's Caleb and Robbie?"

Jamie said, "Caleb took some dishes to the car, but I haven't seen Robbie in a while. Did you check the deck?"

Kenzie peered outside. "He's not out there."

Grace pulled out a stool. "Take a seat and I'll ask Caleb."

She sank down and propped her foot up. "Ah," she sighed, "that feels good."

"I'm going to fix you an ice pack. It looks swollen," Jamie said. "Better yet, do you have any frozen peas?"

"Top shelf. There's a big black X on the package so I don't accidently cook them." Kenzie took a long drink of water.

Jamie pointed to the living room. "Recliner. Now."

Kenzie winced. Very slowly she hobbled to the other room and sank into the chair. Jamie waited while she slipped the boot off and laid the bag of peas over her sock-covered ankle.

"Your tree is pretty this year." Jamie sat down on the sofa and smiled as she looked at the twinkle lights.

Kenzie sighed again and said, "Who says a tabletop tree can't be perfect?"

Grace rushed into the room, rubbing her hands

together. "Jeez, it's freezing out there. Caleb said Robbie took off about an hour ago."

Caleb came in behind her. He looked from Jamie to Kenzie. "Robbie left without saying goodbye?"

Kenzie said, "He just left. Without a word?" She started to get up from the chair.

Grace stopped her. "What do you need?"

Her voice cracked. "Did Robbie take his Christmas gift? It was under the tree. Right in the front."

Grace pushed her back in the chair. "Sit. I'll look." She held up a plaid wrapped box. "It's still here."

Kenzie choked back a sob. "Do you think he forgot it, or he didn't want it?"

Jamie sat on the edge of the recliner. Draping her arm around Kenzie's shoulder, she urged, "Call him."

Kenzie shook her head. *I will not cry in front of my family again.*

CHAPTER 26

Free! Kenzie did a very cautious jig as the hospital doors whooshed closed behind her.

Grinning from ear to ear, she strolled to her car, using the cane for extra stability. After buckling in she started the car and pulled onto the highway.

Squinting against the sun, she pushed her sunglasses up her nose and cracked the sunroof. Fresh, crisp air wafted into the car. Tooling down the highway, singing off-key, she saw the exit for the state forest.

On impulse she clicked on the blinker and turned into the parking area at the state park. She found herself lost in wonderful memories. Countless hiking trips with Robbie had started from this very lot. It was deserted now. Light snow created a polka dot pattern on the blacktop. Parked at an angle she studied the beginning of the trail. *Would they hike here next year?* With the sun slipping behind a cloud, a chill danced over her. She closed the sunroof and put the car in gear. It was time to make the long drive home.

It was almost dark when she parked in front of the gym. Through the window she could see Robbie. Eight days before he was officially done. How would she fill the emptiness in her soul?

He watched her carefully walk down the sidewalk and approach the entrance. After a few long strides, he held it open. A smile graced his face, but he didn't feel joy in his heart. "Look at you. Walking without the boot."

Kenzie beamed. "It feels weird, but in a good way."

He would miss her smile. "I'm sure." He closed the door and followed her to the office, and leaned against the doorjamb. "Do you want to grab a bite of dinner to celebrate?"

Without hesitation in a quiet voice, she said, "I'd love to." Kenzie leafed through the mail and looked up. "What time do you want to head out?"

Was she thinking this was just like any other night they had dinner together, he wondered. "I can be ready whenever."

Pen poised over her calendar she said, "Let me just jot down my PT appointment. I see Ally at four. I'm officially in training for the Shamrock."

Concern filled his voice. "Do you think you should?"

"I'm planning on the half marathon and if I can't run, I'll walk." She lifted her chin defiantly. "I'll crawl across the finish line if I need to."

"I thought it was just the 5k?" He touched her arm, reveling in the small connection. He didn't wait for Kenzie to respond. "Do me a favor—keep Ally in the loop while you train. I'd hate for you to have a setback after all this time."

"Burns, are you worried about me?" she teased, but he could see her eyes remained clouded.

He could hear her annoyance as she dismissed his concern so easily. His voice was a touch frosty. "Some habits are hard to break." Feeling they were treading on subjects better left alone, he said, "Italian tonight?"

"Sounds good." She grinned. "Feel free to spread the word."

He scuffed the floor with his sneaker. "I was kind of hoping we could have dinner, alone." His eyes rose to meet hers. A jolt raced through him. "Before I leave, I'd like to put things on solid ground with us."

Wistfully she said, "I'd like that."

Cheryl rushed into the room like a whirlwind. "Sorry I'm late. It's been one of those kinds of days. The little one is sick and I had to find a sitter, pick up some cough syrup and it's been rush, rush, rush." Oblivious of the tension in the room, she shrieked, "You're wearing two sneakers!"

Kenzie turned her foot, proudly showing off her kicks. "It's been, what?" She looked at Robbie. "Almost ten weeks?"

"That's Kenz for you. Pushing through recovery that takes most people twelve plus to under ten." Robbie wanted to continue their conversation about the half marathon, but held his tongue. "I'm going to get my coat."

He hurried across the room. The murmur of female voices made his heart constrict. What had possessed him to ask Kenzie to dinner? It was torture to be here every day. Tonight, all that would separate them was a table, wine and romantic lighting.

He shrugged into his coat and took a deep, calming breath, then ducked into the office. "Ready?"

Kenzie glanced at the wall clock. "I need a few minutes. Can I meet you there?"

With a curt nod, Robbie slipped out the back. Was she

thinking of standing him up? No, she'd never do that. She was his Kenzie.

After wandering aimlessly around the park, he made his way the short distance to the restaurant. He pulled his jacket closed against the chill, glancing at the cloud-filled sky. It felt like snow. *We'll have a quick dinner so Kenzie doesn't have to drive in a storm.*

Robbie entered through the main entrance. "Hey, Tony. I'm meeting Kenzie for dinner."

Tony pointed to the back "She's at her favorite table."

How did she get there so fast? I must have spent too much time worrying about nothing. He paused mid-step. "Any chance you could bring us a bottle of merlot?"

Tony held up a bottle with a cork partially exposed. "She's one step ahead of you."

Robbie grinned. "Isn't she always?" He stretched out his hand. "I'll take it."

Tony handed him the bottle. "She ordered appetizers too."

He smirked. "Did she order my dinner?"

Tony chuckled. "Not yet." He headed toward the swinging kitchen doors.

Robbie zigzagged around vacant tables. He saw Kenzie. In his mind's eye, he took a picture to remember how she looked in this exact moment. Her hair was a little longer than she usually wore it, he liked the waves. Her blue eyes were bright and he marveled at how she had no idea how beautiful she was. Even if she didn't love him, he loved her with all his heart.

"I brought the wine, and I understand you ordered food."

Her eyes sparkled and they locked on his. Their connection was electrifying.

Her head dropped to the side and she said, "Sorry, I'm starving."

He took a seat and poured the wine. "Glad your appetite has returned." He gave her a tentative smile. "I forgot to ask, did your mom go today?"

The glass hovered on her lips. "No. I wanted to be by myself." With a laugh she said, "But you know she was the first phone call."

He set the bottle on the table. Mundane tasks quieted his nerves. "This place holds a lot of memories."

Kenzie glanced around the room. "My parents used to come here when they were first married. It's a landmark to the townspeople." Her eyes met his over the rim. "I'm glad we're doing this."

He took a sip and set the glass on the table. "I'll have to admit I do have an ulterior motive."

Her eyes widened.

"Kenz. I don't want to move…" He paused, "…without clearing the air."

Her eyes dropped and she refolded her cloth napkin. "The last few weeks have been awkward," she agreed.

He searched her face. "I have to tell you the truth." He wished he could wipe the regret from her eyes.

Kenzie held up her hand. "Me first."

With an imperceptible nod, he took a drink, hoping she didn't notice his hand shaking.

Kenzie smoothed the tablecloth before continuing, "I've been a demanding, impatient and ungrateful friend, and I'm sorry."

Inwardly he groaned at the word *friend*. "Considering the circumstances, it's understandable."

Her finger traced the rim of the glass. "It's sweet that you want to chalk it up to the accident. The truth is, I didn't like feeling helpless; sitting on the sidelines has never been for me. I lashed out at the people I love."

Robbie tucked his finger under her chin and tilted it up. "It's in the past."

Almost inaudible, she said, "Well, not really, since the consequences of my actions drove you away."

"You were right. It was time for a change." His eyes never left her face. "Is there more to your apology than I know?"

Kenzie grabbed a breadstick and crunched on it. "I'm in love with you."

Robbie felt his mouth go dry and he choked, "You're what?" His heart hammered and blood seemed to stop flowing to his brain. He was at a loss for words. Time seemed to stand still. Stammering, he said, "I don't think I heard you correctly."

In a whoosh she said, "I love you, not like a friend. Well, I do love you like a friend, but it is so much more than friendship. When I think about not seeing you every day, my heart aches."

"Kenzie." He wiped his damp palms on his pant legs. He couldn't believe she was saying this now. Why couldn't she have said this a month ago? "I don't know what to say."

Her cheeks went scarlet. "You don't have to say anything. I just thought you should know." She waved to Tony standing by the door. He came rushing over. Her voice cracked. "Could I get the check?"

Tony looked from Kenzie to Robbie.

Robbie said, "No, we're eating here."

"But…" she stammered.

Tony slipped away as Robbie leaned forward and took her hand. "We need to finish this conversation, and if you still want to leave, you can. But I'm not going to make it easy for you."

Kenzie slumped into her chair. "I thought you'd be happy I have feelings for you. Important, life-changing feelings, and you haven't said anything."

"I never in a million years dreamt you'd say that. Why now?"

She whispered, "Oh, and in case you're wondering, I know everything about our hike."

He held his breath. Could she be alluding to what he remembered vividly? "What do you remember?"

"Our hike to the summit, and after when we…" She gulped her wine. "It changed my life."

Robbie stared at her. All he wanted to say was *I love you* and pull her into his arms.

Kenzie's words came out in a rush. "Anyway, in a few days you're leaving and I have no idea when I'm going to see you again. It's okay if you don't feel the same way. I've had a lot of time to think, and I've decided to stop living half a life."

He caressed her fingers. Now wasn't the time to say those three words. Making a snap decision he was still going to leave. Maybe, if she felt the same again in a few months, they'd have a chance at a real future.

He haltingly confessed, "You're in every memory I have, good and bad. We've shared a lifetime. I want us to be those people again, the fun-loving friends who accept each other, flaws and all."

Kenzie's mouth dropped open. Shock filled her face. "You're telling me you want to part as the best of friends, despite what I just said?"

He pulled his chair closer. Holding her hand over his heart, he said, "I'm going to be brutally honest. I don't remember a day I haven't been in love with you. I've watched you grow from a tomboy to a beautiful woman. You dated lots of guys, and each time I'd pray you wouldn't announce you wanted to spend your life with one of them. I held you as you cried over the jackasses who couldn't see how amazing you are."

His breathing was labored. "We've hiked side by side, slept under the stars together, huddled next to a campfire and held tarps over our heads when it rained. Through it all, you never saw me as anything more than your buddy, your partner in crime. Until the day we hiked the summit. What we shared made me fall for you all over again, and I would have given anything for it to be me and not you who got hurt. And then you challenged me to figure out what I wanted in my future and, if necessary, make a change."

Stunned, she pulled her hand away. "Wow. Why didn't you ever tell me?"

He slowly shook his head. His voice thick. "I didn't want to lose you. Something was better than nothing."

Kenzie visibly shrank, tears filling her eyes. "Robbie…"

"You were right. We need to put some space between us." Robbie knew his words were harsh, but he couldn't do this, not right now, He could feel his heart split in two.

Her face fell and she blinked away fat tears.

"We need time to figure out what we want for our future. But before I leave, I want—no, I need for us to agree that we will always be best friends." His fingers grazed her arm. "Kenz?" he implored.

She gave him the tiniest of smiles. "For a quiet guy, you sure had a lot to say."

He gave her his hand. "Kenzie MacLellan, will you be my best friend again?" For the first time he could remember, he couldn't read her expression.

She squeezed tight. "Through thick and thin."

He kissed her hand and pulled her to her feet. Hugging

her tight, he murmured in her ear, "I'm never farther away than the phone."

She turned her face into his broad chest and nodded. He could feel the dampness through his shirt. He tightened his arms around her and held her as she cried.

CHAPTER 27

C hristmas was bittersweet. Kenzie got through the holidays by the skin of her teeth. Her sisters hovered, knowing her heart was broken. Robbie had left without saying goodbye. The new year came quietly while Kenzie forced herself into a new routine.

"Cheryl, I'll be back in about an hour. I've got physical therapy."

Cheryl paused as she wiped down the water bubbler. "How's that going?"

"Ally's tough, but she supports my training. I'm hoping today she'll release me to the treadmill."

"Does she think you're pushing too hard?" Concern flitted across Cheryl's face.

Kenzie placed a hand on her arm. "I have classes to give and a certain employee needs to get some certification under her belt." She grinned. "Have you been studying?"

Cheryl brushed a stray lock of hair from her eyes. "I have. Who knew there was so much to learn about training people? I thought you encouraged them to work harder and counted repetitions."

Kenzie snorted. "I can see how you would come to that conclusion. Good to know you're a quick study." She tapped her watch. "I'm out of here."

"Don't worry, I've got everything covered." Cheryl went back to work and Kenzie took one last look over her shoulder. She thought things were running smoothly, but the gym didn't have the same vibe. She missed Robbie.

After making the short drive to the medical center, Kenzie hopped from the car and hurried inside. The bone-chilling cold stung her face, but the warmth of the office was welcoming. She checked in with the receptionist and took a seat.

"Kenzie?" Ally stood in the doorway to the small waiting area. Kenzie stood up and noticed Ally closely watching her walk. "How is the ankle feeling?"

Kenzie smiled. "Pretty good. The cold makes the wrist and ankle ache, but I'll survive."

"You've got a great attitude." They walked into the mini gym and Ally picked up the chart. She pointed to the table. "Have you been doing your exercises faithfully?"

Kenzie took off her coat and hopped up. "Every morning and then ice at night."

Ally jotted a note down. Without looking up, she asked, "Swelling?"

She shrugged. "Minor, mostly at the end of the day."

Ally made a few more notes and closed the folder. "Why don't you start with the bike and do a few minutes to get the blood circulating?"

Kenzie sat down and, with zero tension, began cycling. She joked, "This sure isn't spin class."

"What's going on at the gym, with Robbie gone? Any issues?"

Kenzie adjusted the tension by one degree. "You mean with classes?"

Ally leaned against a chair. "I was thinking more about how you're doing emotionally. You two were pretty tight. I was surprised he moved."

"He wanted a change." Kenzie picked up the pace, going faster as she tried to avoid the stab in her heart.

"Hey, take it easy, this is a warm-up." Ally checked the timer. "You can move to the treadmill with zero elevation, and slow."

Excited, Kenzie scrambled off the bike. Her first step, she stumbled. She caught herself on the handlebars.

Ally's hand flew out to steady her. "Easy. Are you having pain?"

Kenzie shook her head. The familiar ache had settled in her chest. "I wasn't paying attention and tripped, no big deal."

She stood on the rails of the treadmill while Ally adjusted the speed. "Go ahead and step on."

Kenzie took her first step with her right ankle and began the very slow pace. She gave Ally a sideways look. "Seriously, is the belt even moving?" She grumbled, "A snail moves faster."

Ally laughed, leaned over and inched the speed upward. "So, have you talked to Robbie since he moved?"

Kenzie shot her a look. "You're pretty curious about Robbie. I can give you his phone number if you want." Inside, her heart thudded. She silently prayed: *Please don't ask for it.*

Shaking her head, Ally smiled. "The man has eyes for one woman, and no matter who flirts with him, he's nothing but respectful, friendly, and definitely doesn't flirt back."

Kenzie grasped the side bars, steadying her gait and her hammering heart. "He never flirted with you?" She had accused him of something that was all based in her jealousy. Her stomach contracted. She really was a hot mess.

"Not for lack of me trying." Ally laughed. "I guess I shouldn't admit that since we're becoming friends."

Kenzie smiled. "A friend who could whip this chick into shape for a race?"

"You're still insisting you're going to run a half marathon in less than two months?"

With a flick of her head, Kenzie flashed a broad grin. "Have you met me? I'm one of the most single-minded people on the planet."

"I'd say stubborn like a mule." Ally cautioned, "If Dr. Barton agrees, I'll do my best, but you need to promise to listen to your body."

"Does this mean I can start training?" Kenzie bounced on one foot while the treadmill kept up its snail's pace.

"You need to keep coming to PT, but yes, you can use the treadmill. But no running yet." With a firm finger wag, Ally said, "Walking only."

Kenzie grinned. "This is the best day in a long time."

"Don't get ahead of yourself. It's still a long road before you'll be cleared completely. It typically is three to four months after a fracture before you get full range of motion and the ankle is strong enough to withstand the stress of running."

"Yes!" Kenzie pumped her fist in the air. She nodded solemnly. "I can pace myself."

Sternly, Ally looked at Kenzie. "Remember, you can't fool the expert. I'll be able to tell based on swelling and range of motion."

Kenzie eyed Ally. "I'll make a deal with you—if you get me ready to run, I'll give you a gym membership for a year."

Ally grinned. "Now there's incentive for me to keep you

on the straight and narrow."

Kenzie laughed out loud as she moved the treadmill speed up. "This feels great."

Kenzie groaned and rolled out of bed. She dressed quickly, grabbed her insulated bag from the fridge and hurried out the door. It was her day to open, and a potential new trainer was coming in for an interview.

She muttered, "What I really need is a spin class instructor." She pulled out her phone and sent a text: *Hi friend, just checking in. K*

Before returning her phone to her pocket a response pinged in, a big smiley face. *At least he's still texting me.*

When she arrived at the gym, the interior lights burned bright. "Did I forget to turn them off?"

Parking the car, she hurriedly unlocked the back door. Silently pulling it shut behind her, she crept along the hallway, her heart in her throat. Did she dare hope by some miracle, it was Robbie? She peeked around the corner.

Deflated, she cried, "Cheryl, what are you doing here?" She patted her chest. "You scared me half to death."

"Good morning." Cheryl looked up from the computer and grinned. "I wanted to get a jump on the day. With the interview scheduled, I thought you might be pushed for time, and Ollie spent the night with a friend."

Kenzie dropped her bags next to the desk. "Next time shoot me a text so I don't have a heart attack." She studied Cheryl. "You're in a good mood today. Did something happen?"

A shy smile spread across her face. "Maybe."

Kenzie leaned on the counter. "Do tell." Grinning, she said, "You met someone, didn't you?"

She giggled. "It's not a big deal."

"Are you kidding? You're giddy. Fess up."

Cheryl's eyes sparkled. "Yesterday I had a flat tire and was waiting for the tow truck. When it pulled up, this good-looking guy got out. Do you know Artie Zablonski?"

"From A-Z Auto?"

"That's him. We started talking and, well, he asked if I'd meet him for coffee this Saturday."

"That's awesome. But what are you going to do with Ollie?"

"I'm going to trade sitter time with one of the other single moms."

Kenzie beamed. "If you run into a problem finding a sitter, holler. I'm happy to give Cupid a helping hand."

Cheryl's cheeks pinked up. "Are you becoming romantic?"

Kenzie laid her hand over her heart. "Let's say I understand the value of striking while the iron is hot or the opportunity may be lost."

Cheryl cautioned, "It's just coffee."

"Who knows where it might lead?" With a wink, she said, "Now, if you want to talk outfits, call one of my sisters. They're so much better at that stuff than me."

"I'll keep that in mind." Impulsively, Cheryl hugged her. "You're the best boss I've ever had."

Kenzie pretended to zip her lips. "Don't let that get around. I prefer to be thought of as the tough chick."

Cheryl laughed loud and long. "Tough as a marshmallow."

Kenzie trained daily, pushing herself to the brink of agony and taking every class she could. Unable to fill Robbie's shoes, Mac's Gym became a family affair. Caleb took over the weight room, stopping just short of personal training. Grace was holding spin classes and her parents were covering the desk so Cheryl could be a floater. However, the biggest hole Robbie left was in Kenzie's life. There was nothing anyone could do to help it heal.

She slowed the treadmill to a crawl, letting her pulse return to normal, and flopped to a mat, drinking in gulps of air.

Jamie leaned over and poked her sister. "Are you going to make it?"

Dripping with sweat, Kenzie pushed herself into a sitting position. "Who thought this would be so hard? I wasn't out of commission that long."

"No, but your injuries were bad enough—a concussion and two broken bones, one requiring surgery to boot." Jamie threw her a towel. "We don't have to run the Shamrock. I've been thinking we should postpone until next year, until you've had time to fully recover."

Kenzie narrowed her eyes. "I've never quit before and I'm not starting now."

Jamie lowered herself to the floor. "Sis, you're being stubborn, and frankly, the family is worried about you. What if you cause a stress fracture, or worse? You'll be back on your butt, only this time it'll take longer to recover."

Kenzie's body went vertical, along with her temper. "I don't care what you think. I'm running."

Jamie stood up. In slow, measured words she asked, "Have you talked to Ally or Dr. Barton?"

In a frosty tone, Kenzie said, "I have. They both agree. I know my limits."

Jamie crossed her arms over her chest. "Then maybe you should turn up your hearing aid."

Kenzie limped to the water cooler. Refilling her bottle, she took a long drink. Exasperated, Jamie said, "Look in the mirror. You can barely walk normally after a thirty-minute run on a treadmill."

Kenzie slowly twisted the cap on her bottle. Draping the towel around her neck, she carefully chose her words and dropped the volume of her voice. "Jamie, I know everyone is worried and I appreciate it. I really do."

"I think I hear a but coming." Jamie crossed the sunlit space and stood in front of her sister.

Kenzie's shoulders sagged, her voice flat. "All I have is training. My heart is hemorrhaging. I regret not telling Robbie sooner that I love him, and because of my pride, he's gone." Her voice caught. "I miss him like crazy. Everywhere I look I see him, or expect him to walk in the door. Pushing my body makes me feel something other than the ache in my heart."

Jamie's voice softened. "Have you talked to him?"

Kenzie shook her head slowly. "A couple of texts here and there, all superficial stuff. I grab the phone to call and tell him something funny, but I stop myself. It's been four weeks. I don't know what I'm going to do after St. Patrick's Day, but for today my focal point is to train." Her resolve cracked. "I'm hanging on by a thread."

Jamie pulled her sister into a hug and kissed her cheek. "Then we have a race to get ready for. Grace, you and me; we're in this together."

"Just like always." Kenzie held Jamie tight. She whispered, "Please tell me it *will* get better."

"I promise, it will." Jamie loosened her hug and held Kenzie at arms-length. Teasing, she said, "And for the record, you need a shower."

In one fluid motion, Kenzie pulled Jamie tighter and laughed. "I needed that."

～

On impulse, Kenzie drove to Burlington. She needed to see Robbie. Their silence had gone on too long. She stopped in a bakery. Purchasing two to-go cups of coffee and a couple of scones, she walked down the street to where Robbie was working in a large franchise gym. Taking a deep breath she gathered her courage and walked inside.

Looking around the small lobby, she thought, *this is a bad idea*. Just as she was getting ready to leave, she sensed he was standing behind her. "Kenzie?"

She turned and an intense feeling of joy filled her. "Robbie." She held up the cups. "I thought I'd drop by with a snack."

A knowing smile filled his face. "In the neighborhood, huh?"

Grinning, she responded, "Sort of."

He steered her to a padded bench. "I don't have a lot of time. I have a client in ten minutes."

Disappointed, all she could think to say was, "Oh."

"But this is the best surprise I've had in a long time."

She handed him a coffee and brushed the hair off his forehead. "You need a haircut, Burns."

He pecked her cheek. "I've missed you too."

At a loss for words, she took a sip of coffee.

He looked at the white bag in her hand. "What's in there?"

"Scones." She fumbled with the bag and pulled one out. "I couldn't help myself. They looked good." She smiled.

He got up and crossed the lobby. After speaking with the guy covering the desk, he came back. "Wanna get out of here for a little while?"

She looked at the guy and then at Robbie. "You said you have a client."

With a nod he said, "Mark will cover for me if I bribe him with the scones." His goofy grin soothed her nerves. "We can go for a walk, or better yet we can find a place to sit and talk." He glanced at her left foot. "I don't want you to slip on some ice."

"If you're sure." Her heart raced. "Don't you need a coat?"

"I'll be right back." He jogged through the lobby and disappeared from sight, returning within moments with a winter jacket. He tossed the full coffee cups, pulled on gloves and said, "Ready?"

She waited for him to open the door. "Lead the way."

Arm in arm, they strolled down the sidewalk. Kenzie was sure he took her arm in part so she wouldn't slip. He stopped at a coffee shop. "Hungry?"

Her eyes twinkled. "When am I not?"

He pushed open the door and said, "Good point."

Spying an empty table, he steered her toward it. He kept glancing her way, sure he was hallucinating. Other than the occasional text, they hadn't spoken. Hurt, pride, Robbie wasn't clear as to why they hadn't talked at all. All he knew it was a long and torturous month.

After ordering coffee and muffins, he watched Kenzie nervously unfold napkins for them both.

"So, this is a nice surprise." He thought it was a good way to break the ice. Tap dance around the most obvious question he wanted to ask: did she miss him as much as he missed her?

"I woke up this morning and called in a few favors, and here I am. I decided it had been too long since we've seen each other."

He looked at her and said, "You could have called me."

She blushed and looked adorable doing it. "I guess I could have, but I wanted to see you in person."

He took her hand. "I'm glad you did."

The waitress delivered their order and moved to another table. Kenzie added cream and handed the pitcher to Robbie. "How's it going here?" She swirled the coffee. "Do you have a lot of clients yet?"

"Fair. It's different." He shrugged. "How's things at Mac's?"

"Steady. You know how it is this time of year." She picked up her cup. "Jamie and Caleb are working on their house every chance they can."

"Kenz." It was time they cut through the small talk. She looked up. Those crystal-blue eyes broke through his defenses. "What are we doing here?"

Never breaking their connection, she murmured, "I'm not sure."

The hardest thing he did was wait for her to continue.

"I wanted. I needed." She looked away and then back. "I miss you."

A lump lodged in his throat. "I miss you too. But what should we do about it?"

"I want us to start talking to each other again, maybe hang out from time to time. As friends."

There was that word again. Friends. "Is that all?"

"It's a starting point."

She toyed with her spoon. He knew she only fidgeted when she was really anxious. He laid his hand over hers. "I think it's a good place to start." He picked up her hand and turned it over. Tracing the lines on her palm, he said, "We should make plans to have dinner next week."

She visibly relaxed. "Are you asking me out on a date?"

He folded her fingers over her palm. "Yes, I'm asking you to have dinner with me, our first official date."

He felt his heart go mush when Kenzie said, "Yes, I'd love to have dinner with you."

~

Kenzie and Robbie planned a romantic dinner tonight, which just happened to be the most romantic night of the year. She peered into the mirror to check her makeup. Thinking of her vision the day she tried on the dress she pulled the door open and withdrew the gown. Holding it in front of her, she closed her eyes. She could see Robbie in a tux holding out his hand to her.

Her phone rang. Glancing at caller ID, she saw it was Robbie.

"Hello there." She could feel a smile slip across her face.

"Hi, I'll be at your place in under ten minutes. We have reservations at the Cranwell for seven."

She whistled. "Pretty fancy and very close to home."

"We deserve the best, don't you think? And in case it snowed I didn't want to have to change our plans." His deep voice made her blood hum. How was it that after all these years of friendship he'd have this kind of effect on her?

"I'll be ready."

"See you soon." The phone disconnected.

Kenzie carefully hung the dress on the closet door and smoothed down the skirt. She picked up Gran's picture from her dresser. "Gran, what should I do? I'm fighting for love and my future."

She slipped into her coat, wanting to keep her dress a surprise until they got to the inn. The bell rang and she hurried to the door. Kenzie pulled it open and Robbie was standing on the step holding a deep red vase with the biggest bouquet of mixed roses she had ever seen.

"Happy Valentine's Day." He took a step forward and lightly kissed her lips. "I think it's time I bought you roses, and there is every color to cover every aspect of our relationship. Dark pink is for enchantment, yellow is for friendship, light pink is for grace, orange for fascination and of course red is for love."

She accepted the bouquet and buried her nose in the petals. "They are lovely and very unexpected." Even in heels she had to stand on her tiptoes as her kiss lingered on his mouth, savoring the moment.

Color flushed his cheeks. "Are you ready?"

Setting the vase on the table, she took his outstretched hand. "Yes, I am." They strolled under the stars to the car. "It's a beautiful night. The night sky is incredible."

"They're dim when compared to your eyes."

Kenzie's eyes locked with his. "My goodness, you're the romantic tonight." She clasped his hand tighter.

Robbie helped her into his truck and then hurried around to the driver's side. He backed down the driveway. "So, anything new?" he asked.

She wanted to laugh but understood this was a very different time for them. "Jamie and Caleb are painting at the house."

"Good. I'm sure Grace is getting excited about the big move."

"She is. And how's Jo and George? Work's been busy so I haven't seen them recently."

As he parked the car he smiled. "They're good." He took her hand. "I have a suggestion."

Her heart skipped. "I'm listening."

"Let's agree that our families are good, work is fine and

the weather is typical for this time of year." He kissed the underside of her wrist. "Tonight is for us."

"I'd like that." She waited while he opened her door and helped her into the car. She had never experienced this kind of date with any man and she was going to go with whatever transpired.

Soft music played on the truck radio as they rode in silence while holding hands. It seemed all too soon the drive was over and Robbie was helping her out of the truck. Arm in arm, the couple entered the inn. The hostess greeted them. After Robbie gave her his name, she escorted them to a table that was secluded in a dark corner by the window.

Kenzie slipped off her coat while he held her chair.

"You are stunning." He drank her in from head to toe and nuzzled her neck. "Your dress, the way it moves as you walk is captivating. The sapphire color matches your eyes." He glanced with appreciation at her bare shoulders while her arms were covered in a filmy sapphire fabric. The dress nipped in at her waist, accentuating her curves. His eyes stopped at her feet. He swallowed hard. "What can I say, I'm a sucker when you wear heels too."

"I seem to recall you said blue was my color."

Robbie took his seat, at a loss for words.

The waitress came over with a bottle of champagne on ice and a plate of oysters on the half shell. After pouring them each a glass, she slipped away.

"Did you arrange this?" Robbie had thought of everything.

"I ordered dinner for two. I figured if we weren't distracted by ordering, we could concentrate on us."

She took his hand. "Champagne?"

They clinked glasses. Robbie said, "To romance."

Kenzie responded, "To love."

CHAPTER 28

Ready or not, Racin' the Shamrocks had finally arrived. Kenzie heard a horn toot from her driveway. She slung her heavy shoulder bag over her body and hurried into the cold, gray dawn.

Grace waved from the driver's seat and held up a thermos. "Coffee." She grinned. "Enough to get the blood humming and warm your muscles."

Kenzie opened the back door, tossed in her bag and hopped into the front seat, then looked around. "Do you have an extra mug?"

"That thermos is yours." Grace held a matching one. "This one is mine."

"Thanks, squirt." Kenzie unscrewed the top and took a tiny sip. "Have you talked with anyone this morning?"

Grace backed out of the driveway. "I checked in with Mom and Dad, who will be at the finish line, and Jamie and Caleb stayed at Steve's place last night. They'll meet us at registration."

Looking over the top of the thermos, Kenzie asked, "And Jo?"

"We're going to swing by and pick her up." She glanced at Kenzie. "Is that okay?"

Kenzie looked up towards the heavens. "I'm relieved. I haven't talked to her since Robbie moved. I've been keeping my distance as I wondered if she blamed me for Robbie moving."

Grace studied her carefully. "You two need to clear the air because she said the same thing about you."

Kenzie looked out the window. "Point taken."

"Hey, Kenz? Before we pick her up, can I ask you a question?"

Joking she said, "I think you just did."

"Har, har." Grace's voice softened. "Why have you stopped calling me junior doctor?"

Kenzie felt her cheeks grow warm. "Our mother very kindly pointed out that I was being insensitive since being a physician's assistant is something you're passionate about."

Grace's head bobbed. "All right, so what does one have to do with the other?"

Kenzie's shoulders slumped. "I thought you weren't living up to your potential, that you'd be a great doctor and you had settled."

Grace slowed the car and stopped along the side of the road. "And you don't think that way anymore?"

Slowly shaking her head, Kenzie said, "I realized you had to follow your path and not what I think is best." She grabbed Grace's hand. "I'm really proud of you."

Grace grinned. "You have no idea what it means to me to hear you say that. I love helping people. Being a PA means I get to take care of patients but not get all caught up in the other stuff a doctor has to do, and my student loans are a lot smaller too." Giving Kenzie's hand one last squeeze, she put the car in gear and turned on her blinker. "I'm sure Jo's wondering where we are."

After a short silent drive, Grace slowed and pulled down the gravel road leading to Racing Brook Stables. Kenzie pointed toward the porch. "There she is."

Opening the door, Jo said, "Hey, girls," and slid to the center of the back seat, leaning forward. "Who's ready to go for a little run?"

Kenzie turned in her seat and grinned. "You woke up on the right side of the bed."

Jo settled back, her energy palpable. "We're having an adventure, our first race, and I'm looking forward to brunch at Steve and Yvette's afterward."

Grace glanced in the rearview. "Mom's bringing smoothies with fruit, greens, chia seeds and coconut water and I'm sure she'll have a bunch of other stuff too."

Kenzie beamed. "Look at you, prepared for post-race." She teased, "You did your research."

Grace glanced at her. "It'll be more critical for you than us lowly 5kers."

"What's Grace talking about? You're not running with us?"

"We'll start the race together, but when you guys finish the first leg, I'm going on to finish the half."

"The half what?" Jo asked. Grace caught Jo's eye in the rearview mirror and did a slight shake of her head. "Kenzie? What are you planning?" Jo asked.

Kenzie looked out the window and avoided Grace and Jo's penetrating glare. "What I always do, I'm running the half marathon."

"That's over thirteen miles!" Jo exclaimed. "Are you nuts? Did you forget about your ankle?"

Her shoulders rose and fell as pastures slipped by. "I'll be fine. I've run these a bunch of times."

Jo poked Kenzie's shoulder. "Does Robbie know about this?" she hissed.

"What difference would that make?" Kenzie's words were razor sharp. "I'll be fine. One way or another, I'll cross the finish line, and hopefully you'll all be there cheering me on."

Jo grew quiet. The tension in the car was thick. Finally, Kenzie said, "I'll be careful." She glanced at Grace and then Jo. "I have no desire to get hurt again."

Grace's cell rang and she pushed the button on her steering wheel. "Good morning, Jamie."

Jamie's voice came through the car speaker loud and clear. "Morning, all. Where are you?"

Grace said, "We should be pulling into the parking lot in less than fifteen minutes."

Jamie said, "We're headed down to registration and we'll meet you there."

"Okay, see you soon." Grace disconnected the call.

Each girl remained quiet in preparation for the upcoming event. Nervously licking her lips, Grace said, "I'm not going to lie. I'm nervous. What if I get a cramp or something?"

"Squirt, do your best. If you need to walk or slow down, it's okay. You've trained, you're strong and you can do this," Kenzie reassured her sister,

Jo piped up, "We've got this. We'll cross the finish line and then be there to cheer Kenzie on."

Grace pursed her lips. "I'm going to run the half marathon, so you're not alone."

Kenzie snapped her head around. "No way. You need to train for that distance." She noticed Jo wink at Grace's rearview. "What's that for?" she demanded.

Jo fumbled in her tote bag. "Um. Nothing. I have some-thing in my eye."

Kenzie's voice was sharp. "You're not a good liar."

With a quick retort, Jo said, "You're overly suspicious."

Kenzie chuckled. "We have a long history. When you and Grace get together, you have a secret language."

Jo snorted. "It's called self-preservation; you and Robbie always had your own way of communicating."

For a fleeting moment Kenzie let her mind drift to thoughts of Robbie and their very romantic Valentine's night date, to all the other dates they've had in the last four weeks. *Focus!* She admonished herself. *You have a race to run. You can fantasize about the man after you cross the finish line.*

Grace slowed the car and turned her blinker on. She announced, "We're here."

She was thankful to put this car ride in the history books. Kenzie wouldn't admit it, but she had doubts she'd finish the race. "Go toward the back; there should be more parking."

Grace leaned forward, peering out the windshield. "Who would have thought there'd be so many people, especially with the weather being cloudy?"

Kenzie patted her arm. "You're going to be happy it's overcast once we get started. The temps might hit fifty."

Grace eased into a parking space. "I've got layers. I'll be fine."

"You will." Kenzie unbuckled her seatbelt and pushed open the door. "Give Jamie a call and let her know we're here."

Jo volunteered, "I'll call."

She wandered away, and Kenzie's eyes followed her. "Where's she going?"

"She's probably asking about brunch. You know Jo likes to plan ahead for her meals. She's always hungry."

Suspicious, Kenzie watched Jo from a distance. "I guess."

Grace popped the hatch, then pulled her bag from the back and unzipped it. She grabbed her running shoes and sat in the car hatchway to lace up.

Kenzie joined her while still keeping one eye on Jo, skeptical that was all there was to it. "Scooch over." She pulled on her runners, adjusted her knitted cap and pulled an extra fleece on over her gear. "Jo, are you coming?"

Jo jogged over after lacing up her shoes and bounced around on her toes. "Sorry, I was checking in with Dad. He said he was coming too."

In a monotone voice, Kenzie said, "That's great. It's quite the family affair." Except for Robbie, why wasn't he here too? Pushing that thought from her mind she knew she had to concentrate on the race. It was imperative she not let herself get distracted. Finishing the race was her priority today.

They hurried through the parking area, and Kenzie scanned the crowd. "Look, there they are." Waving her arms, she called out, "Jamie, Caleb!"

Jamie raised a hand and hurried in their direction, with Caleb, Steve and Yvette trailing behind her. "Hey, guys." Jamie clapped her hands together and grinned. "Who's ready to hit the pavement?"

Kenzie, Grace and Jo held up their hands, and the group did a round of high-fives.

Kenzie pointed to the crowd, moving in one direction. "We should check in and get our bibs. We'll give the rest to Yvette." She grinned at her. "You might be sorry you volunteered to be our pack mule for the day."

Jamie and Caleb pulled open their jackets to show off their numbers. Jamie said, "We're ready."

Steve did the same and Yvette said, "If I'm going to be a Sherpa, Grace, can I have your keys? I'll drop everything in the car."

Grace passed them to her. "Thanks."

The group made their way to the check-in station and were handed their packets and bibs. Kenzie pinned hers to her long-sleeve T-shirt with Grace and Jo following suit.

Without sounding bossy, Kenzie said, "We should do a light warm-up as we'll be gathering at the starting line in less than twenty minutes."

Each person grew quiet, focused on their own race.

Kenzie did some light jumping jacks and stretched. *I can do this. I'm strong. I can do anything I set my mind to.* Saying this mantra over and over to herself calmed her nerves, and she ignored the subtle ache in her left ankle. She was oblivious to people around her and then it was time to move to the starting line.

"All right everyone, don't start off at top speed. Find your rhythm and pace yourself." Kenzie threw her arms around her sisters and drew Jo in too. "We're going to do this, ready…"

And the four girls shouted, "Wee Scots!"

Caleb looked at Steve and said, "I'm good with being chopped liver."

Steve grinned. "How about steak tartar?"

They fist bumped. "Even better."

Kenzie checked their bib numbers. "We're in the second corral."

The girls were elbow to elbow with fellow runners. Kenzie glanced at Grace and Jamie. Remaining calm, she said, "Remember everything we've talked about. Run your race, no one else's. Don't look around to see what anyone else is doing, just focus on you and your breathing, your stride and the road in front of you."

A cowbell rang out in the chilly morning air. The crowd inched toward the starting line. Kenzie's pulse quickened.

"Have you changed your mind? Are you going to stop at the 5k finish line?" Grace asked.

Kenzie could tell Grace was worried. Shaking off her nerves, she said, "I'll see you at the finish line."

Jamie bounced on her toes, her energy feeding off the crowd around her. "I can't believe we're doing this!"

The air vibrated with excitement, the tension was palpable. As each throng of people in front of them left, their group shuffled closer to the front of the starting line. Kenzie slipped her earbuds in, but didn't turn the music on. She wanted to be able to hear her sisters.

Her heart fluttered. One foot over the timing strip, and she was off. Her adrenaline kicked in as she found her stride, taking care to not push too hard, too fast.

She could sense she was surrounded by her family and friends as she settled in. Their unspoken support propelled her forward as the first mile slipped past, ignoring her ankle twinge. As they approached the two-mile mark she glanced at Grace first and then Jamie. They wore their game faces. Her sisters were determined, each in their own way, and she had little doubt they'd finish. They rounded the bend and the first finish line was in sight. With a quick thumbs-up to her sisters and the guys, she lengthened her stride and pulled away, focused on each breath and each step. Clearing her mind, she kept her pace; one foot and then the other.

She glanced at the mile marker. Inwardly she groaned. *Only seven miles, just over halfway. How am I going to finish?* Doubts began to take hold. Pushing them aside, she kept pushing herself.

Her ankle screamed. Kenzie focused on her breathing. One foot and one breath at a time. *I will do this.*

Another mile marker. *I will do this.* She kept up this mantra. *I will do this.*

Mile marker ten came into view. She faltered and her stride shortened and slowed. Steeling herself, she kept putting one foot in front of the other. She would not think about the pain radiating up her leg. She stumbled.

A strong hand tightened around her arm and hauled her upright.

Her eyes widened. "Hey." She kept her breathing controlled and steady. Shocked and confused, she wondered, what was Robbie doing here?

"Hey yourself." Robbie was a half step behind her, letting Kenzie set the pace. She was slower than she wanted, but speed didn't matter—she just had to finish.

Her shoulders started to slump, her form was suffering. She heard Robbie's voice encourage her. "Alignment. Form."

Mile marker eleven. Her confidence was coming back. *I will do this*! Mile marker twelve. She sensed Robbie, silently reassuring her, encouraging her to keep going. He was by her side, stride for stride. She picked up her pace. Pushing through the pain, her stride lengthened. She focused on the road, one foot and then the other. She could see the finish line just ahead. She was going to make it; she would finish with Robbie by her side.

The final yards, her running shoes slapped softly on the pavement, sweat running down her back. Her left foot came down over the finish line. Tears flowed unchecked down her face.

She finished. Her arms shot up in victory. Flinging her head back, eyes heavenward she screamed, "I did it!"

Slowing to a walk, her eyes found Robbie's. Her emotions ran the gamut, elation to confusion.

Shrieks penetrated her fog. Jamie and Grace threw their arms around her, jumping up and down. "You did it!" Jamie shouted.

Grace looked down. "You're in pain." It wasn't a question. It was a statement.

"I'm fine." Her voice shaky, she said, "Robbie?"

His arm was draped around Jo's shoulders. A slow, lazy smile crept over his handsome face. "Yeah, Kenz?"

Her eyebrow cocked. "When did—why did—how long?"

His eyes held hers. "I've been behind you since the beginning."

Her breath caught and she rubbed the tears from her eyes. "Why?"

"I was pretty sure you'd run the half, and when Jo confirmed it I knew where I needed to be, just in case you needed a partner." He held up his hands and with a sweep of an arm he announced, "And look, here we are at the finish line."

Kenzie leapt into his arms and held on with every ounce of energy she had. She whispered, "I wouldn't have made it without you."

CHAPTER 29

Chaos ensued. Kenzie's parents and George appeared, and the rest of the gang gathered around the couple. Kenzie wriggled free of Robbie's arms, not because she wanted to, but she had to face it—they had taken steps towards repairing their relationship but were not where she wanted them to be, yet.

James clapped Robbie on the back. Heartily he exclaimed, "You're a good man, running the race with my Kenzie."

Robbie shook his hand but didn't respond.

"Robbie." Kenzie's voice was soft almost inaudible. "We're all going back to Steve's. Are you coming?" There was a tingling in the pit of her stomach as she waited for his answer.

"If you're sure?"

Kenzie held out her hand. Without hesitation, Robbie took it and she absorbed his warmth, his strength. Her smile widened, reaching her eyes. "Grace drove me."

His finger followed the curve of Kenzie's cheek. "I'll meet you there."

Jo said, "If you girls don't mind, I'll ride with my little brother."

Kenzie reluctantly let go. "We'll see you there." She limped across the parking lot. Looking back over her shoulder, she watched Robbie hurry toward his car with Jo. An idea rolled around her brain.

"Earth to Kenz." Grace poked her in the arm. "The car is this way."

She adjusted direction and slugged back another bottle of coconut water.

Grace pointed to her foot. "How bad is your ankle? And be honest."

Kenzie linked her arm with Grace's and leaned against her as they walked. "Let's just put it this way—I want to find a chair and prop up my feet, but I'm not taking off my shoe."

Grace grimaced. "Swelling."

Making slow progress over the rough ground, Kenzie said, "You have no idea. The only thing keeping my entire foot from going basketball size is compression socks and running shoes."

Grace's understanding nod comforted her. "Did you bring something you can change into?"

She looked at Grace from the corner of her eye. "I take it you're going to examine it no matter what I say."

With a laugh, Grace said, "You got that right. Why not take advantage of personal medical care?"

Snorting, Kenzie said, "No lectures, okay?"

Using the key fob, Grace unlocked the car. Relief coursed through Kenzie. "You won't tell anyone you basically carried my butt to the car, will you?"

Grace touched her fingers to her lips. "Your secret is safe, but you know Mom and Jamie are going to notice instantly."

Resigned to the truth of that statement, Kenzie said, "Yeah, I know."

Grace held the passenger door open and eased her down to the seat. It took a minute before she slid her leg inside. Grace shut the door and jogged around to the driver's side. Slipping behind the wheel, she pulled out of the parking lot. "I was shocked to see you run across the finish line with Robbie."

A smile played over her lips. "No more than I was."

Quietly Grace said, "He's an amazing guy."

Tears clogged Kenzie's throat.

Grace glanced her way. "You've always loved him."

She nodded. "More than I realized."

"Ask him to come home to Easton," Grace encouraged.

"I can't do that." *At least not yet*, she thought.

Grace parked on the street and turned the car off. "Kenzie, don't be foolish. Talk to him. Today is the perfect opportunity. And remember, he came because of you."

Kenzie put her hand on the car door handle and opened it. "Squirt, do me a huge favor. Don't push."

"If that's what you want." Grace tucked the car keys in her jacket pocket. "Wait up and we'll walk in together. You can lean on me."

"So I don't fall down and make a fool of myself, you mean?" Kenzie slammed the car door.

"After what you did, completing the race, there isn't a single person in that house who would say you were a fool. Pigheaded maybe, stubborn, obstinate, and a few other words that escape me at the moment, definitely."

Kenzie chuckled. "Don't hold back, Gracie, tell me how you really feel."

"All right, I will. You are the smartest, strongest and most inspiring person I know, and I'm proud to call you my sister." She slipped her arm firmly around Kenzie's waist, and the pair made a slow trek to the house. "Remember, when we get inside, your shoe and sock are coming off so I can examine your ankle."

"But…" Kenzie started to protest.

Grace scowled. "No arguing. After all, I'm the junior doctor."

Kenzie grinned and said, "You're a physician's assistant and the best there is."

The front door flew open and Jamie sailed down the steps. "I thought you two had gotten lost."

"Nope, just taking our time," Kenzie said, struggling to keep her face neutral.

Without a word Jamie wrapped a protective arm around Kenzie's waist. The sisters took the front steps, slowly half carrying her up. Once in the front door Jamie steered her to the oversized kitchen and pointed to a comfy chair. Caleb hurried over and pushed a footstool toward it.

Kenzie bit back the pain. "I wish you would stop fussing over me."

"You can barely walk," Jamie admonished. "Is your bag still in the car?"

Caleb put his hand out and took the keys. "I'll get it."

Grace pointed to her foot. "Kenz…it's time."

Mom walked around the corner as the shoe first and then the sock came off. Kenzie's foot resembled an inflating balloon. The deep purple coloring did nothing to keep the look of concern from flooding Mom's face. "I knew you shouldn't have run!" she cried.

Kenzie attempted to reassure her. "Mom, I'm fine. A little ice and elevation and it's back to normal."

Mom pulled her eyes from Kenzie's foot to Grace. "What's your assessment?"

"You can relax, Mom. Kenz has agreed to sit down, elevate her foot and use an ice pack."

Caleb hurried into the room and handed Jamie a duffel bag. Jamie asked, "Do you have socks?"

Kenzie tried to grasp the handles on the bag. "Yeah. I'll get them."

Jamie ignored her and dug inside. She pulled out a pair of soft fleece socks. "Will they fit?"

"They should. I got them when I had the cast." She bent forward and pulled them on. Easing her foot up on the stack of pillows, she winced.

Yvette handed Jamie a bag of frozen peas. "Kenzie, can I get you something else?"

"I'm fine." She grinned. "Thanks for the peas."

"No need to return them." Yvette chuckled.

Robbie and Jo strolled in. Yvette smiled and said, "Help yourself. There are drinks on the bar and Steve is setting up the buffet. We should be eating shortly."

Robbie pulled up a chair next to Kenzie. "Your ankle looks awful."

She smirked. "That's nothing. You should see the other foot."

"You've always had a great sense of humor." He looked closer. "Great shade of purple."

"Part of my charm, Burns." Deep inside of her, something clicked. Her heart fluttered. She knew what she was going to do. Now she just needed the perfect moment.

His smile softened. "You're amazing."

Jo wandered away and Grace took one final look at her ankle while Jamie and Caleb went to help in the kitchen. They were alone in the midst of the party.

Robbie's voice dropped. "It's been good seeing you this past month."

Kenzie's head bobbed. "I've enjoyed our dates too, it's sort of like old times, only better." He smiled and clasped his hands. She longed to hold them. "And how are things with you? Work good?"

"It's okay. I'm getting used to how they do things."

Softly Kenzie said, "I miss you."

"I miss you too." Kenzie's heart grew light. The kaleidoscope of butterflies took flight in her stomach. "Do you think you could help me up and we could go out to the porch?"

He looked around. "Are you sure you should be walking?"

She held out her hand. "I can lean on you."

Robbie's eyebrows shot up. "Absolutely." He took her hand. His warm fingers held tight as she stood, unsteady at first. He didn't let go.

Kenzie hopped on one foot, barely setting her left one on the ground while Robbie kept a steadying hand on her elbow. "Guess I should have brought my cane."

He held the door open and she stepped out into the biting air. Pulling her fleece close, she leaned against the porch railing. A shiver ran down her spine, but not from the air—her nerves were in overdrive.

"Are you cold?" he asked.

"No, I'm good." Kenzie chewed her lower lip. "I was surprised to see you today."

His face was turned to look at her square in the eye. "You haven't run a race without me since college. Did you really think I'd let you do this one alone?"

She shrugged. "Well, I mean, we didn't talk about it, and…"

He laughed softly. "Kenz, are you going to start rambling?"

She dropped her head and looked up at him through her lashes. "I am so sorry about so many things."

"There's nothing…"

Kenzie interrupted him, her eyes grew big, and she felt a flush of heat rise in her cheeks. "Please let me say what I have to say."

He took a step back and grew silent.

"I climbed my first tree with you by my side, we learned how to ride bikes and swim together, we took our SATs together. You were my first crush at the tender age of nine, although you never knew it." She smiled and continued, "Through all these years, you have been my best friend. But things are vastly different now."

Robbie's brows knitted together, clearly confused. "Kenz, where are you going with all of this?"

Her voice wavered. "Give me a minute, I'm getting there." Her heart urged her forward. "I've borrowed you for school dances and we've been each other's dates when we needed a partner."

Grinning, he said, "You *are* the best wing man ever."

She held up her hand and implored, "Burns, will you please let me finish?"

He placed his hand over his heart, his face serious. "You have the floor."

She blinked back the tears that threatened to fall. "We've worked together, played together, and there are times you scared the hell out of me. That's why I didn't discourage you to spread your wings. I didn't want you to stay in Easton because you felt you had to."

He reached out and took her hand. "That's not why I stayed. It's where I wanted to be, every day, with you. I left because it seemed like you wanted me to leave."

Standing on her good foot, Kenzie placed her swollen one on the bottom rung of the banister before continuing, "Which brings me to my question. I was wondering if I could ask you to borrow something. Well, it's more of a long-term thing. So I wanted to say…"

Confusion filled his eyes. "Do you need money?"

She shook her head and laughed. "You just can't help interrupting, can you?"

He held his palms up. "Sorry."

With a shake of her head, she said, "You certainly are making this difficult for me."

His eyes twinkled, but he remained silent.

"Here goes." She pulled herself to her full height, took a deep breath and said, "Can I borrow your last name?"

"What? You want to borrow the name Burns? For what?"

Kenzie's mouth fell open, stunned. She couldn't believe he was so damn dense!

His shoulders popped up and down. "Long-term? Kenz, what are you talking about?"

She began to hop away and he grabbed her arm.

"Kenzie?" His voice softened. "Talk to me."

Her voice caught and her eyes bored into his. Haltingly she said, "Robbie, I want to borrow your name for the rest of my life…" Her voice trailed off.

He cleared his throat. He had to fight a grin as he blinked hard. "Let me get this straight: are you asking *me* what I think you are?"

Her smile broadened. "I know we've only officially been dating a month, but if you're still in love with me, would you consider letting me have the honor of being Kenzie MacLellan Burns?"

He sat on the railing and pulled her toward him. "You're asking me to marry you?"

She grinned. "If you love me, even half as much as I love you, our life will be filled with joy and…"

He gathered her in his arms before she finished her

sentence. His lips crushed hers, and she took what he was offering.

Left breathless, she laid a hand on his chest. "I hate to point out the obvious, but you still haven't answered my question."

The way he looked at her was as soft as a caress. "Well, I never imagined you'd ask me, so wait a second." He dropped to one knee and took her hand.

"Kenzie MacLellan, I'm a little old-fashioned, so if you don't mind, I have a life-changing question to ask you."

The tears she had been holding back streamed down her cheeks. Her heart sang as it became whole.

"Will you make me the happiest man on earth and be my wife? Share my life, share my name and love me for all our days?"

The dam broke in her heart and love crashed over her in waves. "Yes," she whispered, and then louder she yelled, "YES!"

He sprang to his feet, swept her in his arms and twirled her around the porch, covering her face with tender kisses. "You sure know how to finish a race, Mac."

"Burns, you sure know how to run a marathon. You've been in this one since the day our mothers put us in the same playpen."

Kenzie caught sight of their family members peeking at them from behind the curtains. Laughing, she said, "We should go inside and share our news."

Robbie carefully set her on one foot. "One more question?"

She cocked her head.

"Does it have to be a long engagement?"

She laughed. "We've both waited long enough. I think a June wedding would be nice." She tilted back her head as he claimed her mouth with his. A smoldering fire sparked from the passion of his kiss. She murmured, "The first Saturday in June."

Robbie chuckled, "It can't come soon enough." He kissed her tenderly and said, "Kenzie MacLellan Burns. I do like how that sounds."

CHAPTER 30

Today was the day Kenzie would marry her best friend and the love of her life, Robbie Burns.

She heard a soft knock on the door. "Kenz?" Jamie said as she and Grace tiptoed into the room.

Kenzie sat on the edge of the bed dressed in a short blue robe. She grinned as her sisters sat down on either side of her. She patted their legs. "You two look beautiful."

Grace fluffed the skirt on her soft lavender chiffon dress. "It's super comfortable and that's a good thing, as it's going to be a scorcher today."

"I know. Who would have thought early June in Vermont would be this hot?"

Jamie took her hand. "Are you ready to put our wedding dress on?"

"In a minute." Kenzie slipped her arm around Grace's slender shoulders. "After the wedding, Jamie's going to take the dress to the cleaners, and then it's your turn."

Grace's hands fluttered, her smile dipping. "You both found love after wearing it. What if the magic is gone?"

Jamie laid a hand on Grace's arm. "You deserve to have

the joy that we've found, and I believe with my heart you will."

Grace looked at her sisters. "Don't be mad if I don't tell you when I try it on."

Kenzie pulled her up from the bed. "You won't need to; we'll know."

Jamie brushed a stray lock from Grace's face. "I knew the day Kenzie tried the dress on. An image of her popped in my head."

Grace's eyes grew wide. "Did you see Robbie by her side?"

"No, but I knew in here." She tapped her heart.

Grace struggled for words. "I—I don't know what to say."

Kenzie said, "Gracie, promise us you'll put it on and look in the mirror. Don't wait to see what your happily ever after looks like."

Softly Grace said, "I promise."

Opening her arms, Kenzie said, "Group hug." Happiness was bubbling over. "So, who's going to help me lace up this dress?"

Jamie chuckled. "That's why we're here."

Grace took the dress from the closet door and held it out, caressing the soft fabric. "It *is* a beautiful gown."

Kenzie slipped the robe from her shoulders, and together Jamie and Grace held it as she stepped into the skirt. Grace pulled up the straps and Kenzie slipped her arms through them.

She looked in the mirror and caught Jamie's eye. "Do you think Gran would be upset I removed the sleeves?"

"Are you kidding? With your arms, you should show them off."

Jamie adjusted the neckline while Grace tightened the laces. Kenzie placed her hand on her waist. With each tug, the dress took shape around her. "The brooch is on the dresser."

Grace picked it up. "This is beautiful. The thistle and amethyst are perfect on the dress."

Kenzie secured it to the center of the modest neckline. "Well, what do you think?"

Jamie asked, "Did you want to wear my veil?"

"Thanks, but it's not me."

Grace looked around the room. "So, you have something old, the dress and brooch. What's your something new?"

Kenzie held up and wiggled her fingers. "My engagement ring!"

Grace admired it. "It's a beauty. Who knew Robbie had such great taste?"

"He had his mother's diamond ring and Mom gave him a stone, and voila. The two stones represent our past and our future."

Grace fanned her face and teased, "He is so romantic. What's borrowed?"

Kenzie grinned. "He is. I'm borrowing him for the rest of my life."

"Oh, Kenzie," Grace gushed.

Jamie laughed. "Don't make her cry. We have a wedding in just a few minutes."

The carriage ride was short, from the Burns family home to the top of the field. Kenzie saw Dad waiting for her just as he had last fall when Jamie and Caleb tied the knot in this very spot. *Could this be the beginning of a new family tradition?*

As Jo pulled Pirate to a halt and took her place with Jamie and Grace, Kenzie picked up her bouquet of wildflowers and white heather. She took Dad's outstretched hand and stepped down.

With misty eyes, Dad said, "Kenzie, you are beautiful, so much like your Gran."

She fanned a hand in front of her face. "You're not allowed to make me cry."

"Not to worry, I have a handkerchief." He patted his breast pocket.

She tried to peek down the aisle. "Have you seen Robbie? How does his tux look?"

A puzzled look flashed across Dad's face. "Sweetheart, he's a Scot and marrying a Scottish lass."

Beaming, she said, "I'm ready, Dad. It's time to give me away."

Jamie, Grace and Jo were waiting patiently, and Dad grinned. "Ladies, it looks like Kenzie is anxious to walk"— he winked at her—"or run down the aisle."

The music wafted on the light summer breeze. Kenzie pointed in the direction of the arbor. "That's our cue."

Kenzie waited impatiently as Jo, Jamie and then Grace disappeared from her sight. She took her first step, holding tight to her dad's arm, but she felt as if she were floating. Turning the corner, her eyes locked on Robbie.

She sucked in a breath. "Dad, look."

"Aye, lass." Dad's voice was thick with emotion. "Your future husband is wearing his kilt and our plaid is pinned to his jacket, honoring both families."

Robbie extended his hand, beckoning her to join him.

"Dad, I'm going to be the first MacLellan-Burns."

Dad kissed the top of her head, his brogue thick. "Kenzie, I have to admit, this is long overdue."

Kenzie took another step, and she thought she heard Gran's voice. *Kenzie, you've done well.*

She paused and looked up to the deep blue sky, whispering, "Thanks, Gran, for the nudge."

She took the final steps toward her future and joined hands with Robbie.

The End

Turn the page for a sneak peek at *Blue,*
Book 3 in *The MacLellan Sisters Trilogy.*

BLUE

CHAPTER 1

Grace smiled as she saw the *Welcome to Glasgow* sign on her way to the car rental counter. This trip was just what she needed after her sisters' weddings.

She was signing her name on the credit card receipt when she was struck from behind and shoved forcefully into the counter. Holding her midsection, she groaned just as a woman wrenched the garment bag from her hand and took off at a dead run.

"STOP! HELP! THIEF!" Grace grabbed her tote bag and ran after her. But high-heeled sandals and the slim skirt made it hard for her to stop the thief. The gap between Grace and her luggage was widening.

A man raced past her as Grace kept her eyes on the bouncing garment bag until the thief ducked behind a cement pillar in the parking garage. Her heart felt like a lead weight in her chest. How could she have let this happen? She slowed to a walk and stopped, her tote bag dragging on the ground as she turned to make her way back to the rental counter.

To her shock, the man who had run past was walking toward her with her garment bag slung over his shoulder.

With heaving breath, her eyes widened. Those eyes, that face, that man. She had seen him before. Mr. Green Eyes from the plane on her trip to Scotland last fall with her sisters. She hadn't realized how tall and heart-stoppingly handsome he was, with streaks of gold running through his dark brown hair, a chiseled jaw, a sensuous mouth and those beautiful green eyes. She would never forget those eyes.

"Miss?" His voice was deep and smooth, with a rich Scottish brogue. "Does this belong to you?"

Grace nodded, stunned. Her words came out in a rush. "Oh, yes. It's my wedding dress. I don't know what I would have done."

With a short bow, he handed her the dress. "He's a lucky man."

Before Grace could clarify her comment, he strode away. She called after him, "I didn't catch your name."

He flashed a smile that caused Grace's heart to race.

"Logan Campbell." And with that he turned.

Clutching the bag to her chest, Grace watched Logan walk out of the airport and out of her life.

***

The landscape changed from city and concrete to lush rolling hills. Clouds hung heavy in the sky with the threat of rain. Grace didn't care. She was right where she belonged. Replaying the scene in the airport, she realized she never said thank you to Mr. Logan Campbell. Her hand smacked the steering wheel. *He must think I'm a boorish American. Not bothering to offer him so much as a cup of coffee, let alone a heart-felt thank you. Nothing I can do about it now. I'll never see him again…well, except maybe on a plane.*

She slowed as she entered the village of Stirling. Up ahead was her first destination: MacMeekin's Bakery. After easing into a parking space, she strolled over the cobblestones, swinging her handbag, and down the quiet street. It was midday, most of the locals were working, and tourists were likely off catching the sights.

The old bell above the bakery door jingled as she entered. "Well, hello, Grace, what a lovely surprise." Mrs. MacMeekin came through the swinging kitchen doors, wiping flour-covered hands on her apron. "Are your sisters behind you, dear?" She crossed to the door and looked down the street.

A stab of sadness hit Grace hard. She had never been in the bakery without her sisters or Gran.

"It's just me today." Grace's smile was half-hearted. "A vacation for one."

The older woman opened her arms. "Welcome home, Grace."

Mrs. M holding her tight almost felt like Gran had wrapped her arms around both of them. A lump lodged in Grace's throat.

With a kiss on her forehead, Mrs. M said, "So what brings you to Scotland?"

Grace cleared her throat and blinked away the tears that hovered on her lashes. "I wanted to get away for a couple of weeks. Enjoy some of your baked goods and wander the Highlands." She felt it best to not mention Gran's letter. At least not yet.

"Well, that certainly does sound lovely." Mrs. M chuckled. "I received a letter from your mother. She said Kenzie married a few weeks ago. Is he a good man?"

Grace grinned. "He's the perfect guy for Kenzie.

They've been best friends since they were babies. And let me tell you, Robbie Burns has the patience of a saint."

Mrs. M pulled out a chair from one of the round tables near the windows and sat down. "And Jamie and her husband Caleb, are they doing well?"

Grace settled in the opposite chair. "They moved into their new home, and I'm betting we'll be hearing the sound of little feet within the year."

Not one to sit still long, Mrs. M hopped up. "Tea and scones?"

Grace nodded. "Let me help you."

With a broad smile, Mrs. M said, "Nonsense. You sit and tell me why you really came back. Something tells me there is a bit more to the story than just needing to visit with your gran's old friend and eating cream buns." She bustled about making a pot of tea and plating teacakes and scones from the glass case. Grace got up and carried the cups and plates to the table while Mrs. M took a small tray and put the teapot, creamer and sugar bowl on it.

Grace waited until Mrs. M had sat down and poured them each a cup of tea. "Do you know how Gran met my grandfather?"

A gleam shone in the older woman's eye. "I do."

"So, you know about the wedding dress and the story that goes with it?"

"Aye." Mrs. M nodded and looked at Grace "Is this the reason for your trip?"

"Partly." Grace took a sip of tea and broke apart a scone. She nibbled on a small piece. Her eyes rolled back. "Just like always, Mrs. M, pure heaven."

Her gaze roamed the small but tidy bakery. She spied a picture of Gran and Mrs. M on the wall, and smiled. "Do you know the wedding dress is enchanted?"

"Yes, Arabel told me the story many years ago."

Solemnly, Mrs. M added, "We were friends for most of our lives."

"After Gran died, Dad sent the wedding dress, the MacLellan plaid and a brooch to us. There was a letter from our Great-grandmother. We didn't know about the family legend that if an unmarried MacLellan woman tried the dress on she would find her future. Heck, we didn't even know about the dress." Grace paused to sip her tea before continuing. "As you can guess from recent events, Jamie tried it on and married Caleb. Afterward Kenzie tried it on and realized she had been in love with Robbie forever, and they married. The dress was then handed down to me." She held up her hands. "And here I am."

"Did you try the dress on, dear?" Mrs. M leaned forward in her chair, her voice slightly breathless.

With a shake of her head, Grace said, "Each of us had one last letter from Gran tucked into our luggage. Jamie found hers right before our last trip here, Kenzie found hers before she went on the fateful hike, and I found mine the day after Kenzie's wedding. Gran told me to bring the dress back to Scotland without putting it on."

Mrs. M held up a finger, hopped up from the chair and hurried toward the kitchen. Her face was unreadable.

"Mrs. M?" Grace called after her. "Is everything all right?"

Over her shoulder, Mrs. M said, "Just one moment, dear."

Grace was confused. Maybe she had forgotten something in the oven? She strained to hear if there was a timer going off, but all was quiet. At a loss, she picked up the last bite of scone and popped it in her mouth, and then washed it down with tea.

Mrs. M walked into the room carrying a creamy white, medium-sized envelope. She handed it to Grace. "Your grandmother asked me to keep this for you. She said when you came in, without your sisters, I was to instruct you to read it after you try the dress on."

"But...I don't understand. Gran specifically said to not wear the dress."

Mrs. M sat down and patted her hand. "I remember her words exactly, as she had me repeat them back to her often. She said, 'Tell Grace she needs to go to the Blue Belle Woods within the week. But before she does, she's to put the dress on and look into the mirror. She will find the future she seeks.'"

Grace's hand flew to her mouth. "Did Gran know how everything would unfold for me and my sisters?"

The older woman's smile was all-knowing. "Your grandmother knew the sequence of events, nothing specific, but she felt it was imperative for you to come back to Scotland and put the dress on, here, where it all began."

Grace's shoulders slumped, stunned while she let this new information sink in. Wait until she called Jamie and Kenzie. They wouldn't believe it—well, no, they'd believe almost anything related to Gran.

The doorbell jingled and Mrs. M greeted her customer. "Grace, have another cup of tea and then I'll pack a box of goodies for you to take to the farm."

With a trembling hand Grace poured tea into her cup, to the point where it began to overflow into the saucer and on the table. Muttering to herself, she grabbed a stack of napkins to sop it up.

What does this all mean? Did Gran want the dress here so it could recharge or something? Maybe there isn't enough magic left for it to help me. Stop it, you're being foolish. Dress or not, if I'm going to fall in love, I will.

Pushing all rambling thoughts aside, Grace added cream to her tea. Mrs. M joined her after the customer left the shop carrying a huge box of pastries. She picked up her teacup. "I hope you'll come to dinner while you're here. Maybe you could bring some pictures of your sisters' weddings. I'd love to see them."

Grace smiled. "You could come out to the farm too. I'm a pretty good cook. After all I had one of the best teachers."

Mrs. M's eyes grew misty. "Aye, your gran was a wonderful cook, and I'd love to come to the farm. I haven't been there since she passed away."

Grace grinned. "Then it's a date." She held up her teacup and said, "Let's toast to Gran."

Mrs. M's look softened. "You are so like her, but"—she winked—"we can't toast to her with tea. I have something more appropriate."

Grace exclaimed, "Mrs. M!"

She batted her twinkling blue eyes. "'Tis only right." She hurried behind the counter and came back with a silver flask and two small glasses. "A gift from Arabel." She poured a splash of Scottish whiskey in each glass. Grace picked one up and held it aloft.

Mrs. M said in a clear voice, "To Arabel MacLellan, a dear friend and a special grandmother. We miss you."

Grace said, "To Gran." They clinked glasses and sipped the smooth, amber liquid. Each woman was lost in her own memories as they finished the smooth whiskey.

Mrs. M set her glass on the table and leaned forward. "What do you have planned while you're here? Other than Blue Belle Woods and having dinner with an old woman."

Grace toyed with her glass. "I'm not sure. Wander through the hills and I'll probably go fishing at least once. Being here alone is going to be an interesting adventure."

Mrs. M patted her hand. "If you get lonely, my door is always open."

Grace squeezed her hand. "Spending time with you is a little like being with Gran again."

With a catch in her voice Mrs. M said, "Dear, that is the nicest compliment anyone has ever given me." Giving Grace's hand one last tug she said, "Now, let me pack up that box for you. I'm sure you're anxious to get to the farm."

Grace's eyes swiveled to the street. "It has been a long trip and sitting on Gran's patio is just what I need."

ACKNOWLEDGEMENTS

Thank you for reading *The MacLellan Sisters – Borrowed*.
I hope you enjoyed the story.
If you did, please help other readers find this book:

1. This book is lendable. Send it to a friend you think might like it so she can discover me too.
2. Help other people find this book by writing a review.
3. Sign up for my newsletter by contacting me at http://www.lucindarace.com.
4. Like my Facebook page: https://facebook.com/lucindaraceauthor.
5. Join the Friends who like Lucinda Race group on Facebook.
6. Twitter @lucindarace
7. Instagram @lucindraceauthor
8. Pinterest Lucinda Race author

ABOUT THE AUTHOR

Lucinda Race is a lifelong fan of romantic fiction. As a girl, she spent hours reading and dreaming of one day becoming a writer. As her life twisted and turned, she found herself writing nonfiction articles, but she still longed to turn to her true passion: novels. After developing the storyline for the Loudon Series, it was time to start living her dream. Clicking computer keys, she has published nine books. Lucinda lives with her husband Rick and two little pups, Jasper and Griffin, in the rolling hills of Western Massachusetts. Her writing is contemporary, fresh, and engaging.
Visit her at:
www.facebook.com/lucindaraceauthor
Twitter @lucindarace
Instagram @lucindaraceauthor
www.lucindarace.com
Lucinda@lucindarace.com

OTHER BOOKS BY LUCINDA RACE:

THE MACLELLAN SISTERS TRILOGY

Old and New

Borrowed

Blue

The Loudon Series

Between Here and Heaven

Lost and Found

The Journey Home

The Last First Kiss

Ready to Soar

Love in the Looking Glass

Magic in the Rain

Made in the USA
Middletown, DE
01 January 2021

30596414R00196